Endless Struggle

Random Survival
Book 3

Ray Wenck
Glory Days Press
Columbus, Ohio

Glory Days Press
Columbus, Ohio

Publisher's Note: This is a work of fiction. Names, characters, places, and
incidents are a product of the author's imagination. Locales and public
names are sometimes used for atmospheric purposes. Any resemblance to
actual people, living or dead, or to businesses, companies, events, institu-
tions, or locales is completely coincidental.

Book Layout © 2016 BookDesignTemplates.com
Cover Design by Mibl Art
Endless Struggle/ Ray Wenck. – 2nd ed.

ISBN 978-1-7335290-2-0
ISBN-10: 1733529020

Dedication

Dedicated to survivors everywhere and the

endless struggle that follows.

Author's Notes

A lot has happened since the first Random Survival was released. I owe a lot to EJ, Jayne and Bill from Rebel e Publishers for taking a chance making the rerelease of books 1 and 2 and this third installment of the thriller series possible.

Thanks to all of those who have supported me along the way, especially my children, April, Jon and Jeremy. A special thanks to Nancy Kueckels-Averill, RN, BSN from Michigan Institute for Clinical & Health Research for her knowledge and assistance with medical equipment.

Thanks as well go out to Tyler, Shay, Jodi, Tanja and Molly for their support and assistance in various aspects of this story and my journey.

Enjoy the ride!

It's been a while since I wrote this story. Now, with it's new cover, some updating to the writing, and he rerelease, I find I like this story even more now than when I first wrote it. Thanks for your continued support.

As always, read all you want, I'll write more.

Chapter One

"DO YOU SEE THEM?" CARYN'S VOICE WAS NEAR PANIC, AGAIN.

"Shhh!" Mel said in a hushed tone, but with a forceful look. "Get down and don't move," she commanded. "And don't make a sound." Her gaze held the tall blonde's, until the woman nodded. Mel moved to a large old oak, crouched behind it and scanned the long spans of open ground they'd just covered.

Both women fought to control their heavy breathing after the long run. Caryn pulled up her knees tight to her chest, wrapping her arms around them. She lowered her head and leaned against the small birch she hid behind.

Looking through her small binoculars, Mel panned along the woods to the south. Something dark flashed between the trees. She spotted four more dark forms moving away from them and knew they had taken the bait. She relaxed and hoped Tara would be safe. The ache in her heart again made her wonder whether separating had been the right thing to do. But Tara had been adamant and was off before Mel could voice her concern or offer an alternative plan.

Seeing Mel stiffen, Caryn must have thought the men were coming for them. "Oh, God!"

Mel heard Caryn's cry. "Relax," she said, more forcefully than intended. "I don't see anyone. We might be okay."

Caryn lifted her head. Tears filled her eyes. Upon seeing the welled eyes, Mel rolled hers. God, the woman was so annoying. "Come on, girl, after all we've been through you have to be well past tears by now."

"I can't help it. I'm not like you."

Mel bristled. She hated being termed different. "What's that supposed to mean? Because I'm gay, is that what you're saying?"

Caryn wiped a sleeve across her face. "No, that's not what I mean ... because you're so strong, and ... and brave. I wish I could be more like you. I hate being afraid all the time."

Mel felt a little guilt seep in. For two weeks now, ever since she'd found Caryn cowering in a basement, Mel had been riding her: she was too slow, too weak, too girlie, and too wimpy. But Caryn was right, she was not like her. This high-bred suburban princess had probably never had to work for anything in her life. But Mel worked ... work of all kinds. But the work that had been the hardest and meant the most was the fight for acceptance and equality. And to Mel that fight was never ending.

She stood and walked to Caryn. Sighing, she sat in front of her, set her rifle on the ground and reached out, taking Caryn's hands. "Look, Caryn, I'm sorry if it seems I'm being mean to you, but if we're going to survive we have to be tough and help each other. If you're afraid all the time and we have to watch out for you, you become a liability and put us in danger. You understand?"

Caryn's tear-streaked face lifted from her knees. Her red eyes locked on Mel. "Then what, you kill me?"

Mel dipped her head frustrated. "No, that's never going to happen. What I'm saying is, if you don't conquer your fears you could get somebody else killed. You don't want that and we don't want that."

"But, how do I conquer them. I've never done the things you and Tara do. I don't want to be a burden, but every time something happens, I freeze up."

"I know it's not easy, but fear can only control you if you let it. You have to force it someplace in your head where you can lock it away. I wish we had extra bullets we could spare to let you practice shooting, but we can't afford to. Besides, the noise might draw unwanted attention."

Mel stood to check the field again. "I think we're safe. They're following Tara. But that might not last. We have to get as far away as possible before they decide to come looking for us." She reached a hand down and helped Caryn up; the heavy backpack the blonde wore made it a strain. Since Caryn was always afraid and not much use for defense, they made her carry the heaviest bag so Tara and Mel had their hands and movements free. The two women stood close. "I promise, Melissa, I'll work on it. I don't want to be trouble for you."

Mel nodded and looked away. She didn't believe for an instant that Caryn was capable of overcoming her fears. But she was a survivor, and from what she'd seen in the past month's travels, precious few of them were left. Mel would not turn her back on Caryn, but she wasn't about to go easy on her.

"Come on, we'll go straight through these woods."

"What about Tara? She might be in trouble."

Mel frowned. She'd been thinking the same thing. Tara had taken off in the hopes of leading their pursuit away from them. Since no one followed Mel and Caryn, it must have worked. But was she safe? They hadn't heard any shots, but that might not mean anything. The men chasing her didn't want to shoot, she was too great a prize but, Tara wouldn't go down without a fight. Mel prayed Tara was safe and made it back to her, to them.

Caryn boosted the pack higher on her back and moved off. After one more look behind, Mel slid the glasses in a pocket and followed. She watched Caryn move. The woman had more physical strength than she realized. Mel knew the pack was heavy, yet Caryn walked upright, showing no signs of the burden. Nor did she complain about its bulk.

She was right about them being different though. Where Caryn was tall and willowy, Mel was shorter and stocky.

Caryn was pretty and her hair color was obviously natural. Mel thought herself plain, somewhat muscular and wore her hair almost military short. Tara was a combination of them.

Tara flew helicopters in the Army. She was on leave, waiting for word of her new assignment when the world changed. To Mel, no one was tougher than Tara. A poster child for the female warrior, she had certainly proved herself since the two had met more than a month ago. A lot of raw power was packed into that small, black frame. She was the ultimate butch woman, except, to Mel's great disappointment, she wasn't lesbian. Still, it was hard for Mel to take her eyes off Tara.

"Should we leave some sort of trail for Tara?"

"She'll find us." Mel pressed forward, passing Caryn to take the lead.

"How? She has no idea where we are."

"Don't worry, she's trained. If we keep walking straight, she'll catch up to us. She led those animals south and when she loses them, she'll double back. Have confidence in her skills. You've seen what she's capable of."

Caryn shuddered. She remembered all right … every night in her dreams. "I know she's good, but I think I'll throw in a prayer too."

Mel gave a derisive snort. "Knock yourself out. It can't hurt."

They continued for perhaps an hour. Behind her, a plastic cap clicked open. Caryn had opened a water bottle. "How much water do we have left?" she asked without stopping.

"Eight bottles, I think."

"Man, we're going to have to find a new supply."

Something touched her back. Mel reached over her shoulder taking the bottle. She drank two large gulps, looked at the remains and took a small sip. With a third of the water left she handed the bottle back.

Early September had stayed August hot. The trees still a thick and green canopy made it difficult for anyone to see them. However, the reverse was also true. They might not notice anyone in pursuit until too late. A squirrel darted up a tree. Overhead light pierced the green umbrella. Birds chirped, lending the feeling of normality. And everything was normal in the world, except for the people; both the lack of and the survivors.

They'd met their share of people along the way. Some were very nice and offered refuge; some, like the band of men they met the night before, had their own agenda. The three women were hopeful when they first came across the encampment, but after looking closer, they noticed the camp was made up of mostly men and a few women. One of them looked to be twelve to fourteen. They all looked haggard and unkempt, their eyes hollow and haunted, expressions blank. But, it was the look of fear and the ever so slight shake of the head of the tall, dark-haired woman that had caught Tara's attention.

They thanked the men, whose eyes wandered freely over the three women, begging off their invitation to spend the night in the safety of the compound, saying they had to be elsewhere. The men seemed to accept their excuse, but early in the morning, Tara spotted the posse, and the chase began.

"Caryn, would you hand me a granola bar, please." To get the bar, Caryn had to stop and take the bag off her back. That stopped their progress. "Never mind, I'll get it." She went behind Caryn, unzipped a pocket and dug inside. She pulled one out and was about to zip the pocket closed when she stopped. "You want me to get you one?"

"No, thanks. I'll have one when we break."

"It might be a while."

"That's all right, I'll survive."

Mel closed up and took the lead. She crunched and tried to remember the last time she'd seen Caryn eat something.

Mel rolled that thought around for a while. The pack held two narrow honey and oat bars. Mel finished one and half of the second. She held it behind. "I can't eat no more. Finish this for me."

"No, that's all right. You should eat it."

"Why's that?" She made a sudden stop and turned. Caryn ran into her.

"What?"

"Why should I eat it instead of you?"

Caryn shrugged. "You need it more to keep up your strength."

"And you don't? When was the last time you ate?"

She shrugged again.

"You've been purposely skipping meals, haven't you?"

"It's like you said, I'm a burden. You and Tara deserve most of the food."

Mel looked up and muttered, "I can't believe this." Her eyes had a hard edge when she dropped them. "You think you're a burden now? How much more of a burden will you be if we have to carry you? We won't leave you. So you'll just hinder our movements and our defensive capabilities. You think you're doing the right thing, but you're not. That food is for all of us to share. We're a team. Now, eat this before I cram it down your throat."

With a timid hand, Caryn took the bar.

"And you'd better eat all of it." She turned and walked ahead again. Behind, the sound of the crunch was hard to hide. She smiled. A few minutes later, Caryn said, "Thank you."

"No problem."

They walked on until dusk and found a place to make camp, hoping Tara appeared soon.

Chapter Two

THE BLANKETS THEY EACH CARRIED WERE STRETCHED SIX FEET apart in an eight-foot clearing. They never risked a fire, but at night the woods were chilly. Mel watched Caryn while she set up her bed and went through the pack to find food. Caryn's jeans hung on her to the point of defying gravity. Mel shook her head. As much as Caryn annoyed her, grudgingly she had to give her respect. She might be a wimp, but she'd survived, so far. And sacrificing her food portions so she and Tara had more went a long way, in Mel's mind, to overshadowing her many weaknesses.

As Caryn doled out their meager meal, Mel said, "Caryn, we'll find other food. I appreciate what you're doing, but not eating your fair share will make you weak and more of a burden than you ... uh, you won't have the strength to keep up the long hikes we take."

"I know I'm a burden, Mel. I promise I'll work on being stronger. I don't want you to feel you can't trust me. I'm very grateful to you and Tara for bringing me along and for your friendship."

The last comment brought a twinge of guilt. Mel nodded, not knowing what to say without being insulting. She looked over what she had to eat, compared with Caryn. The amounts looked the same. She popped the pull tab on a can of pineapple chunks and opened a bottle of water. Caryn opened a can of green beans. Halfway down the can, they switched. They split a can of chicken and each ate a granola bar. For dessert, Caryn handed out three ginger snaps.

Mel used a folding shovel to dig a hole deep enough to bury the trash and covered it. By the time she settled back on her blanket Caryn had her backpack emptied, the items organized in front of her. Keeping an inventory of the supplies was her task.

"Four waters, a bag and a half of cookies." As she counted, she replaced the items in her bag. "Four cans of fruit and veggies, one of chicken, one tuna, two bags of jerky, six granola bars." The blanket was empty. "That's it I'm afraid. I figure if we stretch things we can make two more days when Tara arrives."

She zipped the various pouches and put the pack to the side. "I wish Tara would get here, I'm worried about her."

"She'll be all right," Mel said, but in truth, was worried too.

They sat in silence, lost in their thoughts. Mel broke the spell. "She'll be all right," she repeated, as if trying to convince herself. "Let's get some rest."

CARYN STRETCHED OUT ON HER BED, PULLING THE TOP blanket over her. As she did every night, she offered up prayers for her husband and children. Most nights the memories of her family brought silent tears. She finished with one for Tara and Mel, then prayed for strength and that their journey be safe.

As usual, her thoughts and the sounds of the night kept her awake long after Mel began her soft snoring. Eventually, exhaustion took her under, but it didn't stop her dreams. She ran blindly, in a panic, through an unending thick forest. The branches ripped at her skin, but her fear kept her racing onward. Dark shapes pursued her. No matter what she did, they always found her and did horrible things.

In the morning, she woke as exhausted as when she went to sleep. Mel still snored. Caryn sat up and stretched. Her back felt tight. Standing, Caryn went through a series of exercises to loosen her sore muscles.

Reaching into the pack she pulled out a roll of toilet paper and a small bottle of hand sanitizer and walked away from the camp. Mel was stirring when she came back. Caryn dug out a granola bar, a bottle of water and her remaining water from the night's meal. She placed the full bottle and granola bar next to Mel and sipped her water until it was gone.

Mel shot up to a sitting position when she woke, confusion on her face. Swinging her head around, she took in the surroundings as if trying to remember how she got there. She always woke with a start, taking several minutes to remember where she was. She rubbed her face and twisted her trunk from side-to-side to loosen up.

With a sudden thought, Mel looked around their camp with a purpose. "Tara hasn't made it back?"

Caryn shook her head. "No."

"Damn!" She stood and circled the camp.

"Maybe she couldn't find us."

"Yeah, maybe." Mel continued trying to peer through the trees.

Returning to her pack, she dug inside and came out with her roll of toilet paper. Noticing the water and bar, she said, "Let's eat on the move. Be ready to go when I come back," her voice hard, the words sounding angry.

"Okay."

Mel stopped and looked at her. A twinge of regret hit her. She shouldn't take out her worry about Tara on Caryn. Noticing the empty bottle, Mel said, "Where's your bar?"

"I-uh, I was up early and ate already." She busied herself rolling her blankets to avoid making eye contact.

"I hope you did. Remember what I said last night. I need you strong and able to keep up. You can't do that without fuel."

"I know." She placed the roll on top of the pack and tied it in place. She looked back and Mel had gone.

Ten minutes later they started the day's walk. The morning pace was brisk. Caryn worked hard to keep up. Thirty minutes later they hit a dirt road. Mel held up a hand stopping at the tree line. Caryn moved up. Across the road was a cornfield that stretched farther than the eye could see. The road to the left was long and flat. To the right, the lane disappeared behind several small rises and dips.

"Do you see anything?"

"No, but if we cross this road, we'll be in the open. We can be seen from a long way. We'll have to run across as fast as we can. Can you do that?"

"Of course."

"Okay, get ready." Mel gazed left and right once more. "Go."

The two women raced across the road toward the safety of the cornfield. On the far side of the dirt track, the ground took a slight dip. Caryn caught the edge and went sprawling. Extending her arms to break her fall, she hit the ground and rolled until the backpack ceased her momentum.

She turned on her hands and knees and tried to stand. Mel ran back, grabbed under her arm and pulled her to her feet. Caryn ran off balance. Mel let go when they entered the cornfield, and Caryn stumbled to her knees.

"Damn girl, I can't take you anywhere." She meant it as a joke, but it didn't come out that way.

Caryn fought the tears back. "I'm sorry. I tripped on something." She started to get to her feet but became aware of pain in her left hand. Looking, she found a long cut running across her palm, her hand slick with blood. She stared at the wound unable to move.

"Here, get up and let me help you with that." Mel peeled off her pack, took out the toilet paper and gently wiped away the blood, exposing the wound. The cut stretched about three inches. Mel opened her water bottle.

"No, Melissa, we can't afford to waste water."

"We can't afford for you to get an infection either." She poured some water on the cut and wiped it again. "This may hurt. You've got some dirt inside. I'm going to try to get it out. She held the hand tight and dragged the paper inside the cut. Caryn winced and did a dance.

Done, Mel examined the cut closer. Finding two spots that needed more work she poured more water and finished cleaning. Taking the first aid kit out of Caryn's pack she applied antiseptic cream, gauze and tape. "That should do it for now. We'll check it later. Maybe you should take one of these antibiotics."

"We don't know what they're for, though."

"Does it really matter? I mean, it can't hurt, right? If it helps a little, it still helps." Mel handed her a pill and the remaining water. Caryn took the pill and finished the water.

Commencing their trek through the field, neither woman was tall enough to see over the stalks. As they went, Caryn reached into her pocket and pulled out a plastic grocery bag. She tore ears of corn from the stalks and filled the bag. Her hand throbbed, but she pushed the pain aside.

They walked on into the early afternoon until Mel called for a break. They slipped off the packs. Mel flattened some stalks to give them room to sit while Caryn readied lunch. That's when someone, or something, crashed through the stalks at high speed coming straight toward them.

Chapter Three

"STAY DOWN," MEL SAID. SHE DROPPED TO ONE KNEE AND aimed the rifle in the direction of the noise. She tensed as who or whatever it was came closer. Scooting back to have more room to shoot, a drop of sweat dripped from her forehead. Glancing at Caryn, Mel was surprised to see the woman wasn't whimpering or crying.

As Mel brought her eyes back to the sights, a dark figure burst through into the small clearing. Mel tightened her finger on the trigger and was less than a half-pound pull from firing before she realized the intruder was Tara.

All three women gasped. "Oh, God, Tara, I almost shot you." She stood and moved toward her. As she got close, Tara's eyes rolled up and she fell. Mel managed to catch her before she hit the ground and lowered her. Blood covered her ACUs. They were still wet.

Mel lifted the uniform top, exposing a gash in Tara's side. She'd been stabbed. "Caryn, quick, I need the first aid kit."

Caryn crawled forward with the kit. Mel grabbed it and flung the lid open. Caryn gazed at the wound. "Oh no, Tara … is she …?"

"I need your help." She caught Caryn's eyes. "Can you do it?"

Caryn swallowed hard and nodded.

"Wash the wound for me."

The two women worked fast. With Mel's steady lead they had the wound cleaned and disinfected as best they could with what they had. Mel rolled Tara on her side to see the back. "She's cut all the way through. Lucky it's a slice on her side and not a puncture. That would be harder to deal with. She needs stitches, though."

Caryn dug through her pack, pulling out a needle and thread. "You can use this but it's black thread."

Mel took the spool and attached needle. "Well, I guess it's a good thing she's black then, huh?" She threaded the needle and turned Tara on her belly. "I'm going to start on the back, but I need your help."

"Ah, okay," her reluctance clear.

"Hey, this is important. It's a good way for you to work on being brave."

"What do you need me to do?"

"Pinch her skin together. Yeah, right there."

Mel inserted the needle and pushed it through. Tara groaned. The long needle had to be pushed through to be pulled out the other side. "I never sewed before." Her hand shook as she lined up the second stitch. "Should I make the stitches close or farther apart?"

"I think if you want to get it to heal evenly they should be tight."

"But what if she gets an infection inside? Wouldn't it be better to have a few stitches so we can open her up if necessary?"

"It's thread … if we need to open her up, it's easy enough to cut. I think it should be tight so the wound heals better. Plus it will keep out the air and any bacteria if she's closed up completely."

Mel nodded as she lined up the next entry point. "Good thinking." For some strange reason, she couldn't stop the needle from shaking. She lowered her hand for a second and blew out. What was wrong with her? It couldn't be the sight of blood, she'd seen enough that it shouldn't bother her. The reason came to her: her concern for Tara.

Caryn noticed and seemed to understand. As Mel touched the needle to the edge of the wound, Caryn covered her hand with a gentle touch. "Why don't you let me do that?"

Instant relief flooded Mel. "Are ... are you sure you can?"
"Yes. Let me do it."
She took the needle and with an expert touch guided the needle through and out.

By the time they turned Tara on her back her groans had become louder. Afraid she would wake, Caryn increased her pace. Five stitches later Tara's eyes flew open, she gasped and grabbed Mel's wrist. "What the hell are you doing to me?" Her milk chocolate skin glistened with perspiration.

"Relax Tara, Caryn's stitching up your wound."

"I feel like I'm on fire."

"I'm sure you do," Caryn said, "but I've got about eight more to finish. You think you can take it?"

"Please, girl, who you talking to?"

Mel smiled. "All right then, Butch, here we go."

Caryn shoved the next stitch through. Tara inhaled sharply, her eyes growing larger. She sucked and blew air in short blasts as though practicing Lamaze breathing. With the next stitch, her hand shot out and found Caryn's thigh. She squeezed, digging her nails in. Caryn fought hard not to cry out. She moved her leg to shake off the grip, but nothing helped.

"Halfway done, you want to rest?"

"Get it finished."

"Yes," Mel said, "please hurry." She wiped the sweat from Tara's forehead and smiled. "Tara, you might want to release your grip on poor Caryn."

"No way ... if I hurt, someone else has to share my pain." To emphasize the point she squeezed harder.

"Ah! I'm going as fast as I can," Caryn said with a gasp.

Five minutes later, Caryn said, "I'm done, I just have to tie this off so the stitches don't get loose."

Using the point, she lifted the last stitch and pushed the needle through. Making a loop she made a knot and pushed it down as close to the skin as possible. Leaning forward, she bit the thread free. Running a hand along the wound, she said, "That's the best I can do."

"Nice work, Dr. Caryn," Mel said.

Caryn shook two pain pills from a container and gave them to Tara with a bottle of water. Tara swallowed the pills and the whole bottle of water in one long drink. Putting her hands behind her head, she lay down and closed her eyes.

"So, what happened?" Mel asked.

"They were faster than I thought. They outflanked me. Eventually, I had no choice but to stand and fight. They weren't trying to kill me. I was no good to them dead. That gave me an advantage because I sure as hell had no such restrictions. They tried closing the circle around me and I ran at one and cut him. It allowed me to break free, but one of the men tackled me. I punched him in the throat. Some guy jabbed me with a bayonet when I tried to get up. As you can see, I wasn't punctured so I got up and stabbed him."

She took a few deep breaths. "I took his rifle and ran. A coupla guys kept chasing me. I fired to keep them back, but it was the only bullet the guy had, can you believe that? So when the next fool got close, I threw the rifle at him like a spear. I don't know if I hit him because I ran like mad, but they stopped chasing me. A few of them fired at me, but that was the last I saw of them."

Tara released a long breath. "I'm so tired. I need a long nap."

"I suppose we can hang here for a while but, Tara, we're running low on everything. We have to start looking for food and water."

"Okay, but I need to rest. Give me an hour then wake me."

"All right."

An hour later it was apparent an hour wasn't enough. They couldn't wake Tara.

Chapter Four

"SHE'S GOT A FEVER," CARYN SAID. "WE SHOULD'VE MADE her take an antibiotic before she slept." Pulling out a pill, she said, "Melissa, can you crush this?"

Mel took the pill and looked at it. "How small?"

"As fine as possible." Caryn took out three chewable baby aspirins and placed them under Tara's tongue while Mel ground the antibiotic between two knives without much success. "I can't crush it."

"That's okay, put it on her tongue." Caryn opened Tara's mouth and pulled her tongue out. Mel placed the tip of her knife above Tara's tongue and scraped off the crumbled drug. Very carefully Caryn poured some water on the tongue. Tara coughed and woke. She peered through glassy eyes.

"I don't feel good." Her body shook. She was burning up, yet said she felt cold.

Caryn dabbed the sweat from Tara's face. "You rest, we'll watch over you."

Tara didn't reply, but slowly her eyes closed. Two minutes later she was asleep again.

"Now what?" Mel asked.

"I guess we stay here for the night. I don't think we should move her." She wiped Tara's face again. "If she was attacked last night and only finding us now, that means she's been bleeding for a long time." She lifted Tara's legs and slid her backpack underneath. "She's lost a lot of blood and might be in shock." Unrolling both blankets, Caryn covered the injured woman. "I'll bet she hasn't eaten since we were all together. She's weak. We'll have to watch her."

Mel glanced around the small opening. "Okay, I'm going ahead to see if I can find any food or a place to stay while Tara heals."

Caryn nodded but didn't look happy about being left alone.

Mel read the look. "I won't be long. I promise. We need food and have to know what else is around."

"I know. Go. We'll be all right."

Caryn sat back wrapping her arms around her neck. Her eyes glazed over and she began rocking. She was afraid enough already without being left alone. Falling into a trance, Caryn had no desire to look around for fear she might discover someone there. She'd rather not know if she was about to die.

MEL WALKED ON MOVING THROUGH THE STALKS, TRYING NOT to move them much. Someone would have to be high enough and actively looking to see the stalks move, but she didn't want to take a chance, her thoughts focused on the events of the past two days. There had been one problem after another. The men who chased them, being stuck as Caryn's protector, and now, Tara getting injured kept them from making any real progress.

Of course, who knew where they were going? The decision to move east had been Tara's. She insisted there was an air national guard post somewhere in this direction. There she hoped to find a helicopter allowing them to travel farther and faster and find other outposts that might be safer than the ones they'd run across so far.

Mel was so lost in thought, she walked for longer than intended. Jumping as high as she could to see over the stalks, the only thing that came into view were trees about a hundred yards off to the right. She altered her course. Aware she should be starting back, Mel decided she had to see what was around the trees first.

Perhaps thirty minutes later, the field ended. She poked her head out and scanned the area. Almost straight in front of her was an old farmhouse. A large wooden barn, a silo and a good-size outbuilding stood behind the house. A small windmill between the structures wound in slow continuous circles. To the right, thirty yards distant from the barn were the woods. Another cornfield went off on the far side of the house. A long gravel driveway ran from the backyard to the street to the left.

Mel watched for signs of movement. Taking a long scan, she ran across the driveway to the house, stopping alongside. There she waited to see if anyone responded. Sliding along the house toward the back, the windows above her were too high to see into. She climbed the rear steps, squatted below the door's window and duck-walked forward. At the door she rose and peeked inside. Nothing moved. Feeling braver, she leaned over the porch railing to peer in the back windows.

The interior was dark. She glanced behind her, rifle ready, as a sudden chill ran up her spine. No one moved to intercept her. After a long moment, she relaxed a bit.

If no one was inside, this was a great place to stay until Tara recovered. Mel walked around to the opposite side of the house. Without going inside, Mel was as sure as she could be the house was empty. Her mind made up she began the trek back. Not sure how far she'd traveled, her excitement made the return pace much quicker.

A sudden rustling, not far to the right, made her stop and duck. Whatever it was, advanced fast. A large deer broke into view, not eight feet away. Startled, Mel lifted her rifle and squeezed off a shot, too late and hurried to be on target. The shot missed and the deer disappeared.

"Damn, girl, what were you thinking?" She looked around to see if the shot had drawn attention, not that she could see anyone approaching. She decided not to wait to find out.

By the time Mel found her way back to the clearing it was late afternoon. She was surprised when she burst into the opening unexpectedly. Caryn, however, was shocked. The poor woman sprang to her feet and backed away doing a strange dance.

"Oh, dear lord, you scared me?" She was breathing so hard Mel thought she might hyperventilate.

"I kinda scared myself. I didn't expect you to be right there. I thought I still had a ways to go."

Caryn let her calm down before saying, "Well, I'm glad you're back. I was worried. I heard a shot."

"That was me. I saw a deer. It was a dumb thing to do. If those men are still out there, it'll lead them here. How is she?" Mel asked.

"About the same. She moaned a few times but hasn't woken. I can't tell for sure but the fever seems the same."

"I found a great place for us to stay. It's about an hour and a half from here. Do you think we can move her?"

"I suppose, but how? She can't walk."

Mel gave that some thought. "I know. Put her on the blankets and we'll carry her like she's on a stretcher."

"That's a good idea. But it will be dark soon."

"Then let's hurry. We should get as far as we can."

Caryn slipped on the backpack. Mel took the blankets off Tara and spread them out next to her. The two women took hold of Tara's arms and legs and lifted her to the blankets. Then, grabbing two corners each, they lifted their wounded comrade. Caryn stumbled forward a step from the weight but regained her balance.

The walk was slow. Several times Caryn called for a break. As the sunlight faded it was clear to Mel they wouldn't make it halfway to the farmhouse. As dark settled, unable to see where they were going, they made camp. Too exhausted to open cans, they decided to have water and granola bars. Caryn gave Tara more pills. This time, she didn't wake to swallow them. Caryn left them under her tongue to dissolve.

Unable to do anything more for their friend and exhausted from the hike, the two women were quick to sleep.

Chapter Five

"MYRON, SERIOUSLY, BE QUIETER," REBECCA SAID.
Myron hung his head, embarrassed. "Sorry," he whispered. He hated it when Becca corrected him. In truth, he'd been daydreaming. Myron didn't have the focus that Becca and her brother did, and little interest in hunting; especially when it took this long to find something to shoot.

Hours ago they parked and started the hunt. Bobby had the ridiculous idea of driving miles away from the house in search of game. He woke Myron before the sun was up, a sin as far as Myron was concerned. No one should be up before the sun. It was an insult to the great ball of fire in the sky. But then, Bobby played the race card. "Your Indian forefathers would have risen earlier than this. They would've thanked the sun for another good day to hunt. Now get up or we leave you behind."

As if that wasn't bad enough, Bobby added the one thing he knew would work. "What will my sister think of you deciding to sleep in rather than be with her?" Not fair! Now he was traipsing through a cornfield, half awake because Bobby had seen a deer. Hadn't that been an hour ago? That deer had to be long gone by now.

Bobby raised a fist and they stopped. He turned his head, aiming an ear to pick up any sound. His eyes squinted as if that helped his hearing. Turning to his sister, he bent down and cupped his hands. Becca didn't hesitate. Placing a foot in his hands and her hands on Bobby's shoulders, she extended upward, above the corn stalks. Her head turned scanning the golden tops. She stopped and held a spot. A breeze lifted her hair in a stream behind her.

Dropping down she said, "She's about thirty yards in that direction." She pointed. Bobby nodded. "We'll move parallel to get closer then cut across to get ahead." He looked at Myron. "Complete stealth now, all right?" Myron's face flushed, but he nodded. Being singled out upset him, but he didn't complain. That would make him look weak. Instead, as Bobby and Becca moved toward the deer, Myron determined to be as quiet as possible. He would not be responsible for losing the deer. At least he wouldn't have to kill the animal. Both Bobby and Becca carried rifles, handguns and knives. He carried a longbow and quiver and a knife. Though he wore a handgun it was at Becca's insistence. He hated firing it so never took it out of the holster. He had never been able to kill any animal he tracked, not until several months back. Myron had drawn and fired without thought when a crazed killer was about to end Becca's life. The arrow took the man in the throat. Myron had been emotionally upset, but not as much as he thought he'd be. After all, he didn't really have a choice.

Now, with a half dozen kills, Myron was more confident that he could take a life, if necessary, but only then. The deer wasn't a threat to anyone, so he wanted Bobby or Becca to have the honor.

Twenty minutes later the pace slowed. Bobby lifted his fist again. He looked back, confusion clouding his face. Leaning back toward Becca, he motioned Myron closer. "There's a lot of movement coming from the left and right. Unless there's a herd out here, there might be other hunters. We need to be very careful or we might stumble onto someone. If we surprise whoever it is, they may shoot first."

"Why don't we turn around then?" Myron asked.

Becca made a face. Myron didn't redden this time. Becca lived for this type of excitement and when the bloodlust was upon her, she was as much animal as her prey.

Bobby said, "Because it could be a bunch of deer. If we can take down two or three, we'll have meat enough to last a long time. Sis, you check the sides. Myron, you watch behind us."

Myron nodded, not agreeing at all. Now that he had responsibility for their safety, he felt nervous. Staying low, Bobby moved forward again. He stopped three rows later, listened then altered course. Ahead, something big moved. Bobby signaled again. The sound of trampling stalks was close. Seconds later, he turned ninety degrees to the left. They crept along on a course parallel to the movement.

Whatever was moving was no more than eight to ten rows to the right. Bobby's sudden stop with no signal took Becca and Myron by surprise. They ducked as Bobby had. He leaned back and whispered, "There's something else moving up behind whatever this one is." He pointed toward the sound they'd been following. "They're making more noise than the first group. Either they're together, or the first group is making so much noise they can't hear the other group approaching."

Becca said quietly, "What do you want to do?"

Bobby gave the question thought. "You two stay here. I'm going to take a quick look."

Becca grabbed his arm. "No, I'm going too." Her eyes flashed with fire.

Bobby pulled her arm off his and held it tight. "I need you here in case I get in trouble. Besides, you know damn well, I can move quieter than you. This is the smart thing to do. Now, think smart."

She looked hard into her brother's eyes, drew in a breath, and nodded.

"I'll be back, but if you hear a commotion, move closer, but don't give yourselves away until you're sure you can do whatever's necessary."

Bobby didn't wait for a response, wanting no discussion. On his belly, he crawled through the stalks.

BECCA WATCHED UNTIL SHE LOST SIGHT OF HIM. WAITING wasn't in her nature. She'd do what her brother said, but her patience had limits. If he wasn't back in fifteen minutes, she was going after him. Looking back at Myron, she smiled. He returned it but his lips quivered. He was nervous. It would be better if she went after her brother without Myron. She smiled again. Becca doubted he'd argue with her about being left behind. His fingers, wrapped around the notched arrow, tugged on the bow string then released. He did that several times. Becca reached out, placing a gentle hand on his to relax and reassure him. Once more he blushed. She winked at him. As she turned her face away, the hardness returned.

BOBBY SLID SNAKELIKE THROUGH THE RIPENED CORN. HE moved forward ten stalks, then right one row. Whatever he was tracking was not moving fast. He closed the gap quicker than anticipated. Five more minutes and something dark moved in front of him. He froze and waited. Fleeting glimpses failed to reveal a clear picture of what he faced. To his surprise, the moving thing changed direction and came right at him. He drew in a quick breath and readied his rifle.

A heartbeat later a deer burst through, coming from his left side. Bobby swallowed a startled cry. The animal towered over him. Bobby aimed but didn't fire as the frightened deer saw him and bolted through the corn. As the deer disappeared, Bobby smiled. There must be a herd of deer.

A scream lifted over the stalks dispersing in all directions.

Chapter Six

THE DEER LEAPED FROM NOWHERE, LANDING NOT THREE feet from Mel. She started and backed up, still holding the blanket with Tara on it. Caryn, however, dropped the blanket and screamed, her hands flying toward her face.

The weight shift told Mel Tara was down. She was glad she'd insisted on carrying the front section with Tara's head. Even in her feverish sleep, Tara groaned. The deer, more afraid than they were, leaped as high as the stalks and disappeared.

Mel lowered Tara to the ground and wiped her face with a sleeve. "Jesus Christ!" she said. "That scared the piss out of me. I think that deer enjoys scaring me. That's the second time it's jumped out of nowhere." She looked at Caryn, who squatted with her arms covering her head. The poor woman was likely to die of a heart attack if she couldn't control her fear.

"Caryn, you okay?"

Her hands trailed down her face. "I'm sorry. It was so sudden I-I … I don't know how much longer I can do this."

"Hey! Stop talking like that." Mel moved closer and knelt next to her. "I won't allow you to give up."

"Mel, I shake all the time. I'm trying to fight my fears like you said, but I can't live like this."

Mel put a comforting arm around her. "Caryn, when life was normal did you go to church?"

"What?"

"Did you believe in God?"

"Yes."

"God saved you for a reason. If you give up, you'll never know what that reason is. Maybe this is your test for your eternal soul. For whatever purpose, he brought the three of us together. Let's see what he has in mind, okay?"

Caryn's eyes filled with tears. "Okay," wiping her eyes as Mel stood. Caryn grabbed her arm. "Melissa, thank you."

"No problem. I'm going to make a bigger clearing. You get us some lunch."

While Mel snapped stalks, Caryn crawled to Tara and felt her face. "She's still hot."

"The house shouldn't be too much farther. We'll take a quick break and start again. I think it's not more than a half hour away."

More crashing stalks behind them made Mel stop and look in that direction. She smiled, remembering how scared she had been when the deer first landed in front of her as if it had dropped from the sky. The poor creature must be trying desperately to find its way out of the field.

She sat down and accepted a granola bar and half bottle of water from Caryn. She took a bite but stopped chewing when multiple trampling sounds seemed to be coming their way. Caryn stopped eating too. Her eyes opened wide as she realized whatever was out there, was coming at them.

"It sounds like a bunch of deer. Get up in case we have to dodge." Mel backed to the edge of the clearing. Caryn ran to her but then looked down at Tara. The tops of the stalks swayed, disappearing as if a strong wind blew them, then snapping back in place. The animals were close.

"Oh, my God! They might trample Tara," Caryn said, and threw herself on top of the defenseless woman, just as three armed men broke into the clearing.

Mel's mouth dropped open. The rifle was five feet away. She ran for it, but one of the men was closer and snatched it. "Looking for this, sweetheart?"

Caryn looked up. "Oh, no!" She scrambled backward.

The man on the right had a shotgun leveled at them. He let out a loud high-pitched laugh. The man in the center had a broad smile. "Found ya!" Then he shouted. "We got 'em. Over here." He lifted his rifle above the corn as a beacon.

The three men stared without speaking. Their excitement broke into laughter, the conclusion of a successful hunt. A minute later, three more men stepped into the clearing, now fast becoming too small.

One of the newcomers, a tall man with wild black hair covering his head and face spoke, "So, we caught up with you. Thank you for volunteering to become new members of our clan."

The others laughed. He looked down at Tara. "What's wrong with her?"

Caryn found her voice. "You animals tried to kill her."

"Ah, this is the one you couldn't handle," he said to the man with the shotgun.

"Hey, Brian, she took us—"

"Shut up, Lucas."

Brian looked down at Tara. He nodded to the man on his right. "Glen, see if you can wake her."

The man stepped forward and squatted. Caryn started forward, but Mel gripped her arm hard and held her back.

Glen shook her. He slapped her face when she didn't respond. He looked up at the leader. "She's got a temperature. I don't know if she's worth the trouble."

Brian shrugged. "We'll leave her then. We've got two of them. If anyone wants to stay behind to have some fun with her, go ahead."

"No, you can't," Caryn shouted. She broke free of Mel, grabbed Glen by the shoulders and flung him away from Tara. "Leave her alone!" She stood, arms outstretched, a guardian for right.

No one moved for a moment, then Brian smiled and stepped forward. He stood inches from Caryn. Her face twitched with angst, but as afraid as she was, Caryn held her ground.

"You're her mighty protector, eh?" His smile melted away, leaving an evil image. Caryn's entire body shook. In a flash,

Brian's hand exploded against her face sending her sprawling near Mel's feet. She rolled to a sitting position, with one hand on her face, determined not to cry.

"You are ours now. You will do as we say or pay the price." He turned to the group. "She needs to be made to understand her life is no longer hers. Who wants her?"

Three men stepped forward anxious to be first. Brian held up a hand. "Not you, Lucas." He looked between the other two. "One can have her now, the other when we get back to the camp."

The two suitors looked at each other. One nodded and stepped back. The winner grinned and stepped forward.

Mel dropped next to Caryn. "Don't fight him. He'll hurt you. Let it happen and I promise we'll find a way to escape."

Two men pulled Mel away from Caryn.

Caryn tried to stand, but the man was on her. "No!" He knocked her down and began tearing at her clothes while the others cheered him on. Caryn fought as hard as she could. Her efforts earned her another slap. She couldn't hold back the tears now, but she refused to give in. The would-be rapist hit her again. "Give it up and I won't hurt you."

Mel turned her head not wanting to watch. Lucas grunted and reached behind his back. He stepped forward clutching at some unseen thing. His steps became uneven, his legs lost control and folded under him. He fell face first, an arrow protruding from his back. Shocked, the men looked and didn't seem to comprehend.

To the right of the struggle, cornstalks moved. With her arms pinned, the inevitable imminent, Caryn turned her head not wanting to look at the man's sadistic grin. Through tear-clouded eyes, she saw a form fly from the corn descending above her.

Chapter Seven

BECCA TOOK A RUNNING START AND LEAPED IN THE AIR WITH all her strength. Her face displayed the anger and hatred for what these animals were doing. She vowed they would never defile another person.

As she fell toward her target, her face held little resemblance to the beautiful woman who had entered the cornfield. Landing, her knife held high, she plunged it into the rapist's back trying to drive the blade through his body. Becca yanked him from the woman's almost naked body, as a gunshot sounded followed by a thud. "The woman said 'no,' asshole." She pulled the blade free and ripped the razor edge across his throat.

Shoving the body to the side Becca advanced on her next target, aware a third body was already on the ground. The man she stalked had his rifle leveled at her. Before he could fire, a bullet tore through his head. Gunshots filled the small clearing like rain. As the man fell, Becca stepped on his body, using it as a springboard. She bounded into the air and landed on a man firing into the stalks. Grasping his head, she pulled back, punched the blade into his belly, then again. As she dragged him backward, Becca lifted the knife upward, carving through his intestines.

Letting him fall she looked around the clearing for her next target, her breathing audible, blood dripping from her knife. Five bodies filled the area. Bobby and Myron stepped into the clearing. "Where's the sixth one?" She spun around, her body tense and ready to spring. "Don't tell me you let one get away."

"It happened, Becca. Let it go," her brother said. "Our intent was to stop them. We did. It's over."

"Over for now." She felt the adrenaline rush begin to flush from her body. Bending, she pulled the nearest dead man's shirt free and wiped her knife.

Bobby said, "Are you all right?"

Mel nodded, tentative. "Who are you?" Her hands, now free, reached slowly toward her rifle.

Bobby glanced at Caryn, who struggled with her clothes, too emotional to make much progress. He averted his eyes. "Why don't you help your friend? We'll talk afterward."

Mel nodded and went to Caryn. The shaken woman grabbed Mel's arm, put her head against it and sobbed loudly. Mel sat down and wrapped strong comforting arms around her. As she did, she took in their rescuers. Had they stepped from the pan to the fire? With the three saviors' eyes looking elsewhere, she snagged her rifle and dragged it to her.

Becca instructed Myron to strip the bodies while she checked Tara.

"What've we got, Sis?"

She lifted the unconscious woman's shirt exposing the bandage. "She's either been shot or stabbed, maybe both. Whatever, she's running a fever." She looked up at her brother. "She's got an infection. We need to get her back to Doc."

Bobby looked at the sky, surprised at how late it was. "We're a long way from the truck. Carrying her will make it longer." He looked at the other two women. The larger one was helping her friend on with her pants. The blonde was still crying, but no longer loud.

He waited until she was dressed before asking questions. To his sister, he said, "Do we have anything to help with the infection?"

"All I've got is pain killers."

"Will they help with a fever?"

Becca shrugged. "I don't know, but it can't hurt."

The two women finished. The blonde stood, still looking at the ground, the remnants of her shirt pulled around her. The other woman came forward.

"I want to thank you for helping us. We've been traveling a long time and have met few people willing to help with anything. It's nice to know some good people still exist." She stuck out her hand. "I'm Mel."

"I'm just glad we got here when we did." He took her hand. "Bobby. I-I, hmm, were we in time?"

Mel looked at Caryn. "Well, as far as that goes, yes, but, the attack was just as bad. She's not used to dealing with the type of people this new world has created."

"I wish we could've been here sooner, but we didn't know what was going on. We approached with caution." He looked at the blonde again. "Myron?"

"Yeah, Bobby."

"Let me have your jacket, all right?"

"My jacket?"

"Excuse me a minute," he said to Mel. He went to Myron and whispered in his ear. "Be a gentleman. That woman's been through enough. She shouldn't have to walk around in tatters."

Myron glanced at the blonde. "Oh, oh, yeah, sure." He peeled off the lightweight jacket and handed it over.

"Thanks, buddy."

Mel was leaning down next to Becca checking on her friend when he returned. Bobby hesitated, not sure if he should approach the shocked woman. He decided the sooner she covered herself the quicker she might recover.

Bobby approached with caution not wanting to spook her any further. He reached out with the jacket. "Ah, miss?" She didn't seem to hear. Bobby took another step. "Miss, I have a jacket for you."

Caryn lifted her head. Her eyes looked glazed. Bobby saw the tear streaks and the red swollen cheek. Then, in a blink, the woman's eyes took on the look of fright. She backed away and screamed.

Mel came running. She hugged Caryn and cooed to calm her.

"I'm sorry. I was trying to give her this jacket so she could cover up."

Mel took the jacket and placed it around Caryn's shoulders. "Here you go, honey. The good man brought it for you. Remember, there are still good men."

Caryn looked at Mel as if she didn't understand the words. "He saved us, Caryn. He's one of the good guys. He won't hurt you. Here, let me put your arms in the jacket."

Caryn didn't move, but let Mel dress her. She buttoned up the jacket and Caryn grabbed the front and pulled it tight around her.

Mel guided her toward Tara. "Caryn, Tara needs your help. You're the only one who can help her."

"Tara," she repeated like a parrot.

"That's right, Tara. She needs you."

Mel helped her squat near Becca. Caryn looked at her. Becca smiled. "Hi, honey, how can I help?"

Caryn reached out and touched the unconscious woman's forehead. "She's really hot." As if that knowledge had power, Caryn became alert. "Mel, we have to do something."

"Can you give her more pills?"

"For the fever, yes, but if there's an infection, no."

"Where were you going when we found you?" Bobby said.

"There's a farmhouse not far, that way. We were going to rest there and try to help her."

Bobby nodded. "Is there a driveway that runs in that direction?" He pointed.

Mel nodded. "Yeah, It's a long one. It ends at a street."

Bobby looked at Becca. "If you can get them to the farm-house, I'll go back to the truck and bring it there. Then we can get her to Doc."

"Wait, what?" Mel said.

Becca said, "Mel, your friend needs serious help. Help we can't give. We have a doctor at our compound."

"But, what if we don't want to go?"

"Mel, it should be obvious we're not here to hurt you. If you don't want to stay, you're always free to leave, but let's save your friend first."

"How many men do you have?"

Becca laughed. "Is that what you're worried about? We have more women than men. We also have quite a few families. Please, trust us, if only for your friend's sake."

"What do you think, Caryn?"

She looked up. "Tara needs help. She might die."

Mel nodded. "Okay. Let's do it."

"Myron, contact my dad and let him know what's hap-pened."

Myron said, "Okay," and reached behind him. His eye-brows pinched together as he turned in the opposite direction patting his back. He turned in a circle trying to look over his shoulder, like a dog chasing his tail. He stopped and the wide eyes and open mouth told Bobby the reason.

"You lost the radio?"

"I, uh, guess. No, wait, I might have left it in the truck with our overnight bags."

Bobby sighed. "All right. I'll call when I get to the truck." Nothing was ever easy; not a simple hunt, or a radio call. He hoped all the setbacks were behind them, but for some reason, that didn't seem likely.

Chapter Eight

"ARE YOU SURE YOU DON'T WANT ME TO GO?" BECCA
ASKED. "No, the fewer men around Caryn right now, the better, and might help her recover. Try to keep Myron out of sight. If you can find anything cold to put on her to keep the fever down, that might help for a while."

"Okay, brother, be careful." She hugged him.

"I'll be back soon."

He left the clearing at a jog.

Mel and Myron packed up their belongings, then picked up the blanket stretcher. Ready to go, Mel noticed Caryn standing over the body of her attacker. In a sudden burst of anger, she kicked the body repeatedly until Becca stood next to her.

Caryn stopped. She couldn't take her eyes from the dead man.

Becca said, "Get it all out, Caryn. Let it build up and take one more ferocious kick, then we have to get Tara to safety."

Caryn looked at her. As Becca watched, a transformation came over the woman. Caryn looked at the body again, wound up and delivered a solid kick. "Bastard!"

"Yep, but he's a dead bastard now." Becca put an arm around her and guided her toward the corn. "We need to hurry before it gets dark."

"Okay." Her body straightened as if a new resolve had been reached.

The caravan moved out at a slow pace. After thirty minutes Becca relieved Myron. Twenty minutes later they reached the road.

"Let's set her down," Becca said to Mel. With her burden relieved, Becca walked forward to see the farmhouse. After studying the area, she said, "Myron, carry the stretcher." She turned to Caryn. "Can you carry the front?"

"Of course I can." Her tone was indignant. "Why are you asking me that? Do I look feeble? Am I inept?"

Mel put an arm around her. "Caryn, she didn't mean that? I think she has some plan that's all."

"Sorry if I insulted you but save the attitude for when we're safe inside." She pointed at Mel. "I need you to lead them through the corn until you're even with the house." Nodding at the rifle, she said, "Can you hit anything with that?"

"Most things."

"I'll cross and make sure it's safe. If I run into trouble, I'll need you to cover me." Looking at Caryn, Becca said, "That's why I asked you about carrying your friend because she has a rifle. See, nothing personal."

Becca gave another long look at the grounds around the house. "Okay, I'm moving out now." She ran across the road in a crouch, stopping behind a tree on the other side of the driveway. Dusk had fallen, dragging darkness behind it. Becca wanted to get inside the house before she couldn't see anything.

Peering around the trunk, she picked her next safe spot and raced to it. Moving from tree to tree Becca ended twenty feet from the house. She pulled out small binoculars from her pocket and aimed them at the windows. Satisfied no one was watching she ran to the porch. There she squatted and peered through the windows. The door was locked. She'd have to break a window to get in, but if anyone was inside they'd be alerted. Becca saw no other option. She had to be faster than anyone who challenged her.

Sliding to the farthest window from the door, she used the butt of her handgun to smash the glass. She swept the gun around the frame to clear as many shards as possible then stepped through. Once inside, she ducked at the end of a sofa and waited. Minutes later, when nothing moved, Becca walked through the house.

Upstairs were four bedrooms and a bathroom. The smell hit her like a hammer when she opened the last door in the hallway. Becca pulled the door closed and gagged. Dropping to her knees, trying not to retch, she fought to draw in air and force the stench from her nostrils. Someone had died in that room. No, she corrected herself, someone was dead in that room.

Feeling stronger, Becca went back downstairs. It could've been worse. There could've been a zombie. In a pantry, she found a case of bottled water. Opening one, she drank it down. Out the back door, in the fast fading light, Becca signaled the others, hoping they could see her.

No one moved, so she put two fingers in her mouth and whistled. Seconds later the procession was in the open and moving toward the house. Becca kept watch, scanning the land around the house and the outbuildings.

She put her arms under the wounded woman as Caryn and Myron climbed the stairs. Inside, they laid her on a couch and sat down to catch their breath. Becca dug out water for each person, then rooted through the cupboards. She smiled on discovering cans of assorted soups, veggies and fruits filled one shelf in neat, organized rows. The shelf above contained boxed foods, from cakes and cornbread, to rice dishes and mac and cheese.

Back in the living room, Becca found everyone collapsed, exhausted from the trip and the ordeal. "The good news is there's plenty of food. We'll have to find a way to cook some of it or eat it cold. It's up to you."

No one spoke.

"Well, it's there when you need it. Oh, don't open the last door upstairs. There's a body in there."

Becca looked outside and found a propane grill on the ground to the side of the back porch. Grabbing two cans of chicken and rice soup with pull tabs, she poured the contents into a pot. Taking a wooden spoon, she went outside to heat up dinner. Ten minutes later she determined the propane canister was empty.

"Damn!" She looked at the soup, sighed and ate it cold.

Chapter Nine

DARKNESS SURROUNDED BOBBY BY THE TIME HE REACHED the road where they'd left the truck. He stepped onto the cement and headed east. The truck shouldn't be far ahead. As he walked Bobby replayed the events of the day. They started off hunting deer. Instead, they bagged three women. But that was all right. They might have struck out on finding food, but they saved three people.

A sound filtered through his thoughts. Bobby stopped to listen, not sure what he heard. As a precaution, he moved to the side of the road, just outside the cornstalks. After minutes passed he felt foolish and started walking again but stayed in the long grass next to and below the pavement. This time, he stayed focused. A minute later someone barked out a laugh, followed by a second, high-pitched laugh.

Bobby ducked and froze. At least two people were somewhere in front of him. Were they near the truck? He waited and heard what sounded like the creak of a door opening. Fifty yards away the interior light flashed on, extinguished by the closing door. The brief illumination silhouetted three forms. A flash of panic shot through him. They were stealing the truck.

Staying crouched, Bobby moved faster. As the engine coughed, he broke into a run. The engine sparked again without catching, but the third time the motor turned over. Red brake lights flashed twenty yards in front of him. He couldn't let them take their ride. The wounded woman depended on Bobby getting her to Doc.

Climbing to the road, he increased his speed as the headlights flicked to life. The truck pulled forward. "No!" Bobby said. He pulled up and aimed the rifle at a rear tire. But without a spare, the truck was unusable. The truck increased speed. Bobby kept running, closing the distance. But, as he grew tired and the truck accelerated, he stopped. Trying to steady his breath, he lifted the rifle, took careful aim at the driver's head through the rear window and fired. However, as he squeezed the trigger, the truck made a sudden left turn. The bullet whizzed past without making contact.

He felt hope fade but took up the chase again. Leaving the road on the opposite side, he cut diagonally across the corner of land toward the intersecting road. Ahead, the taillights shone brightly against the blackness. The two red dots seemed to float in mid-air moving away at a steady pace. The gap grew, yet still Bobby gave chase. Two blocks away, Bobby was about to give up when the brake lights flashed on. He slowed his pace and watched as the truck turned left, the lights disappearing. The thieves had either turned onto another road, in which case the truck was gone or, they turned up a driveway, where Bobby had a chance to take the truck back.

Keeping his eyes on the approximate spot where the truck vanished, Bobby increased his speed again. He passed several houses, giving him renewed hope. The distance melted away. He walked rifle in hand and ready as he drew close. He moved to the right to be across the street from whatever he might find. As he did, he passed a sign that said, County Road F. His heart sank. A crossroad. He stood staring down the darkened length. No red dots danced before him. His heart and hopes sank. Now what?

He decided to continue down the same street in case he'd been wrong about where the truck turned. A short distance further, across the street, he could make out a driveway. Bobby crossed to it. With only dim starlight above he couldn't see a house anywhere close. Bobby kept walking down the street. A few minutes later he stopped.

Bobby exhaled a long breath. The truck was long gone by now. He turned to walk back, his head hanging. It would take the rest of the night to find Becca. By that time, the wounded woman might be dead.

As he passed the driveway, a quick flash of red froze him in his tracks. He stared up its length. The lights did not show again.

Had he imagined it? No matter, he was going to check it out anyway.

Holding the rifle waist high and pointed forward, Bobby advanced at a slow steady pace, his eyes trying to pierce the darkness ahead. If he couldn't see them, they couldn't see him. The driveway apparently went a long way. After a while, a large, darker shadow loomed off to the right. The closer he got the more he realized the structure was most likely a house.

The voices made him freeze, then drop to the ground. In front of him was another smaller building he guessed was a garage. Since that was where he saw the lights, Bobby headed there.

The voices sounded louder. Realizing they were coming toward him, his pulse quickened. Bobby rolled off the drive into the grass on the side. There he aimed the rifle in front and waited.

"I'll check it out in the morning," someone said.

"That's cool. I can't believe someone left it there," a second man said.

A flashlight sparked to life, the small cone danced along the path twenty yards in front of him.

A third said, "That means there's someone alive out there somewhere."

The first man said, "Maybe we should go looking for whoever it is."

"Whatchu gonna do then? It's hard enough to find food for us. Best just to let them be."

"Yeah, but what if it's a woman?"

The light turned, moving away from him. The men laughed. One made a comment Bobby couldn't hear.

The men walked away, following a path that led toward the house, their voices trailed off in the distance. The light played on steps and a front porch. It stopped for a moment, illuminating the front door. Bobby waited, giving them time to get inside. Thinking it safe now, he climbed to his feet and moved forward. Twenty-five yards further, he was outside the garage. A sliver of light seeped out through a covered window. A generator rumbled someplace close, explaining the light glowing inside.

Bobby slid along the wall until he was next to the window. He peered through the slim space the piece of cardboard didn't cover.

It took a moment for his eyes to adjust before Bobby saw a man in mechanics coveralls, leaning over the engine. His back was to him so Bobby took the opportunity to scan as much of the interior as he could. On a work bench across from him sat their three backpacks. Each one held extra food and water as well as a change of clothes. They also held extra ammo and various equipment they might need for an extended stay.

He had been foolish to allow his sister to talk him out of carrying the bags. "We're only going for a short hike," she had argued. "They'll just slow us down and make too much noise going through the stalks." Yeah, like big foot Myron didn't make enough noise anyway. The thought of Myron brought him back to his big blunder. Bobby leaned sideways and scanned the bench. To his great relief, he saw the two-way radio.

Bobby remembered telling his father they might be gone overnight so he wouldn't be worried about them not returning until the next evening. No help would be coming. He was on his own and a woman's life depended on him. Now, he had to find a way to get the truck back, without getting killed.

Chapter Ten

AFTER EATING HER COLD MEAL, BECCA WENT INSIDE. THE blonde was kneeling next to the unconscious woman. The other woman sat on the sofa at a ninety-degree angle to the first, her head in her hands. Myron was exploring upstairs.

"How's she doing?" Becca asked, trying to recall her name. The blonde, Caryn, that was it, turned.

"Not good ... she's burning up and I can't help her."

The other woman lifted her head to listen.

Becca had an idea. "Myron!"

"Yeah,"

"Check the bathroom for any medicine."

"K."

Becca went into the downstairs bathroom. She found Band-Aids, toothpaste, nasal spray and all the normal things one might find in a medicine cabinet, but nothing that would help the ailing woman.

From there she searched the kitchen. In a cupboard, she found vitamins, aspirin, and various bottles of supplements. Becca took four aspirin and one vitamin and ground them to powder between two tablespoons. She took them to Caryn. "Put this under her tongue." The woman took the spoon. While she opened the injured woman's mouth, Becca lifted her shirt to look at the wound. Pulling off the bandage, she studied the angry red skin that surrounded the cut. A faint odor rose to her nostrils. She crinkled her nose.

"We're gonna have to reopen this," Becca said. The other women looked at her. "I'm no doctor, but we need to disinfect the wound somehow. It stinks like she's rotting. We need to find any disinfectant we can. Do you have anything?"

"I'll look," the stockier woman said. She opened her pack and sifted through it. Becca went back to the kitchen. In a knife block, she found a pair of scissors. Returning to the woman, who Becca now felt was near death, she carefully snipped the threads. As she pulled the wound apart, she turned her head. The smell almost made her gag. Pus seeped out. Becca ran back to the kitchen as much to get paper towels as to breathe clean air.

Behind her she heard, "Oh Mel, what are we going to do?"

If Mel responded, Becca didn't hear.

Returning, she wiped the pus away, as Myron descended with an armful of medications. He placed them on the table next to the sofa. Caryn rummaged through the pile. "Iodine," she held up a bottle. "Here's a spray disinfectant."

"That's good," Becca said, "but I need something to clean this wound out with. We can spray that afterward."

The other woman spoke up. "We can use soap or we have some anti-bacterial cream."

Becca thought. "Let's use both. I'll use the soap, then the iodine, then the spray and the cream." She looked from face to face. "Well, it can't hurt, can it?"

Since all she got was shrugs, Becca took charge. "Myron, find something to put water in, then bring soap and a washcloth." She turned to the woman on the couch. "Can you find a thermometer and some clean white clothes, like t-shirt material?"

Mel nodded and ran upstairs. She returned, her arms filled with white t-shirts. "Must have been the only thing the man wore." She laid them next to Becca.

Myron brought the soap and towels. Caryn placed a large bowl on the floor and opened and poured water. Everything in place, Becca looked over the gathered items. "Can anyone think of anything else we might need?"

Caryn said, "What about needle and thread to sew her up?"

Becca shook her head. "I think we should leave it open for a few days. We might need to repeat the process. I hope my brother gets here fast. Myron, go upstairs and keep watch. We don't need anyone sneaking up on us." She pulled off her jacket and tossed it to him. "Take the binoculars from the pocket."

Myron nodded, took one look at the injured woman and paled. Averting his eyes, he went upstairs. Becca smiled inwardly knowing she had just done him a favor. She didn't need him fainting. Releasing a deep sigh, she put the washcloth in the water. While she rubbed a bar of soap with the wet cloth, she said, "I need someone to hold the wound open."

Without hesitation, Caryn leaned forward, gripped the two sides and pulled them apart. The odor was more pungent now, causing all of them to blow out a breath.

Becca dribbled water over the infected area, then slid the cloth inside. Holding and pulling on each end, she dragged the rough material back and forth over the wound. She repeated the process three more times. Then, using a cup, poured water inside several times. She had no idea if that would help or not. At this point, she was winging the treatment. Using a t-shirt to wipe away the blood, she blotted the flesh dry.

Next, she opened the bottle of iodine and poured some onto a paper towel and wiped it over and around the jagged edge of the wound. She wasn't a hundred percent sure of the benefits, if any, of the iodine, but would rather take the chance on it helping than not use it. For a brief second, the woman moaned. Becca took that as a good sign. Becca sprayed the disinfectant inside, then applied a generous coating of the anti-bacterial cream, figuring, at this point more was better.

Using some white medical tape, Becca artfully placed strips across the cut to hold the ends together. Taking a large gauze pad, she pressed it against the cut and taped it in place. Finished, she sat back and breathed out. Wiping her forehead, she was surprised at how much sweat had formed.

The other two women stared at her. "I guess that's the best we can do for now. Maybe we should empty this bowl and fill it with fresh water. We can take turns keeping a compress on her head."

The women nodded.

"Oh, by the way, my name's Becca."

Chapter Eleven

"HAS ANYONE HEARD FROM BOBBY OR BECCA?" MARK asked the group sitting around the dining room table. Their heads swung from the puzzle they'd been working on, to him. No one spoke at first. Caleb said, "We've all been here for an hour or so." The others nodded.

"Besides," said Darren, "we don't have a radio."

"What about when your groups went out scavenging? Did anyone report anything unusual?"

Caleb said, "No, no one said anything. You want me to ask?"

"How many teams did you send out today?"

"Three. All to the north. The hauls are getting lighter. We're finding less and less usable stuff. Some canned food, but little ammunition or medical supplies."

Mark knew that would happen at some point. Early in the Event, as the massive and mysterious deaths across the nation was now called, collecting supplies had been easy and plentiful. Whatever survivors were left all did the same things: hunt for food and clean water. That hunt was endless. He couldn't begrudge them their share of what they needed to survive. However, this community was growing and their needs were greater than ever. That was why he insisted on growing their own produce and moving toward more natural sources of energy, like windmills and solar panels.

Only time would tell if it would be enough. The trick was to stay ahead of the problems and try to anticipate their needs. They may never have enough to feel comfortable for a long period, but he knew, now, and for the near future, barring any unforeseen catastrophe, they were safe. He'd know more when winter hit. If the community survived the first winter after the Event, he'd have more confidence in their long-term survival.

"Shift your teams west tomorrow. Increase to four teams and add an extra person to each. Tell them to be alert for any ..." He paused. "Well, for anything out of the ordinary."

"Okay," the tall, young man said. "You think there's a problem?"

"Not sure, but I'd rather err on the side of caution."

Caleb nodded and moved off to carry out his orders.

Mark stood frozen, staring at, but no longer seeing the young men and women around the table. It was late, Bobby should have called by now. His thoughts went back to the conversation between him and his son before they went hunting.

"No matter what you decide to do, you call – understand?"

"No problem, Dad. Even if we come home instead of staying the night, we'll call."

Mark nodded at his son. Nervous about letting them go, he had to trust they knew how to take care of themselves. They'd certainly proved they could months before, battling first a crazed killer and then a roaming army. But he was their father, he was entitled to worry.

Becca had come around the truck and given him a hug. "Don't worry, Daddy, I'll watch out for the boy."

He'd snorted. "And who's going to watch you?"

"That's why I brought Myron."

"Now I am worried."

"Shhh! Daddy, he might hear you. You know how insecure he is, especially around you."

Mark had looked past his daughter, through the truck's windshield, where the wild-haired young man with the black-rimmed glasses sat watching them. He'd smiled and waved at the boy. Myron had given a tense smile and tentative wave in return.

Myron was a few years younger than Becca and obviously infatuated with her. He followed her around the camp like a puppy. His daughter insisted nothing was going on between them; he was just a friend, a very good friend who had saved her life. Not that he should worry about whatever relationship they had. He knew his daughter well enough to know if he said "No," she'd go out of her way to show him who was in charge of her life.

He couldn't help but worry, she was and always would be his little girl. Even though that little girl had killed more people than he'd ever know. He worried about that too. But she was twenty, hmm, twenty what? A brief stab of panic lanced through him. Had he missed her birthday? Was she twenty-two now? What the hell month was it anyway? Keeping track of days was so much more difficult now.

Performing a mental calculation, he relaxed. October. Her birthday was in October, still a month away.

"Daddy! Stop." She must have mistaken his faraway look for concern. "We'll be fine." She planted a kiss on his cheek and jumped in the truck next to Myron while Bobby took the wheel.

Mark went to the driver's side window. "Did you check the batteries?"

Bobby gave an exasperated look. "Dad! We'll be all right."

Becca winked at him. "He's such a child sometimes, but I'll take good care of him. Don't worry, Daddy. I love you."

"Love you, too," he said, as Bobby backed down the drive.

Mark had waved long after they were gone, unable to put aside the feeling of dread that descended over him. He shrugged it off. They were going hunting for much-needed winter meat. He had no reason to believe they were in any danger. In fact, since their skirmish with that invading army, there had been no sign of danger from anywhere.

Then why hadn't he been able to shake the feeling of dread?

Now, he stood remembering the truck disappearing from view, afraid it was the last he'd see of his kids. Why hadn't they called?

Lynn came into the room. "Lynn, have you heard from …"

"No, they haven't made contact. I've had the radio with me the whole night."

"Damn! I told them to call no matter what they were doing."

"They probably just forgot." She put a comforting hand on his arm and smiled into his worried eyes. "They're all right." She handed him the radio. "Maybe they're out of range. You told me yourself that even though they say the range is fifteen miles, they probably only have an effective range of eight miles."

He smiled. "I did say that didn't I?"

She lifted on her toes and kissed his cheek. "Call Juan to do a relay," Lynn said, then went into the kitchen. Mark walked through the living room and out the front door. On the porch, he looked into the darkness in the direction his children had driven and lifted the radio.

The Perez family lived about five miles to the southwest of where he stood. Many of the families in their small community lived within a five-mile radius. Each household had two-way radios, walkie-talkies, for emergency use. To Mark, it was an emergency now.

"Juan, this is Mark." He waited a few seconds and tried again. "Juan, pick up, it's Mark." Again he waited, but this time, before he could try again, a groggy voice responded, "Mark, what's the problem?"

"Juan, did I wake you? I'm sorry."

"It's all right. What's the emergency?"

"I need, uh, I wonder if you would try to reach my kids, Bobby and Becca. They seem to be out of range for me."

"Do you think something happened to them?"

"No, no, I, uh, I ... I'm not sure. They haven't checked in, so I don't know."

"Okay, I'll call." Mark waited while Juan sent his message. "Bobby or Becca, check in, please." Mark could hear static on his end. Juan repeated the call twice more with no success. Then something changed.

"Hello ... hello ... Bobby? Hello."

Mark waited, anxiety getting the better of him. Then Juan was talking to him. "I'm sorry, Mark. No one answered." "What was that at the end? Did you get someone?" "Well, I thought I did. Someone clicked me, I thought I heard someone grunt then the connection went dead, as if someone yanked out the batteries."

Mark ended the call as the feeling of dread from earlier returned. He shook off his negative thoughts. His kids were not children anymore. They were smart and strong. He had to have confidence in their abilities. They were safe, he told himself. They had to be safe. If he didn't hear from them by the morning he was going out searching, even though he had no idea where they were.

Cold tentacles of fear wrapped around him again.

Chapter Twelve

AS BOBBY WATCHED, THE MAN MOVED TO A WALL WHERE HE pulled down a ratchet. He fitted on a socket then leaned over the motor from the front. Bobby panicked when he saw the man fit the tool to a bolt. If this man removed parts, he'd never get the truck out of there.

His eyes darted over the garage trying to form a plan. The only idea Bobby came up with was a quick frontal assault. The mechanic was twisting with quick vigorous strokes. Bobby had to act now. He ran to the front of the building and peered into the darkness beyond. If anyone was out there, he couldn't see them. He had to take the chance.

Moving to the large overhead garage door, Bobby wondered how to get it up and get inside, still maintaining surprise. He was about to try when he noticed a slim blade of light sneaking from the interior to his right. He examined the source and found a door. Bobby twisted the knob until it stopped. As gently as possible, he pushed the door.

Bobby stepped inside in a hurry, in case the door squeaked, which it did. Afraid of making more noise he left the door open. Raising the rifle, he moved behind the truck and up the driver's side. Reaching the upraised hood, he stepped away and aimed the rifle. The man was nowhere in sight. A wave of anxiety swept over him.

"Put the gun down."

Bobby risked a look. The mechanic stood near the tailgate with a shotgun aimed at him. Thinning gray hair lay plastered to his head, grease-stained coveralls hung loosely over his frame. Bobby tried to swallow, but his mouth had gone dry.

He lowered the rifle and his captor took a step forward. "Drop it on the floor."

Bobby complied. "Now drop the handgun and the knife."
Again, Bobby did as instructed. His eyes focused on the shotgun barrel as it moved closer to his face. He became aware of the other man's strong sweat and nicotine odor and turned his head to take a breath. "Come to kill old Bill, did ya?"

Bobby shook his head. "No, no, I-I just wanted to get my truck back."

The mechanic laughed. "It's not your truck anymore. You shouldn't have left it on the road."

"Okay, let me go then and I won't bother you again."

"Oh, one way or the other you won't bother me again. Empty your pockets."

Bobby didn't move. The shotgun barrel touched his forehead. "That's all right, don't move. After I shoot you, I'll go through your pockets anyway."

Bobby sighed. He pulled everything out of his pockets, set the stuff on the workbench to his right and pulled his pockets inside out. He stood with his hands up. The older man motioned him back with the gun. Bobby backed up.

The mechanic looked over the pile. He chuckled as he held up a lighter; laughed out loud when he picked up Bobby's pocketknife with the assorted tools. Then he picked up the truck key. "Ah, this will make things easier." He opened the driver's door and leaned in. Reaching for the ignition the mechanic slid in the key.

Bobby watched. His captor bent inside the truck and the shotgun pointed upward, his excitement over his findings making him less cautious, if only for the moment. Bobby lunged for the door, slamming it against the man's arm, his yelp of pain lost in the blast. The shotgun blew chunks from the ceiling that rained down on them.

Bobby slammed the door again. Keeping it pressed against the arm he twisted the barrel, ignoring the heat, until he wrenched it from the man's hands. Bobby backed away from the door. The mechanic shoved it open, holding his bruised arm. Lurching at Bobby, he reached for the barrel. Bobby whipped the gun away and drove the butt into the older man's forehead, dropping him to the floor. He moaned once then lay still.

Fearing the other men were coming after hearing the blast, Bobby worked in haste, piling all their belongings into the truck. Then he looked at the engine. He knew little about working on engines, but Bobby figured if the man was trying to take off a part, something must be loose. Reaching inside, he grabbed every part he could until he found the alternator was loose. He tried to remember if the truck would still work but decided he couldn't take the risk. He found the ratchet on a bench. Giving the bolts quick turns he tried moving the alternator and decided it was tight enough.

He tossed the shotgun and a toolbox inside, grabbed his lighter and penknife, then reached in to start the truck. It roared to life. He ran to the door he'd come in through. Peeking through, voices drifted toward him, fast approaching.

Bobby muscled the overhead door up and ran back to the truck. He jumped into the seat, slammed the door, and shoved the stick into reverse. The truck leaped backward. As it cleared the garage, two men arrived. Seeing a stranger driving they aimed handguns.

Increasing his speed, Bobby kept the vehicle moving in reverse, down the long driveway. Though difficult to see in the dark Bobby fought to keep on track. He needed to turn the truck around to get more light on the path. Two bullets punctured the windshield. He ducked on reflex and swung the wheel hard. The impact with a tree jolted him. Without looking, he knew the men were getting close. Shifting, the truck flew forward with bullets pinging into the sidewalls. One round came through the open window, passing inches in front of his face. He yelped as if hit, his mind registering nonexistent pain.

At the street, Bobby made a sharp turn and accelerated down the road. More shots followed him. He allowed a sigh of relief. However, the relief fled in a hurry when the rear-view mirror showed headlights as they gave chase.

At the first intersection Bobby cut the lights, slowed, and made the turn. Guesstimating how long he had before his pursuit reached his road, Bobby flicked on the lights and raced for the next turn. Seconds later he shut off the lights. He had a vague idea of where the next road crossed.

The lights following made the turn too. He had to take the next turn without using brakes. He took his foot off the accelerator and coasted to the next turn. Not enough speed had bled off. The turn was sharp. Bobby fought the wheel to stay on the cement and not flip over. Managing to keep the truck out of the drainage ditch, he rode on the berm for a long way before being able to swing the truck back on the road.

The pursuing headlights appeared faster than last time. They were gaining.

In the dark, Bobby wasn't sure if he could outrun them. He needed to get off the road without being seen. He came up with an idea, if the area to cooperated. He'd make a turn and with luck find a house to hide behind. If it worked, he'd be safe. If not, well, he'd be trapped and have to fight his way out. He shook his head knowing the plan could go wrong fast, but he saw no other way. His plan just had to work.

If not, he'd be forced to flee leaving the truck. "No," he said. "That's not an option."

Chapter Thirteen

MEL STUDIED BECCA AS SHE LOOKED OUT THE WINDOW. A question had been fighting for air ever since they settled in the house. With Myron upstairs keeping watch and Caryn sleeping on the second couch, now was a good time to let the question free. Before she spoke though, Becca muttered, "Where the hell is he?"

"You think he's in trouble?" Mel asked.

Becca turned. "I don't know, but he should've been here by now, unless he decided to run for the compound and bring Doc here." She pulled aside the curtain and continued her vigil.

That made Mel freeze. She stood. In the dim candlelight and flame of the hurricane lamp, Becca was a dancing shadow. "Becca, I have to ask you a question."

"Sure," she said but didn't turn around.

Mel's hand slid down the rifle barrel. "If we go to this compound, are we gonna be allowed to leave?"

Becca looked back at Mel. "Huh? Why wouldn't you?"

Mel said, "Those men who were chasing us?"

"Yeah?"

"They were from another compound. There were a lot of men, but only a few women. The men asked if we wanted to come in but one of the women behind everyone else shook her head. She looked terrified. I'm sure she was trying to warn us away. I told them we'd stop on our way back. We left in a hurry, but they sent those men to bring us back."

"Mel, we are a collective of maybe forty people. Only about fifteen of us actually live there. Everyone else has their own house. There are no fences to keep anyone in. If you don't like it, you are always free to go. The only reason I offered was because your friend needs a doctor. If you prefer, we'll just take her. She can decide to stay or leave when she's well."

"How do I know we can trust you?"

Becca turned fast, making Mel jump back and lift her rifle. Becca looked at the woman. The tension Mel felt must have shown on her face. The wild crazed look on Becca's face faded, but her tone still held anger. "Seriously? How about because we saved your lives? We've asked for nothing. Maybe a little gratitude would be nice. But, I'll tell you what … when my brother arrives you can choose to stay or go." She looked back out the window. "If the dummy ever gets here, of course."

She turned back to Mel. "I'll say this though, if I see that rifle come up at me again, you and I are gonna have a serious problem."

Mel didn't respond. She pointed the gun down and backed away. Her legs touched the couch and she sank to the floor. She was confused. Her gut told her these people were different, but she was responsible for Caryn's and Tara's safety. How much free trust could she allow?

"One of us needs to sleep. You want first or second watch?" Becca said.

Mel thought a moment. She was too awake now. Besides, she'd angered Becca, sleep might not be a good choice. Her gaze drifted to the knife hanging from the woman's belt and strapped to her thigh. The image of Becca flying through the air and cutting her assailant's throat made her shudder. "I'll take first watch."

Becca nodded and checked her watch, one AM. "Wake me at three."

"Okay." She waited for Becca to climb the stairs before taking up position at the window.

UPSTAIRS, IN THE FRONT BEDROOM, BECCA FOUND MYRON asleep on the bed. It was what she expected to see. She smiled. He was a good-looking boy, but he was four years younger than her. She liked Myron but preferred to keep him as a friend. Brushing black hair from his pale round face, Becca smiled then went to check the other rooms.

In each room, Becca looked through the window. From what she could see in the darkness, nothing moved. Taking the room across from Myron's, Becca lay down and placed her hands behind her head. Her thoughts returned to Mel. The picture of the woman holding that rifle loosely pointed at her was not one she could erase. Becca would have to watch her. Trust went both ways.

With that in mind, she got up and dragged the small dresser in front of the door. It didn't hurt to take precautions. No sooner had she closed her eyes than she heard a knock at the door. She looked around, rubbed her eyes and looked at her watch. It was nearly four.

Jumping to her feet, Becca picked up her weapons and slid the dresser from the door. Keeping her head away from the opening, Becca said, "Didn't I tell you three?"

"I let you get another hour's sleep."

Becca pulled open the door and stood facing Mel. Mel did not have the rifle with her. "Okay, you can sleep here if you want, or the next room. If I were you though, I wouldn't open the door to the right, unless you want to sleep with a corpse." She stepped from the room and stretched. "Anything happen?"

"Not that I could tell in the dark."

Becca nodded. "Well, it'll be light soon. Pleasant dreams." She said it in a tone that offered the other woman anything but. She smiled as she trotted down the stairs.

Chapter Fourteen

"STOP!"

The SUV braked to a stop at an intersection. The three men each looked in a direction. Nothing moved.

"Damn!" the driver said. "We lost him."

The larger man in the passenger seat, said, "Maybe, but I think we're chasing a ghost." He spun in his seat and looked back through the rear window. "How many houses have we passed in the last two blocks?"

The man in the back seat with the long beard shrugged. "I don't know … maybe ten, twelve."

"I think that guy ducked up one of them driveways as soon as he made that last turn. The front seat man said, "We need to go back and check each one of them houses."

The driver swung left on the cross street, backed up and drove off the way they'd come. "Where do you want to start, Mack?"

"Go back to the first house after we turned. We'll go down the street and check the houses in order."

A minute later the SUV swung up a driveway that wound through thick trees. The headlights lit up a large log cabin. They parked and got out. All three men held guns. Mack said, "Jerry, you go around to the left. Jacky, you take the right."

The two men moved off while Mack stepped closer to the front of the house. We'll find him, Mack thought. And when we do, he's gonna take a beatin'.

BOBBY GAVE A SIGH OF RELIEF. HE HAD MADE THE

PERFECT move, turning the corner at the intersection, then whipping the truck up a winding driveway that cut through trees. He parked near the house, shut off the engine and waited. Several minutes ago the racing engine of the pursuit car roared past. He'd wait another few minutes then take off in the opposite direction.

His thoughts turned to his sister and her new wards. He hoped they were all right. Becca would be worried by now. Bobby smiled, picturing her pacing and swearing.

He was about to start the truck when something caught his attention from a distance. Leaning his head out the window, Bobby concentrated as the sound grew louder and closer. A second later he knew the SUV was coming back.

Bobby got out of the truck and jogged down the tree-lined driveway. He was just in time to see the vehicle drive past. But what made him more fearful were the tires dragging in protestation across the cement. They were stopping. How did they find me? He couldn't decide if he should run back to the truck or go to the street to see what was going on. Curiosity won out. Bobby slipped into the trees and worked his way toward the street.

No one was on the road. Have they turned the corner or are they searching houses? Whatever they were doing it was time to leave. Jogging back to the truck, Bobby slid into the seat and started the engine. Just as he edged in front of the house, he saw lights cutting through the trees to the left.

Backing up and hiding on the side of the house, he slid out of the truck and went to the front corner of a log cabin-style home and followed the light trail. The vehicle was at the house next door. As the other engine shut off, with a start, Bobby realized his was still running. He ran back to the truck battling with the decision to stay or run. Either way, they'd find him. Reaching inside the cab, Bobby turned off the motor.

Pulling out the rifle and his knife Bobby stalked around the back of the house stopping at the rear corner. The houses were a good distance apart, separated by trees and brush. However, the natural barrier wasn't thick enough to prevent light from showing through. Headlights shone on the neighbor's house. He scampered into the woods dividing the two properties and approached with stealth as if hunting a deer. Halfway across, voices seeped through the trees. A few steps further and the spot-lit house came into view. He veered toward the vehicle.

Bobby stopped at the edge of the trees, behind the SUV. He looked at the house. One man was on the porch. Dropping low, Bobby crept to his pursuer's vehicle. Taking the knife in both hands, he plunged it into one tire. To him, the pop sounded loud enough to be heard for miles. He held his breath for an instant before moving on. Crawling underneath the SUV, he repeated the process. To Bobby, the escaping air hissed like a tea kettle.

"There's no one here, Mack."

Bobby froze.

"Yeah, not here either," someone else said.

There were three of them for sure. But if they had finished with their search they'd be coming back to their ride. Bobby crawled backward. Clearing the bumper, he crouched and made for the trees, although not as silent as when he came.

"What was that?"

"I didn't hear nothin'."

"Quiet, I heard it too."

The men were too close, making Bobby afraid to move. Three sets of eyes scanned the woods. Bobby lay behind a medium-size trunk. If they moved into the woods they couldn't help but find him.

The three men edged closer. They stood at the tree line not fifteen feet away. A lone flashlight flicked on and scanned the area around him. The moment felt eternal.

"All right, let's check the next house." The light shut off.

Once the three men got in the SUV, Bobby legged it. It wouldn't take them long to discover the flats. Behind him a voice shouted, "What the hell?"

Breaking into the open, he raced around the log cabin, jumped inside the truck, and started the engine. He shifted and pressed the pedal down. As he shot toward the drive-way, all three pursuers broke into the clearing, not twenty feet from the truck. Bobby slid down in his seat as the guns roared, peppering the truck like hail.

"Get his tires," someone yelled.

The bullets tore into the truck's body. Blindly, he reached for the handgun on the other seat but couldn't find it. Diverting his gaze for an instant, he almost rammed into a tree when he misjudged a curve in the driveway. The wheels rode up and bounced over the big roots before regaining the road. He'd crash on this road without using lights. He either had to slow down or turn on the lights. A bullet shattered the rear window and his decision was made.

The lights illuminated the path. Bullets pelted the truck. He weaved again following the driveway. The firing ceased for the moment. But then, something banged on the rear of the truck. Bobby glanced back. One of the men had gained the truck bed. The man steadied himself then stood. He raised the gun, aimed …

Bobby hit the street making a sharp left. The shooter took flight, sailing over the sidewall and landing on the cement road.

The truck tilted, wheels spun, but caught. The engine revved. Bobby kept an eye on the mirror, but he appeared free of pursuit. Now if he could find his sister. His fear abating, he snorted a laugh. What he just faced was nothing compared to what his sister would bring down on him for being late.

With a slim blade of light rising over the horizon, Bobby set about finding a familiar road.

Chapter Fifteen

WITH SUNLIGHT PEEKING THROUGH THE WINDOW
BECCA became more agitated. If Bobby was lost, she
was gonna make him pay. If something had happened to her brother, she'd hunt down whoever
hurt him and they would pay. One way or another,
someone was gonna pay.

Caryn stirred on the couch. She rolled over and
stretched her arms and legs hard. Rubbing her face, she
sat up and saw Becca. "Good morning," she said.

"Morning," Becca replied without looking. Her eyes
focused down the long driveway. The sunlight revealed
the street a quarter mile in front of the house, running
east and west. Except for a few trees, the ground was
open all the way to the road.

"Is something wrong?"

Becca blew out a breath. "You might say that." She
spun on Caryn. "Since you're awake, you stand watch."
She picked up her weapons and moved toward the door.

"Where are you going?"

Becca pulled the door open. As she stepped through,
she said, "To look for my brother." The door closed, cutting off further questions. She leaped from the porch and
jogged across the driveway to the cornfield. Moving inside the stalks to where she could see the area outside
the field, yet still have cover, Becca walked toward the
road.

Twice she stopped to rein in her anger. Crashing
through the stalks made her presence obvious to anyone
watching. She tried to caution herself. If Bobby was in

trouble, it wouldn't do him any good if she got captured too. Still, she moved in a reckless path until she reached the end of the field.

The east-west road stood ten yards in front of her. Becca pulled out the binoculars, aiming it along the road in both directions. Nothing moved. She sighed. Now what? She glanced back at the house, the decision about choosing weighed heavily on her. With all her being Becca wanted to go find her brother. She knew deep in her heart that he was in trouble. Bobby would not be so lost he'd be unable to find the house. Something had happened – something bad. But, other than head for where the truck had been parked, she had no idea where to start looking.

Maybe the truck broke down. No, he'd have hiked back to tell me. A chill crawled down her spine. Glancing back at the house once more, she made her choice. After checking the road again, Becca dashed across and into the small copse of trees on the other side. From there she could see the upper story of the farmhouse. She thought of Myron. Guilt swept over her, but she shrugged it off. As long as they stayed inside and out of sight, Myron and the others should be all right, at least until she found Bobby and came back.

Keeping to cover, Becca moved in the direction she thought the truck was parked. In truth, it was all guesswork. They had traveled so far in the dark to get to the house that Becca wasn't exactly sure where the truck was. She just knew it was out there, someplace. But, with Bobby's life possibly in danger, she had to find the spot. What to do from there, however, she had no idea. It wasn't the first time she made plans as she went.

BOBBY PICKED UP THE RADIO. HE WAS SUPPOSED TO CHECK in with his father if they planned on staying out overnight. Turning it on, he grunted in anger at finding the radio dead. Pulling off the back panel the reason became obvious – the mechanic must have taken the batteries out.

Slapping the unit down on the seat Bobby cursed. Knowing his dad, he was already out looking for them. But, because they had driven quite a way from the area where he said they'd be hunting, his father had little chance of finding him. Regardless of how mad his dad was, Bobby still had to find Becca, or he really would be in trouble.

With caution, he pulled the truck toward the street. He had pulled between two semis in a commercial lot so he could use the two-way radio. There'd been no sight of pursuit for more than two hours. Bobby got his bearings and turned right. The road he needed should be a few miles to the west.

Barking a quick laugh, he wondered how his sister was coping. She wasn't always the friendliest of people when she got nervous. Then whatever happy thought he had fled, realizing when he showed up, he'd be the one she unleashed on. Oh well, he had to find her first. Bobby hoped she had sense enough to stay in the house until he arrived, even if he was a few hours late.

Checking the road once more, he pulled out of the lot and turned right. A short distance later he paused at a north-south intersection but decided it wasn't the right one. At the next one he turned south, but at the next east-west cross street he stopped. So much of the land looked the same it was difficult to discern if they'd passed those fields or woods before. Guessing, he turned west.

Midway to the next intersection Bobby recognized a farmhouse. They'd passed by it yesterday. Now he had his bearings. Thirty seconds later he found where they had parked the day before. With a smile, he headed for the next cross street.

"BOBBY!" BECCA SCREAMED WITH ALL THE VOICE SHE possessed, but the distance increased. She stomped her foot. "Damn!" As she stood watching the truck disappear around the far corner, her anger at missing her brother faded. At least she now knew he was alive. Where he'd been all night still had to be answered, but knowing he was all right would make the explanation easier to swallow.

Then, with a sudden jolt, she realized where he was going. Becca turned and crashed back into the corn. If she hurried, she might be able to catch him as he turned onto the next road. She ran on, no longer caring how much noise she made. Her only concern was getting to the road before her brother passed.

Gasping, she pulled aside the last stalks revealing the road. Elation hit her. She smiled and looked both ways. The smile evaporated quickly when she saw the truck pass on the southbound road. "Dammit!" She had one more cornfield to cross before she hit the road that passed the farmhouse. Exhausted from her sprint through the first field, Becca stumbled up a slight incline to the road. She stood on the cement, hands on knees, catching her breath. "I'm gonna smack you, brother, if I ever catch you." With that, she drew on her reserves and started through the next cornfield.

Chapter Sixteen

BOBBY HESITATED A MOMENT GAZING DOWN THE
ROAD TO the left. Sure this was the right road, he
turned and drove at a slower pace looking for
signs he was right. A minute later the roof and
chimney of a farmhouse appeared through the
trees.

At the driveway, he stopped. It was a long way to the
house. Much of the approach was across open land.
Bobby studied the windows and grounds. No sign of
activity but this had to be the right place. He aimed the
truck up the drive and crept along. He stopped ten
yards up and gave the house another long look. What
if they already left? Only one way to know for sure.

"THERE'S A TRUCK COMING UP THE DRIVEWAY," MEL
SHOUTED. She lifted her rifle as if to shoot through
the closed window. Caryn came up behind Mel to
get a look. Above them, running footfalls announced
Myron was awake. His rapid steps pounded down
the stairs. "Wait!" he said, out of breath. He gasped,
"Wait!" but there was little volume.

The two women eyed him. "What?" Mel asked.

Myron sucked in air and said, 'That's Bobby. It's the
truck. He found us. It's okay." Myron went to the front
door.

"Hold it!" Mel grabbed his arm. "We don't know
who that is. It could be someone driving your friend's
truck. And with your other friend gone without a

word, I'm not feeling very trusting at the moment. I'm not letting you go out there."

Myron's jaw dropped, but he didn't know what to say. Then with a snap, it closed, and his eyes flared. He yanked his arm from Mel's grip. "That's Bobby out there. In case you forgot, he's the one who helped save you. He's here to give your dying friend a ride to a doctor, who might be able to save her life. If you don't want to go, stay here, but I'm going out there so he knows it's all right." He pulled the door open. "Get a grip!"

He stepped out on the porch and waved his arms over his head.

BOBBY SMILED AS MYRON STEPPED OUT ON THE PORCH AND waved. "Yep, this must be the place." He drove forward parking next to the house. He got out and Myron ran down the steps and embraced him. "Bobby, I'm so glad to see you. We were worried."

"Yeah, I had a slight delay, but everything's good now. Where's Becca?"

Bobby frowned when Myron paled. "Myron?"

"Well, when you didn't show up she went out to find you."

"Myron! Why didn't you talk some sense into her?"

"I'm sorry. I was sleeping. Besides, you know how Becca is when she gets something in her mind."

Bobby sighed. Yeah, he knew very well what she was like then. "How long ago did she leave?"

"Early this morning."

Bobby spun and looked around, as if his sister might suddenly appear. This hunting trip was becoming a deeper nightmare with every turn.

"Okay, let's get everyone ready to move."
The first shots were fired as they started up the steps.

BECCA FROZE. THOSE WERE GUNSHOTS. "OH, NO!"
FEARING the worst, she increased her speed. The stalks fell away, trampled beneath her. Giving no thought to the noise she made, Becca surged forward praying she wasn't too late. Ready for battle, gun in one hand, knife in the other she tore through the corn.

She hit the man from behind, throwing him forward before she could stop her momentum. Becca bounced backward, falling on her butt. In a flash, she took in the obstacle. The man rolled onto his back to see his attacker. Others moved toward her.

Becca could taste the fear but refused to let it render her immobile. Leaping to her feet, she swung the blade in front of her to keep them from advancing. Pointing the gun at one man, she pulled the trigger as someone hit her arm downward. She turned her head to the right and tried to free her arm. The taller man brought her wrist down across his knee. Becca screamed and the gun fell.

Freeing herself by slicing the man's arm, she backed away. Her right arm hung, possibly broken, but definitely on fire. The men smiled and closed in. She fought back the fear, but it became too much for her to handle. Overwhelmed, they pinned her arms behind her.

Her eyes lit on a familiar face.

His eyes sparkled. "Hey, sweetie, remember me?"

The man who had escaped them yesterday laughed. The sound sparked fury within her. Becca stomped on the instep of the man holding her, broke free, and drove forward, determined to at least take him with her when she fell. But an explosion in her head stopped her short.

Chapter Seventeen

BULLETS PELTED THE PORCH. BOBBY DUCKED AND REACHED for the door. Behind him, Myron let out a yelp. Bobby turned as the younger boy fell. Sure it would be the last thing he ever did, Bobby stepped toward Myron and grabbed him under his arms. The wounded boy screamed in pain as Bobby pulled hard and dragged him toward the door.

Just as suddenly as the shooting started, it ended. Bobby gave no thought as to why. He increased his efforts, thankful for the reprieve. Reaching for the screen door, someone pushed it open. He stepped up, into the house and hands stretched out to help pull Myron in.

He let Myron slump to the floor and writhe grabbing his arm. Mel shut the door hard as Bobby went to the front windows. He pushed the curtain aside and peered out. No one in sight.

The shots had come from the cornfield on the other side of the truck. He looked at the vehicle and with a sour eruption in his stomach realized he had left his rifle on the front seat and the keys in the ignition. Stupid. How could he have been so lax?

Glancing back, he saw Mel and Caryn tending to Myron's wound.

"How bad is it?" Bobby asked.

Mel had Myron's sleeve rolled up. She shook her head. "It's nothing but a scratch really. I'm not sure what all the whining is about."

Myron glared at her. "I got shot," he said. "It may not be much to you, but then I don't see you bleeding."

"Hold still while I wrap it," Caryn said.

"The wound is so shallow it's almost stopped bleeding by itself," said Mel.

He glared at Mel with only a slight wince while Caryn put a bandage around the bullet furrow and taped it in place. He sat up and studied his arm.

"Come on, big boy." Mel reached a hand down to help him up. "We got more important problems than your mosquito bite."

She pulled him to his feet and he held his arm. In a soft, whiny voice he said, "Doesn't mean it doesn't burn."

"Everybody get your weapons!" Bobby shouted. "We need to defend this house."

Myron ran upstairs. Mel snatched up her rifle and stood near Bobby looking out the window.

"Did you see anyone?"

"No, but judging by the amount of fire, there are more than five or six."

"Could be just one guy firing on automatic."

"I don't think so." He looked over his shoulder at Caryn standing in the middle of the room. He couldn't hide his irritation. "We need everyone helping here. Grab a handgun and go watch through the kitchen windows. We can't let anyone sneak up on us."

He watched as the scared woman did as commanded. He looked at Mel, who shrugged. Myron came stomping back down the stairs carrying his bow and quiver.

"Myron, I'm afraid that's not going to cut it in a fight like this. Use your gun."

Myron looked from Bobby to his bow and set it down. He slid the gun from his belt and came to stand next to them.

"You two keep a lookout here. I'm going upstairs. While we have a chance, you might want to move some furniture in front of the doors."

He took the stairs two-at-a-time turning toward the front bedroom. At the window, he pulled back the curtains and gave a long look into the cornfield. From this height, he could make out the heads of about a dozen figures milling in a group about ten rows into the stalks. They had trampled out a small clearing big enough to hold them all.

The numbers caused icy tendrils to descend his spine. They easily could overrun them. Why had they stopped shooting? He doubted they all had to reload at the same time. Something must have happened to make them cease firing.

They appeared to be discussing something. Perhaps how best to assault the house. Bobby wondered if, while they were distracted, he might be able to slip out to the truck.

As he tried to decide his next action, to his surprise, two of the men squared off and grabbed each other. They were face-to-face, inches from each other, and by their expressions, both shouting.

Bobby got excited. They might be able to use the altercation to their advantage. Unlocking the window, he slid up the frame and leaned out trying to hear. Although the voices reached him, the words weren't clear enough to understand.

One man, slightly taller pointed to something on the ground. His opponent, a thinner man with long hair, answered. He shoved the bigger man backward. As a space cleared between them, Bobby got a look at the thinner man's face.

"Shit!" The man who had escaped the day before had returned with friends.

The bigger man stepped forward and delivered a punch knocking down the long-haired man. He pointed again to the ground and then at the house. Bobby realized then they might be out of time. He had missed an opportunity.

The larger man gave instructions to the others and they dispersed through the field.

Bobby ran to the stairs and yelled down. "They're moving. Get ready. It's the guy who escaped yesterday. He brought reinforcements. There's about a dozen of them."

He went back to the window.

God, he wished he knew where his sister was. Well, at least she isn't trapped in the house. Maybe she'd be able to do something to help them from outside. He said a silent prayer for her safety and realized a moment later it would not be answered.

The large man bent down below where Bobby could see. He appeared to be dragging something when he stood again. A group of four men reached the edge of the cornfield and stopped. The big man gave a few more commands, lifted his burden and stepped into the open using Becca's half-naked body as a human shield.

Bobby gasped as fear ripped at his heart.

Chapter Eighteen

"YOU, IN THE HOUSE, COME OUT NOW OR I WILL KILL YOUR friend."

Bobby stepped back from the window unable to watch. Panic shut down his mind. He struggled for thoughts and breath. Tears welled and air seemed to have become scarce.

Downstairs, Mel said, "Ah, shit!"

Myron shouted, "Oh, God, no! Hey, Bobby, you seeing this?"

Bobby was unable to get a response out through his dry throat.

Myron ran up the stairs and into the room. He stopped and looked at him. "Bobby, they've got her. They, they – they might have done things to her." He sobbed and stepped closer. "What are we going to do?"

Bobby couldn't form thoughts, let alone words.

"We have to do something." The distraught boy collapsed against Bobby. By reflex alone he wrapped his arms around Myron.

The impact and contact served to break Bobby free from his fugue. "Yes, yes, we have to do something." His brain functioned again as though someone had flicked on a switch.

He pushed Myron back and went to the window. The scene hadn't changed much. The big man stepped forward a few more feet. The other three men took up shooting positions.

"I'm not going to wait too much longer. Someone in there had better talk to me."

"Bobby, you hearing this?" Mel yelled up the stairs.

"Yeah." His mind whirled for a solution. He needed time. He stuck his head out the window. "What do you want?"

The man holding Becca by the back of the neck shifted his gaze. "What I want is for you to come out and give yourselves up. If you don't, I'm going to finish what we started and take this pretty young thing right here in front of you." He nuzzled his face into her neck and seemed to inhale. "We'll all take turns with her until you do come out. If you still don't come out when we're all done using her, I'm going to put a bullet in her head."

To help sell the point, he cupped one of Becca's breasts and gave her cheek a long, slow lick.

Becca made no effort to stop the man. Her legs looked rubbery, as if unable to hold her weight. Her head lolled to one side. They must have beat her senseless.

Bobby shuddered with rage. No matter what else happens, this man will die, he vowed. He shifted his gaze to his sister. Why hadn't she fought him? Her hands and feet weren't bound.

"Well, I'm waiting. What's it gonna be?"

Finding his voice, but working to control his anger, Bobby said, "O-okay, just a minute. We have to talk about this."

"Well, while you're talking," he ripped off the remaining tatters of Becca's shirt and released her. She tumbled to the ground. "I'm going to call first dibs."

"No! No, wait. We're coming."

"You've got one minute."

"Bobby ..." Myron pleaded.

"Quiet and get a grip. You can't help Becca if you're a whimpering heap. Go downstairs and watch from there. Send Mel up here."

Before Myron could speak again, Bobby grabbed his shoulders, spun him around and pushed. "Go," he yelled. "We don't have much time before they start raping her."

Myron moved then, crying, "Ohhhh," on the way down.

Going back to the window, so far, Becca was still alone on the ground. She rolled to her side. He hoped that meant her mind was clearing. His eyes swept the area and a hurried and desperate plan crystallized.

As Mel joined him, he said, "You any good with that thing?" He pointed to the rifle.

She shrugged. "Not bad. What d'ya have in mind?"

"I hope you're better than not bad. That'll get me killed." They stood back from the window so they both saw the man and Becca. "Can you hit that man?"

She leaned forward to take a better look. "It's not that long a shot. I should be able to."

"If you miss, don't stand around looking. Keep shooting until he's down then turn on those guys in the corn."

She nodded. "What are you going to do?"

"I'm gonna give myself up. Take the shot when I get to the truck." He went to the window and yelled, "Okay, don't hurt her. We're coming out."

"Good luck."

"If we go down. You'll be on your own. Do what's best for all of you."

"Best for me is to go down shooting."

"Block the doors and keep moving. Don't let them focus on one spot. You should do all right."

Chapter Nineteen

ON THE GROUND FLOOR, CARYN SHOUTED. "HEY, HEY, HEY. They're moving out here. What should I do?"

In a calm voice, Bobby, belying the turmoil roiling inside, said, "Whatever you do, don't let them inside."

"I'm not sure I can kill anyone."

Bobby shook his head. He had no time to waste convincing the woman. In a matter-of-fact voice, he said, "The alternative is to be repeatedly raped and if you're lucky, killed. Your choice." He entered the living room. "Let's go, Myron."

"Huh?"

"We're giving ourselves up."

"What?"

"Let me rephrase that. We're going to rescue Becca."

"Oh. Well, okay, that's different."

"Tuck your gun behind your back." Bobby did the same. "Try to linger near the porch when we walk out there ... when the shooting starts, give me cover fire, then get inside when your magazine empties."

Without waiting for any comment, Bobby pushed the sofa away and opened the door. He stepped onto the porch and raised his arms high. "Okay, we're coming out."

As he stepped down he noticed Becca was lying on her stomach. He tried to make out her face as he approached, focusing on her eyes. Behind him, Myron let out a faint whimper as he stepped out on the porch.

Bobby walked toward the man who held a handgun at his side. Another man carrying a rifle stepped from the stalks to stand behind the first man. Bobby tried to keep the truck between him and the shooters for as long as possible. At the tailgate, he stopped.

The big man craned his head to the side to look past Bobby. "Tell your friend to hurry up. And where's the others? I know you had a coupla women with you. They need to come out too."

A sly movement at the big man's feet made Bobby flick a quick glance at his sister. Her hand moved ever so slowly under her. He looked up but couldn't help himself. He peeked again. Now her long slender fingers were poking into her pocket. He caught her eyes. They held his. To his great relief she was alert and more importantly, up to something. He had to give her time.

"They didn't want to come out. They're afraid." He prayed Mel was watching and locked on.

"Well, that's too bad for everyone then, isn't it?"

He raised his gun arm and Bobby stiffened thinking he was about to be shot. Instead, the man signaled toward the back of the house and said, "Go get 'em, boys."

Bobby followed his gaze. A group of men broke from the field and ran toward the house.

Now, Mel.

The leader swung the gun toward Bobby. He wanted to scream at Mel. What was she waiting for?

Before any shot was fired, Becca rolled toward the man and buried her small pocketknife into the meat of his calf. The man howled lifting his leg. The gun discharged as he did, striking the tailgate of the truck a foot from Bobby. He ducked and yanked out his weapon as more shots erupted.

A bullet ripped through the leader's chest blowing him backward in a spray of blood. The body bounced and stopped at the feet of the second man who ducked and fired wild shots at the house. The other two in the cornfield began shooting seconds later.

Becca got to her feet, and keeping low, ran for the truck. Bobby felt adrenaline pulsing: he had to cover his sister or she'd be dead for sure.

The second man noticed Becca's flight and aimed at her; Bobby squeezed the trigger as fast as he could. Several rounds struck the man, his body doing a macabre dance before falling backward into the corn.

Bobby continued to fire non-stop while backing for the cover of the truck. Becca closed the gap to safety as Bobby's magazine ran dry. He dropped behind the truck bed and changed out the mags. He popped up to fire just as Becca dove and rolled to a stop at his feet.

He helped her up and in a swell of emotion hugged her. "Thank God!" He handed her the freshly loaded handgun and turned toward the cab. Opening the door, he reached across the seat and withdrew his rifle. By the time he lined up a shot, another shooter was down, lying half out of the corn.

Bobby glanced to the rear of the house where heavy firing was happening. How much longer can Caryn hold out alone? A crash, much like a window breaking, escalated his fears. He looked at Myron, on the porch on one knee taking careful aim at the cornfield. Bobby doubted he could even see a target.

"Myron," Bobby said, "Get in the house and help Caryn. Hurry."

Myron duck-walked to the door, pulled it open and stepped inside just as the glass storm door exploded.

"Becca, I think they're being overrun in the house."

"You go. There's still one more of these bastards in front of us."

"Becca, I'm gonna move the truck. You have to come or you won't have any cover."

She looked at him for a moment then nodded. "Okay. Drive in the back and angle toward the corn. I'll jump out and stalk him from there."

Bobby studied his sister's face. He wanted to argue about her plan but knew by the set of her jaw and the spark of fire in her eyes, nothing he said would change her mind. Reluctantly, he nodded.

Sliding in the driver's seat, Bobby started the truck and shifted into gear. Keeping his head down, he moved forward, watching his sister in the side mirror. She fired a few times then grabbed the side wall and climbed into the bed.

The lone man in the cornfield shot at her, but Mel's fire made him change targets.

With Becca safe, Bobby accelerated, away from the house, driving around a large tree to face the rear porch and reversing until the tail hit the first stalk.

In one move, Becca bounded over the tailgate, into the stalks and disappeared. Bobby turned his attention to the house. One body lay face down on the porch with no one else in sight. Remembering how many men he had seen run toward the house, that meant trouble. Perhaps as many as five gunmen were now inside.

He slid across the bench seat and out the passenger door. Using the truck for cover he sighted on the house with the scope. The door was open, the windows all shot out. Someone had to be alive, though; gunshots sounded from within.

More shots. Someone screamed. Caryn! He didn't have the luxury of stealing up on the house in stealth. Caryn's shrieks were continuous. He had to move now. Keeping low he sprinted for the porch. There he lifted the rifle and aimed at the door. A rifle wasn't the best weapon to use indoors, but it was all he had.

With anxious caution he climbed the steps, never altering his sights from the doorway. On the porch, he moved to the side of the open door and risked a quick peek. Someone fired. The bullet was not directed at him.

Caryn still screamed. It sounded more like she was fighting with someone rather than the moans of pain a gunshot might cause. He stepped across the threshold into the kitchen and paused. Another body lay sprawled in the archway between the kitchen and the dining room.

A slap turned Caryn's screams to sobs. A second, much more solid blow, followed.

"Just tie her up for now until we can deal with this other asshole," a voice said.

Bobby inched closer trying to get an angle to see into the room.

"Okay, she's secure and out."

"Good, now go back through the kitchen and work down the hall. We'll outflank this guy. I'll draw his fire and you take him out."

Bobby backtracked in a hurry. A second later a man came through the archway, not looking in his direction. As he crept down the hallway, Bobby shot him in the back of the head.

As the man went down, Bobby quickstepped to the archway. There he acquired a target across the room, hiding behind a lounge chair in the living room. Bobby aimed and fired. The man fell sideways.

A bullet struck the arch inches in front of his face. He jumped back, his heart racing. Darting past the opening, he hugged the hallway wall. Two more shots hit the kitchen cabinets across from him. Sticking the rifle through the doorway, he squeezed off three shots without aiming, moving the barrel a few inches each time.

The sound of something moving reached him. Seconds later, a barrage of bullets impacted the arch, then everything went silent. No one fired. He waited. Still nothing.

"Myron?"

"Yeah?"

"You all right?"

"Hell, no. People are shooting at me."

Bobby frowned. "I mean are you hurt?"

"No."

"Can you see anyone else?"

"No. There's no one else in the living room. The guy you shot was the last."

"Don't shoot, I'm coming down the hall."

Bobby edged forward. The stairs were to the left. Large, dark-stained wood spindles lined the steps. Behind those lay Myron.

"Cover me," Bobby said. He stepped into the living room. Another body lay on the rug in the middle of the floor. Myron had been busy and by the looks of it, had done well. He slid along the dividing wall between the dining and living rooms. He ducked and peeked when he reached the wide archway. No one.

Changing his perspective, he lifted slightly and looked again, this time for longer. One body lay behind the large wooden dining room table. Despite seeing no obvious threat, the hair rose on the back of his neck. Adrenaline coursed through his veins again as he stepped into the room and checked the few places to hide, each one several times before moving toward the body.

As he cleared the last chair, he found Caryn, her hands tied and motionless. Where had the other man gone? He looked up from the body and saw the open window. Whoever had been inside had fled.

He crouched by the window and used his scope to search for the escapee. In the distance, well beyond the barn, Bobby thought he saw a figure dart into the trees, but if it was the last shooter, he had no shot at him.

He breathed out and lowered the rifle. Another close call. He checked to make sure Caryn was still breathing. Her shirt had been hiked above her bra but that was as far as the act had gone. The sight reminded him of his sister, which in turn brought to mind the man he'd seen arguing with the leader. Was that who had escaped out the window? If so, that was twice he'd gotten away. Bobby was sure of one thing, the man would be back, but next time he wasn't going to escape.

He gently pulled Caryn's shirt into place and cut her hands free. Trickles of blood ran from her lip and nose. Her right eye was bruised and swollen. He couldn't see any bullet wounds. With relief, he knew she'd live.

He knew Myron was all right. Upstairs, the floor creaked as Mel walked around. Now, all he had to worry about – again – was his sister.

Chapter Twenty

BECCA WAS OFF AND RUNNING AS SOON AS HER FEET touched the ground. She went straight out about twenty rows into the corn before turning right. After a few rows in that direction, she slowed her pace. A few steps farther and she stopped to listen.

A cob brushed her chest. She winced and looked at the injured spot. Tiny red scratches and welts lined her torso. She stopped to examine them. The sight enraged her further. Only great willpower kept her from running, screaming straight at where she guessed the gunman to be. She wanted revenge, not just for the pain and her nakedness, but also because she had been helpless to stop the animals from doing what they wanted. She had been afraid. That thought alone enraged her further making her almost like the savages the men were. They were going to pay.

She swallowed the snarl and moved, stalking her prey. Her pace increased in time with the quick shallow breaths she expelled. She stopped again, taking deep calming draws of air before continuing. Shifting the gun to her left hand and despite the pain, she pulled open the pocketknife she'd stuffed back in her pocket when Bobby gave her the gun.

The feel of the knife in her hand, even a small one, brought a sinister smile to her bruised face. The knife was the best way for her to get her revenge. An image of the long-haired man danced before her. Becca envisioned disemboweling him, holding him upright, while the light faded from his eyes. She would enjoy that.

Though gunshots still rang out from the house, she cleared her mind, relegating all sound to distant background noise. An eerie quiet descended over the small patch of ground she concentrated on as if she'd been placed in a void, separate from the world around her. She advanced to the position of the gunman, who still fired at the house. Mel kept him pinned down. Becca hoped the woman was able to see her when she attacked. She should find some way of warning Mel, but the desire for blood was too great. She turned toward the shooter and crouched, ready to spring.

Ahead, someone moaned. Mel must have struck home. Becca lowered to the ground and crawled. The wounded man was not far in front of her.

A bullet ripped through the stalks, striking the ground to her left. She paused. The closeness of the shot sobered her. With as much stealth as she could muster, Becca stood and lifted her knife hand in the air. Even with her arm extended, Becca was barely tall enough to be seen. There was nothing she could do but hope Mel spotted her. She ducked and proceeded.

Another shot from the house hit the ground in front of her. The gunman returned fire, followed by a click. Becca recognized the sound. Now! her mind screamed. She burst through the final rows and found the man lying on his back, slapping in a new mag, and using the body of one of his fallen companions as a shield.

His eyes went wide when he saw her and he screamed. His fingers fumbled on the slide to chamber a round, his legs scrabbling on the ground for traction. Becca snarled like a wild beast and went airborne, both arms extended; the knife aimed downward like a spear point, the gun pointed forward.

Halfway to her target, Becca realized he would get off a shot before she reached him. She pulled the trigger, but her focus had been to embed the knife deep into the man.

The bullet struck the dead body beneath and to the right of the gunman.

The man jumped. Becca twisted and stretched, the blade inches from the man when he fired. Fire exploded along her side. She gasped, but her downward plunge continued. She hit the man. He shrieked on impact. Her forehead struck the man's face cutting off his screams. In a blur of exploding white light and spurting blood, Becca's vision vanished. She rolled, losing the gun, but somehow held onto the knife.

Her weight falling to the side of the man ripped the embedded knife along a rib, opening the man's torso and sending waves of agony through her injured arm. With a shudder, the man ceased moving.

Using the back of her hand to wipe her eyes, Becca yanked the blade free and crawled up to the man. She pressed the knife to his neck ready to slice through to the spine, but he offered no resistance. Her breaths hurt as they rasped in her throat. Her head pounded. She sat on top of the body trying to ease the pain in her lungs.

Becca buried the knife in the man's chest while using both hands to wipe away the blood and sweat from her eyes, clearing her vision. She wanted to spit on him, but was incapable of creating saliva. Pulling the knife free, she wiped the blood off the blade on the dead man's shirt and stood.

The pounding in her skull forced her to bend and put her hands on her knees for balance as a wave of nausea swept over her. Unable to hold an upright position Becca crumpled to one knee, placing both hands on her head as if the pain were the result of a sound wave she was unable to block out, before she blacked out.

"MYRON, IT'S ME. I'M COMING OUT. DON'T SHOOT."
"Okay."

Bobby stepped cautiously into the living room. Tara still lay on the couch undisturbed by the noise of the gunfight around her. Bobby went to her and touched her neck. A very faint pulse still throbbed. The delay might cause this woman's death.

Upstairs Mel fired again. Bobby lifted his head to listen; someone returned fire. He went to the side of the front window and peered out. No targets were in sight but he knew the threat still existed

He went to the stairs. Myron still lay across them, his head down on his arms. "Are you all right?"

Myron just nodded.

Bobby scanned the boy's body looking for signs of injury but could see none. Myron's wound was mental: killing was hard. Soldiers returning from war had posttraumatic stress disorder. Myron must be suffering in the same way. He couldn't treat or field dress that sort of injury, especially not here, not now.

"Come on, Myron," Bobby reached out his hand. "Becca still needs our help."

The boy didn't respond and ignored Bobby's hand, but stood. His face impassive, his haunted eyes locked on Bobby's for a second, then moved on.

"Hey," Mel called, "your sister just attacked that shooter. I can't risk shooting, but I think the guy got off a shot. She might need some help."

The hairs on the back of his neck sprang to life as adrenaline pumped again. Bobby raced to the door, surprised to see Myron right behind him. "Cover me," he said and raced outside.

Without the truck in front, the only cover was a bush ten yards from the porch. Bobby dashed there. No shots tracked him, nor did Myron shoot. Bobby peeked around the bush and studied a ten-foot-wide area along the front row of stalks. A rustling caught his attention. He stared hard at the spot, but didn't see anything.

Bobby dashed forward reaching the corn and squatting. With no other sound, he stood to enter the field and heard a low groan. Concerned it had come from Becca, he disregarded all caution and burst into the rows.

Seconds later he found the three bodies. His heart leaped to his throat and a gagging sound escaped. "No!" He threw himself to the ground next to his sister. Rolling her limp body, Becca's chest looked as though it had been body-painted in red. "Becca!" The word was a sob.

He pushed his fingers against the blood-slicked flesh at her neck. For long agonizing moments he hunted in vain, then, like discovering buried treasure, an exultant cry escaped his lips. He glanced down her chest, noticing the quick, shallow rise and fall. "Oh, thank God."

Something crashed through the stalks near him. He spun, lifting the rifle until he saw Myron. The boy dropped to his knees. "Is she … is she …?"

Bobby shook his head as tears welled. "No, she's alive," he choked, "but I'm not sure how bad she's hurt. There's so much blood."

Lowering her head across his legs, Bobby peeled off his sweat-soaked shirt and wiped away the blood. As her nakedness came clean, he noticed a multitude of cuts and scratches, before discovering the bullet furrow along her side, under her arm. Balling the shirt, he pressed it against the wound.

Myron stripped off his shirt and laid it across Becca's chest to cover her. The two boys locked watery eyes.

"She'll be okay," Bobby said. "She has to be."

Chapter Twenty-One

"Lynn, I have to look for them. They should've been back by now. There's been no word and I can't reach them by radio."

"I know you have to go, Mark. I'm not trying to stop you. But you need to take someone with you. If there is trouble you shouldn't be alone."

He studied the concern on Lynn's pretty face. She was ever the voice of reason and as always, she was right. He nodded. "All right, I'll ask Lincoln if he'll go."

She hugged him. "Thank you."

He brushed back a loose strand of blonde hair and offered a half-smile. After she released him, he jogged across the street and knocked on the front door of the large two-story home. A few moments later the door swung open and a petite woman looked out with a shy smile.

"Hi, uh, Mark. Are you looking for Linc?"

"Yeah, hi, Jenny. Is he awake?"

That seemed to strike her as funny. She smiled. "Of course, silly, the sun's been up for hours now. I think he's in the garage."

"Okay, thanks."

He pivoted and trotted down the stairs. Racing along the house he approached the garage when he heard a crash. "You rotten, piece of shit, come out of there."

Mark slowed and slid the gun from his hip holster. More crashing and cursing came from within. Sounds of a scuffle. Mark moved cautiously to the open side door. There he peeked in. Beyond a pile of wood boards, Lincoln had a grip on someone below him and was trying to pull him up.

Mark stepped in to help. He cleared the wood to find Lincoln wasn't wrestling with an assailant. Instead, he had his foot planted firmly on the bottom of a sink and his hands wrapped around a plastic pipe protruding from the drain. He strained and swore, but the pipe would not surrender.

Mark holstered his weapon and laughed. Startled, Lincoln spun on Mark ready to defend.

Mark lifted his hands in peace. "Easy, big man, I'm not as much threat as that sink is."

"Man, you scared me."

"Having trouble?"

"Ah, yeah, I was trying to put in a new sink for Jenny, kind of a surprise," the one-time pro-football star said. "But the damn thing doesn't want to cooperate."

Mark walked forward and looked at the object of Lincoln's scorn. An eight-inch section of PVC stuck out from the bottom of the drain. "Lincoln, I don't mean for this to be insulting, but do you have any experience with plumbing?"

Lincoln's shoulders sagged in defeat. "Not much, why?" His tone was defensive.

"Were you trying to unscrew this pipe?"

"Yeah,"

"With your hands?"

"Well, yeah. The only wrench I found didn't fit. But it shoulda broke free or budged, a little anyway."

"This is PVC, it's glued in place. It doesn't unscrew."

Lincoln's mouth gaped. He blushed despite his color. The tall black man was clearly embarrassed. "I, uh, I, ah shit, man, I should know better than to try something constructive. I don't know what the hell I'm doing. It's just so boring. There's never anything to do. I wanted to do something nice, for Jenny."

"It's all right, Lincoln. All you ever have to do is ask. I'll be glad to help you, or teach you so you can do it. And if you need tools, we've got plenty, just come and ask."

"I know, Mark, I just didn't want to embarrass myself. I mean how hard should this have been?"

Mark laughed. Lincoln couldn't help but start laughing too. "You just gotta be smarter than a plastic pipe, that's all."

"Yeah, I guess I flunked that test." He looked at Mark, pointing to the sidearm. "So, what brings you here? Not advice on home decorating, I'm guessing."

Mark sobered. "No, Becca and Bobby haven't returned yet. They were due back today. Even if they were going to be late, they should have contacted us on the two-way. I'm concerned and want to go looking. Lynn insisted I take backup."

"And you were wondering if I'd ride along?"

"Yeah."

"You know you gotta smart lady there, right?"

Mark smiled. "Yeah, so she keeps reminding me."

"Okay, give me a minute to grab my things and tell Jenny."

"Thanks, Lincoln. I owe you."

The big man pointed at the sink. "Oh, don't worry. I'm gonna collect on that."

Chapter Twenty-Two

THE TWO MEN MET AT MARK'S TRUCK FIVE MINUTES
LATER. Lincoln carried a handgun with a backup
magazine. Mark's weapons were already in the cab.
Mark waved to Lynn standing on the back porch,
her "Be careful" and "Good luck" already said.

He slid into the driver's seat and drove down the gravel
driveway, turning left.

"Any idea where to look?" Lincoln said.

Mark smiled.

"I'll take that as an 'of course not.'"

About to cross the first intersection, Lincoln called out.
"Wait! Stop!"

Mark hit the brakes and looked where Lincoln was now
pointing.

"Is that them?"

Barreling toward them from the west was a red pickup.

"Well, that was easy," Lincoln said. "But you still owe
me."

Mark continued to watch the fast approaching vehicle.
"They're coming awful fast. Do you see anyone behind
them?"

"What? You mean like chasing them?"

"Yeah.

"No. They seem to be alone."

Mark pulled forward and turned the truck around. The
other pickup barely slowed to make the turn when it
reached the intersection, then bolted up the driveway
spewing gravel.

Mark pulled in behind them as Bobby and Myron leaped from the cab. Two unknown women sat on the bed. Mark and Lincoln got out and trotted toward them.

"What happened?" asked Mark.

"Not now," Bobby said, dropping the tailgate. "We've got wounded."

Mark froze when he saw Becca and another woman lying on mattresses tossed on the truck bed. "Dad, get Lynn and have someone contact Doc."

Bobby's sharp words set him in motion. Lincoln grabbed his arm. "I'll do it. You stay with your daughter."

Mark climbed onto the tailgate and crawled toward Becca. A simple bandage had been wrapped around her chest. He tried to remain calm, but the sight of his unconscious daughter was too much. His throat constricted, but he swallowed the sob.

"She was shot," Bobby said. "But I don't think it's too serious. Looks like the bullet just clipped her side. It didn't go in."

Mark nodded. A gathering crowd had closed in to look. Lynn's voice boomed over the talk. Disregarding names, she barked orders. "You get blankets. You three go to the barn and set it up for an operating room. You, go get my medical kit." She reached the truck and paused as she took in the bodies. "Move people. You know what to do. We've all been through it before."

So true. Mark stretched down a hand to help Lynn up on the bed. Unfortunately, they'd had to deal with wounded people far too often. However, he'd never had to see one of his own children unconscious and bleeding. The sight unnerved him.

"Mark! Mark, help me."

Again, he snapped from his anxiety-induced trance.

"Slide the mattress to the edge," she said.

"Wait, Lynn," Bobby said. "The other woman is hurt worse. She's been unconscious for more than a day. She's burning up. You should take her first."

Lynn looked from Bobby to the other two women to the body of the unconscious black woman. She stepped over Becca and examined her other patient. After a moment, she turned to Bobby. "You and your father get her to the barn, fast."

As the two men slid the mattress to the edge of the truck, Lynn looked at Mel and Caryn. "Are either of you hurt?"

Caryn shook her head.

Mel said, "Nothing serious. We'll keep. Just take care of Tara, please."

Lynn nodded and backed off the truck. Bobby and Mark carefully lifted Tara to a folded blanket and, using it as a stretcher, carried her off. Lincoln and Caleb were already moving Becca as Lynn strode to the barn.

Mark and Bobby placed the injured woman on a large wooden table where a white sheet had been spread. Two bright lights on stands had been placed at the ends of the table. Lynn came in seconds later and checked vitals. Someone had placed her medical kit on a small table next to the makeshift operating table. She pulled out some scissors and cut away the woman's clothes. The wound had festered. If the infection hadn't progressed too far, she could deal with it.

Continuing the examination, Lynn ran an exploring hand down the body, then said, "Help me roll her on her side. Bobby grabbed Tara and pulled her onto her uninjured side while Lynn checked her back. She stopped, bent, and looked closer. "She's got a bullet wound too."

Bobby looked at Mel. "Did you know she'd been shot too?"

The shock on her face was answer enough. "No, we were so concerned about the knife wound we never thought to check anything else."

Lynn probed the wound and shook her head. "This is beyond my abilities. I'll get an IV started, and do what I can, but Doc's going to have to work on her. She doesn't look good. Bobby, go get one of those IV bags that Doc left here. Mark, I need something to hang the bag from."

He nodded and went to find something as Becca was brought in. "

"Set her on that work bench and set up a light for me," Lynn ordered.

Mark passed by his daughter's inert body and touched her arm. As he looked for a pole to use, he released a long breath. This promised to be a long day. He prayed Becca was all right. But he also vowed to hunt down whoever had hurt his daughter.

He found the length of pipe he'd been looking for. He glanced at Becca again, lying there bleeding. His distress turned to anger. Someone was definitely going to pay.

Chapter Twenty-Three

MARK SAT AT ONE OF THE PICNIC TABLES USED FOR FAMILY meals and stared at nothing. His mind had gone blank from the endless prayers for his daughter.

"Mark?" A soft voice spoke in his ear as a light touch found his back.

He looked up at Lynn's weary face. She gave him a reassuring smile and sat next to him.

"Is that coffee?"

"Yes." He handed her the half-empty cup. "But it's cold."

She took the cup. "That's okay. I just need a jolt of caffeine." She tipped up the cup and drained it.

He watched and waited until she set the cup down, aware she would talk when ready.

She looked at him, studying his face. A smile creased hers, lighting her eyes. "Relax. Becca will be fine. She lost some blood and has a lot of scrapes and bruises, but the wound was superficial. I cleaned and stitched her. She'll have a scar, but she'll recover. She's awake if you want to talk to her."

He returned the smile. She squeezed his hand. He leaned forward and kissed her forehead. "Thank you." He stood, took a few steps, then stopped. "What about the other woman?"

Lynn's features clouded. She shook her head. "Not good. Doc's still working on her. I think it's a matter of time."

Mark frowned at the news.

"It's a good thing we spent so much time searching for medical supplies after that last battle. What we collected may save her life."

He nodded and walked toward the barn. Inside, Doc, a tall, slender brunette, who'd been an emergency room physician before the world changed, stepped away from the table. A white sheet covered the injured woman. Her black face looked gray, but her chest rose and fell beneath the cover.

"How is she?"

"About as well as can be expected, considering she's been shot and stabbed. I wish they had brought her sooner. I'd feel better if I had the right antibiotics, the right tools, the proper setting, and some oxygen but at this point, I'm guessing she's got a fifty-fifty chance if I can control the infection that already set in. She needs nutrients too and those are in limited supply. We need to raid more medical facilities to stock up. Especially if people keep getting shot."

"Why don't you make a list of things you need and I'll go hunting for you."

She smiled. "Okay, Mark. I'll do that." She offered a tired smile. "Your daughter will be fine. She just needs to rest and let the stitches mend. Lynn did a good job with sewing her up. The scar should be minimal even though the furrow was wide and fairly deep." She stretched and let out a groan. "I think she had a concussion too, but all things considered, with all we've been through, we've been very lucky we haven't lost more people. And I don't mean just these types of injuries. Anything, from a splinter to a broken leg could cause death without the right medical supplies and equipment."

"Yeah, that's true."

"Of course, that may change when the winter comes. I'm concerned about colds and flu. We may not be able to fight them off."

"Is there anything that might help with that?"

"Well, if they've been preserved, vaccines would help, but without research or lab facilities it's a guess as to which ones to use. All I can do is use my knowledge and my best guess. After that, it's all in God's hands."

"Dad?" A weak voice called out.

Mark looked where his daughter rested.

"Go see your daughter. We can talk later."

"Okay, but I'm serious about you making that list. We might as well try to prepare now. Cold weather will be upon us before we know it."

Mark approached Becca. She reached for him. He took it and gave a reassuring smile.

"You just can't go anywhere without finding trouble, can you?"

She gave a feeble smile back, her face pale and suddenly very childlike. "That's me, the trouble magnet."

He brushed her hair back and caressed her cheek with the back of his hand. "Doc says you'll be fine. You need some rest, is all."

"No argument here. I'm ready to sleep for a week."

"Then why don't you get started? I'll check on you later."

Becca grabbed his arm. "Dad, those people are crazy. They could've let us go, but they didn't. They came after us. They'll be back."

"If they do, we'll deal with them. You just rest and get healed." He gave her another quick squeeze, planted a kiss on her forehead and left the barn.

Outside, lunch was being prepared for the community. Mark walked toward Bobby, busy setting the cooking grate over the fire pit. The two new arrivals stood behind him looking as out of place as they probably felt.

Seeing his father, Bobby stood.

"Bobby, why don't you introduce me to your new friends?'

"Sure, dad, this is Mel and Caryn."

Mark extended a hand and shook both women's. "Nice to meet you both. Sorry, it's under such strained circumstances." He pointed at Caryn. "I see you've been bandaged. I hope your injuries were not too serious."

Caryn shook her head but avoided his eyes.

Mel said, "No, just bruises, scratches, and light cuts. Ah, thanks, for taking care of us."

"I'd like to hear what happened. Would you sit with me a bit and fill me in?"

Mel shrugged. "Yeah, I guess, but, uh, how's Tara?"

"Doc tells me she's still not out of danger. She can give you the details."

"Do you know when she'll be ready to leave?"

Mark eyed the young woman. "I don't think it's anytime soon. At this point, we're just hoping she'll live. You can worry about leaving after we know she'll be able to. Is there someplace you need to be?"

Mel gave a nervous glance at Caryn, but the older woman still stared at the ground.

"I-I just want to make sure we can leave when we're ready."

Understanding came to Mark. "You can leave here whenever you want. You can stay as long as you want. You are not prisoners. We don't operate like that. We do not turn anyone away who wants to join our ever expanding family, but we're not some cult that latches on and never lets go. As long as you follow our few rules you are welcome to stay as long as you want. No one will hurt you, nor are there any requirements or obligations, other than to contribute to the daily chores."

He motioned to the picnic table. "We can talk more about that later. You're our guests until you decide to stay or not. Please, sit and tell me your story. Bobby, join us."

With everyone seated, Mark turned to his son. "Why don't you start with where you met Mel and Caryn? They can fill in the rest afterward."

Bobby described the meeting and ensuing battle. While he narrated, Lynn joined them. She carried a fresh and hot cup of coffee. Finished, Mark said, "Ladies, this is Lynn. She runs the compound. She'll set you up with a place to sleep. If you need anything, just ask her."

"Welcome, ladies," she said, shaking each woman's hand.

Bobby finished his version of events.

"Mel, can you tell us about your journey?"

"The three of us been together about two months now. First Caryn and me, then Tara joined us a week later.

"Tara is in the Air Force. She said there was a base around here where she thought we'd be safe. On the way we ran into a few other people. Most avoided us, some were okay, but didn't want to leave the area in case loved ones showed up.

"Then, we came across this group of people living in an old junkyard. They have it all fenced in, blocked so you can't see inside. They saw us and invited us to stay, offering us food and water. We were short on both and tired. We almost decided to stay, but then one of the few women we saw shook her head at us as if telling us not to enter. She looked so frightened."

Mel shuddered. "I can't help but feel bad for those women. God knows what they must go through. It chills me to think we could've been stuck there with them."

Caryn covered her face and moaned.

Mel patted her arm. "It's all right, Caryn. We're safe now." She glanced, questioningly, at Mark. "I think."

Mark smiled.

"Of course, you are," Lynn assured her. "If there's anything I can do for you, ask." She reached across the table, took Caryn's hands and gently pulled them from her face. "Caryn?"

The scared blonde gazed up. Tears rolled down her face.

"You are safe here," Lynn said. "I promise you. You are not a prisoner or slave. You can choose to stay or go when your friend is ready to travel. No one will stop you. I know that might be hard to believe right now, but give us a chance to prove it, okay?"

She nodded, but the tears continued. She wiped her face and Mel wrapped a comforting arm around her shoulders.

"We'll be all right, Caryn. I'm here with you." To Lynn, she said, "We've been through a lot."

"As have we all," Lynn said.

Chapter Twenty-Four

THE MEAL GAVE MARK A CHANCE TO DIGEST WHAT HIS SON and Mel had told him. By the time the table had been cleared he had an initial course of action. "Before everyone gets back to their chores I need to say something."

The assembled family grew quiet. "This may be nothing that affects us, but it is always better to be prepared. For now, no one is to travel off the grounds alone or without telling someone. In fact, at this point, I'm going to insist you clear any trips with me or Lynn. Also, I need four teams of two to drive to the other families and tell them about the threat."

"Couldn't we just call them on the walkie-talkies?" Ruth asked.

"Yes, but I want a visual on all off-site houses. Just … for safety reasons." He paused. "Again, this threat might be nothing for us to worry about, but we've all been through enough to know it's better to be ready."

"What about the army?" said Caleb.

"I'll go talk to General West. Since losing more than half his men he might not want to send anyone out to check, but I'm going to make him aware there could be an aggressive, roving band in the area. Any questions?"

No one responded.

"Okay, then get your teams, check out a vehicle and get going. I want this done now. Oh, and everyone should have a radio with them, and be armed."

The small crowd dissipated in a hurry. Lynn and Doc stood at the end of the tables. Mark went to them.

"Doc, you want to take a ride?"

"To the National Guard base?"

"To start. Then I thought we'd look for some medical facilities and try to stock up your supplies. Since you know what you need and are looking for, I thought it might be easier to have you along."

She pinched her lips together. "Sure. Let me just check on my patients." She walked toward the barn.

Lynn stepped forward, her arms wrapped around her body. She leaned her head against Mark's chest and he enveloped her, rubbing her back.

"Oh, Mark, will this ever end?"

"I'd like to say yes, but human nature, being what it is, there's always someone looking to take what you've got. Everyone wants to look out for themselves. That's why we'll survive and others not. We stay together, as a team, a family. But, if we didn't have each other to lean on, we might be takers too. Everyone's trying to survive. It's a constant struggle and an endless hunt for things we need to stay alive."

"I guess. It just seems like we finish one crisis and move to the next."

"The more good people we can draw around us the stronger we will be and the less likely others will attack us. These pockets of raiders will be something we may always have to contend with. I'd like to say otherwise, but that wouldn't be realistic."

She inhaled deeply and stood back from him. Her eyes met his. "As always, be careful."

He smiled and kissed her forehead. "I promise."

"Excuse me, uh, Mark," Mel was approaching with Caryn tagging behind. "I didn't mean to interrupt."

"Not a problem."

Lynn moved to the table to pick up a tub of dishes.

Caryn moved next to her. "Can I help you do something?"

"Sure. We can always use more help."

The two women went into the house.

"How's your friend doing?" Mark asked.

"Which one?" Mel said, with mild sarcasm.

"I guess both."

"Your doctor says Tara is resting, but there's no change. It's still 'wait and see.' Caryn? I don't know. She's a nervous wreck and so afraid of everything. Physically she seems okay, but I don't know mentally. She's been through some shit, that's for sure."

"Maybe she just needs to be around a stable environment for a while. Lynn will be good for her. Did you have a question about something?"

"Yeah, the doc said you were going to the army base. I was wondering if I could tag along."

"I don't see why not. I intended taking an extra body anyway. We're going to search for medical supplies afterward, if that's all right."

"That's not a problem. I just wanted to know where the base was for when Tara wakes up."

"Okay, we're leaving in about five minutes. Go get your weapon and extra ammo if you have it."

She lifted an eyebrow.

"Just in case," he said.

She nodded and trotted off to the garage where she had placed her gear. Mark went into the house, grabbed his rifle, a handgun, extra magazines for both, binoculars, and a phone book.

Mel was already waiting outside. He pointed to the somewhat battered white pickup and climbed in the driver's seat. Doc was on her way as Mel slid in beside him. With all three inside, Mark handed Doc the phone book. "So we're not just driving around clueless, look up places that are close, but maybe not in heavily populated areas. Hopefully, they won't have been looted yet."

"Okay," she said. "Road trip."

Chapter Twenty-Five

MARK PULLED UP THE LONG DOUBLE-WIDE DRIVEWAY OF the Air National Guard base and stopped at the gate. Two armed guards stepped from the small booth to the left. One held an M-16, though not pointed, at the ready. The second, a smaller, but higher-ranking soldier stepped toward the truck's open window.

Recognition showed on the man's face. "Sir, what can I do for you today?"

"Hello, Sergeant, I'm here to see the General."

"No appointment, right?"

Mark shook his head. "Just have some information I think he might want."

"Information, sir?"

Mark smiled. He knew he wouldn't get in unless he explained more. "Have your patrols noticed any wandering groups of men of late?"

"As in hostiles?"

"Potentially."

"Can't say that I've heard of any."

"We have. I wanted to apprise the General."

The sergeant nodded as he thought that through. "And who do you have with you today?"

"You might remember the doc here and this is Mel. She's new to our community."

"Let me radio in your request, sir."

"Thanks."

Two minutes later, after having the truck searched and the weapons held at the guard booth, Mark pulled to a stop next to the base offices, a small, two-story, brick building. As they neared the front door, Doc said, "While you talk to the General, I'm going to check in at the infirmary to see if they need any help."

"We shouldn't be too long,"

Inside, they walked down a tiled hallway toward the back of the building. They passed two doors on either side before Mark pushed open the last door on the left. The outer office was manned by a short, thin man in ACUs. He smiled and said, "Good to see you again, sir. General West is expecting you. Go right in."

"Thanks."

They entered the inner office and found a balding, somewhat paunchy, man sitting behind a large metal desk. The office was larger than the outer one, but sparse, in both furnishings and ornamentation.

The General looked up from his paperwork, smiled and stood. "Mark," he said as if he hadn't had advance notification and was surprised Mark happened to walk in the door. He offered his hand over the desk. "Come to enlist, did ya?"

It was an old joke, dating back to a time when the General had tried to press, first Becca and Bobby into service, then Mark. "Not this trip, sir."

"Well, maybe next."

They shook hands warmly.

"Sir, this is Mel. She's new to our family."

"Ah, you brought me a recruit, eh." He smiled like the proverbial sheep-covered wolf and took her hand.

"Not sure about that, but she does have an interesting story to tell. I thought you might want to hear it."

The smile faded for an instant, his narrow eyes darted toward Mark, then back to Mel. Mark knew what the man was thinking. Not another invading army. Not so soon. They had faced one not two months previously. The encounter had cost them dearly. The General had not been able to rebuild his numbers enough to face another large host of invaders.

"Please, sit." He motioned with his hand.

They took seats and Mark said, "Mel and two friends were traveling when they came upon some trouble. I'll let her tell the tale."

Mel cleared her throat. "Me, and two others I met, Tara and Caryn, were traveling. Actually, Tara, is, er, was, in the Air Force, and she wanted to come here."

The General's eyebrows shot up with excitement. "And where is Tara?"

"Easy, sir, she's been wounded. Let Mel finish her story," said Mark.

"Of course. Proceed."

"Well, a few miles from here we passed a community housed inside a fenced-in junk yard. It was difficult to tell how many people were living inside, but if I had to guess I'd say fifty. "

The General's eyebrows lofted again, but this time in surprise.

"It was definitely a male-dominated community. The few women we saw looked terrified and we didn't go in. We continued, but some of the men followed us, their intent clear. They intended to take us back to the compound, basically as slaves. There was a brief skirmish. We were outnumbered, but we managed to escape.

"We hid while Tara led them away. However, when she caught up with us, she'd been shot. She's in bad shape right now."

The General's face fell.

"Doc worked on her," Mark said. "Right now she's recovering, but Doc is cautious about the outcome."

"I see," the General said, clearly disappointed.

"Anyway, they found us again and were about to rape Caryn, when Mark's son and daughter saved us. We fought them off, but one man got away.

"We got Tara to a farmhouse while Bobby went to get his truck. At that point, Tara was unconscious and needed a doctor. But while we waited, they found us again and had more men. We fought them off, but the same man escaped. We made it to safety, but I fear more men will come."

"I thought you should be aware," Mark said. "Maybe notify your patrols to be alert. From the sounds, these raiders might be bold enough to attack an armed jeep."

"Yes, I see how that could be something to look out for. I'll bring that up at our morning meeting. Our patrols have been somewhat limited since the battle. I just don't have the people to cover the area as I did before."

"I understand. I just wanted you aware."

"I appreciate that." He turned to Mel, "But tell me, this Tara, she wouldn't happen to be a pilot, would she?"

Mel shook her head. "I don't think so, but she did say she flew helicopters."

"Well, that's more experience than anyone else here has. I sure hope she survives."

Mark remembered that before the battle, the General was trying to train someone to fly the F-16s they had. The only two people with any experience at all died in that battle. The fighter jets were too valuable to send up with an untrained pilot.

"Well," Mark said, standing, "that's all we came for."

The General stood, not yet ready to say goodbye. "So, how's everyone at the house?"

"We're doing well. Just trying to get ready for the winter."

The General bobbed his head, his eyes looking left as if trying to find something else to talk about. "Yeah, it'll be our first winter here too. I hope it won't be too severe."

Mark waited for the next bit of small talk, but the older man seemed at a loss. He extended his hand and the General took it, ending their conference.

Chapter Twenty-Six

AFTER COLLECTING DOC AND THEIR WEAPONS, THEY
SET out to find the first medical facility on the list.

"There's an Urgent Care in Swanton." She gave him the
address.

"Both of you keep an active eye on the roads," Mark
said. "I don't want anyone sneaking up on us."

The roads remained deserted all the way into the small
town of Swanton. After a few wrong turns and guesses,
they found the one-story building in a small shopping
center. The front window had been broken, as had every
other storefront.

"Someone's obviously been here before," Mel said.

"What do you think, Doc?"

"Whoever broke in was probably looking for food and
water. They might have left the supplies alone. It's worth
a look."

Mark parked and looked around. "Okay, but someone
has been here and still may be, so be alert. Don't go off
on your own."

They stepped from the truck taking everything with
them. Mark locked the doors and scanned the area in a
long, slow circle. No obvious signs of life showed.

They moved toward the building. Doc tried the door and
it opened. "I'll take the lead. Mel, watch our backs."

They entered, single file, into a standard waiting area of
carpeted floor and warm colored painted walls. Though
the floor was littered with glass, the space appeared un-
touched, as if ready to open for business on any normal
day. The reception area window had been broken, the
glass cleared from the frame, suggesting to Mark that

someone had to crawl through to get to the back. The door was no longer locked.

He turned the handle and pushed it in with his foot, keeping the rifle trained waist high. He listened. Nothing moved. With great caution he stepped forward, gazing at the floor to avoid the broken glass.

The reception desk stood to the left, a nurse's station to the right. Short hallways ran left, right, and straight. The floors were littered with the remains of broken bottles, discarded paper, plastic pill bottles and assorted items.

Mark leaned back and whispered, "First we clear the area, then we'll look for stuff." He motioned right, away from the glass-strewn floor, and they followed. The hall ended and turned left. The floor was littered the same way. The left side wall was lined with three doors. Mark guessed they would be examination rooms.

He pushed the first one open; the small space as he expected. Too small to hide anyone, but someone had been very destructive in their search. He moved to the next room leaving the door open. The next two doors stood open, the rooms looked the same as the first.

He retreated down the hall and checked the six rooms in the center hall. Four were examination rooms, the back two had once held supplies and drugs. Both doors had been broken open and lay in splintered heaps. The shelves had been stripped clean of anything that might have been useful.

To reach the final hall on the left, they had to step over and through the broken shards of the reception window. They made more noise than Mark would have liked, but to his mind, whoever had been there was long gone. However, he advanced with care.

Three more rooms stood on the right. One was another exam room. The final two were offices. Each had been ransacked thoroughly.

Mark relaxed. "Okay, Doc, look through the wreckage. Tell Mel what to look for. I'll stand look out in the reception room."

They set about their search which didn't take long. "Whoever went through here knew what they were looking for," Doc said. "There's not much worth taking." She held up a small plastic shopping bag. "Hopefully, we'll have better luck at the next place."

Over the next several hours, they repeated the procedure at a half dozen once-active medical centers and doctors' offices with very little to show for their efforts. They continued in a western and southern direction swinging through Delta, Archbold, Wauseon and Bryant. The latter bringing them close to the area where the deadly gunfight had occurred months ago. The closeness made Mark uneasy, but no one came forward to challenge their presence.

The one major find was a portable ultrasound machine. They set it carefully in the truck bed, wrapped in many sheets to cushion the bouncing.

"We don't have too much daylight left," Mark said. "We're a good hour from home." He looked at the remaining locations Doc had highlighted in the phone book. "We can hit these two on the way back." He pointed. "The others will have to wait for another day."

He headed north. Twenty minutes later they found the next building, a small clinic in a very rural area. A brick ranch stood in the middle of a country block. Few other houses or buildings were in sight. The attached garage had been transformed into the office. The doctor must have lived on site. Neither the house nor clinic appeared ransacked.

Mark stopped in the short driveway and glanced around. An old Mercury Marquis sat parked on the left. He gave that a quick look, but it showed no sign of use or disuse.

In a somewhat excited voice, Doc said, "It doesn't look like anyone's broken in. Maybe we'll find something worthwhile here."

Mark didn't respond. He looked from window to window. Everyone, from clinic to house, had curtains drawn. He studied them for movement.

"Mark? Is there a problem?" Doc asked.

He shrugged. "Nothing obvious."

Mel picked up on his apprehension. "But …?"

Sucking his lips in and staring at the house, Mark said, "I can think of two reasons why no one has been here. Either it's out of the way enough that it hasn't been discovered yet, or ..."

Mel lifted her rifle, catching on to Mark's thoughts. "... someone is protecting the property."

He nodded. "Keep an eye on the windows for any movement."

They got out and approached the clinic. The door had a long glass panel in it with stenciled letters that said, Dr. Warren Smahls, followed by the hours he saw patients.

Mel tried the door, locked.

"Should I break the glass?" she asked.

"No," Mark said, "let's look around first."

He led the way up the narrow walk to the front porch of the residence. Stopping at each window, he stepped forward and tried to peer inside; the lack of any gaps prevented a line-of-sight. The front door was locked too. They circled around the clinic to the back. A rear door looked like the best bet to gain entry into the clinic without being seen by anyone from the street.

Mark turned the knob and pushed hard against the door to test how firm the lock held. The fit was solid. It needed to be with drugs inside. There were no windows on the back of the garage. If one existed on the side of the building it had been covered when the garage had been converted to the clinic. A brick and glass breezeway connected the clinic to the house.

He turned and looked at the open field behind the house. His eyes lit on a small area and his blood chilled. Six graves. The sight sent a painful memory of two other graves flashing through his mind, those of his wife and youngest son. He shook off the image and turned back to the house, his mind whirling.

"I think the best way to get inside will be to break a window on the back of the house. We can force the door to the clinic from there without being seen."

"What's spooking you?" Mel said.

He shook his head. "Just a feeling. The windows are all covered, and no one has hit this location. There's potentially a lot of value inside. Someone had to be aware this clinic existed."

He took another glance at the graves. Nodding his head, he said, "And someone had to dig those graves."

"So, you think there's someone alive inside?" said Mel.

"I think we have to be ready. Those graves may be family members, or – they might be other people who tried to get inside."

"Man, you're giving me chills now," Mel said, with a nervous look toward the house.

"Yeah, I know the feeling."

Chapter Twenty-Seven

MARK WENT OUT TO THE TRUCK AND CAME BACK HOLDING a long-bladed, flat-head screwdriver.

They approached the back door to the house thinking entry might be easier there. He instructed Mel to stand to one side of the door and Doc to stay against the opposite wall, well away from the door. She was not used to being shot at and far too valuable to their community to put in the line of fire.

She held a handgun upward and squatted well beneath what Mark guessed was the kitchen window.

He stood on a cement patio and studied the house. A lone cement step stood below the glass storm door. To the right, just off the patio, was a bricked-in grill with a chimney. Across from that sat a glass-topped table with four chairs. A hole through the table showed where a large umbrella had once been inserted. He imagined the entertaining that must have happened there once upon a time.

Then, like a physical slap to the head, the reason for his uneasiness struck him. "The grass has been cut." He looked around again. "Everything is too neat. Someone's here or was until recently."

Knowing it would be locked, Mark tried the door. He didn't want to break the pane for fear of alerting whoever might still be alive inside. Of course, they were most likely already alert to their presence. He inserted the screwdriver into the slim space between the storm door and the lock, pushed hard, and pried. The latch popped free with little effort. The inner door, however, was wood with a small square window at the top. No matter how he tried, Mark couldn't get an angle that allowed him the leverage to pry the door open. In the end, he broke the glass and reached inside.

The window was high enough to make reaching the lock difficult. He stretched and grunted, but his fingers fell short. Using the screwdriver, he scraped the frame free of broken pieces, placed his foot on the side of the door frame, and levered his body high enough to lean through the opening.

The lock flipped, he dropped down, and quickly, shoved the door open, just as the first shot was fired.

The bullet struck the door. Mark dove and rolled behind an island in the kitchen. Two more shots followed him, pocking the floor where he had been.

"Get the hell out of my house, you bastard."

The voice sounded feeble, as though the owner was sick, or perhaps elderly.

"I'm sorry, sir. We mean you no harm."

"Bullshit. Get your ass gone or I'll add you to the grave-yard."

"We're not here to hurt you. We were just looking for medical supplies."

"Thieves!" the voice shouted, its pitch climbing almost to a shriek.

Something moved, but from Mark's vantage point he couldn't see where.

He crawled to the far side of the island and peeked. Nothing. He took another look then heard a noise behind him. The shooter was in the kitchen moving too fast for stealth.

Mark lurched forward as another round buried itself into the cupboard, past Mark's head. He got to his knees ready to spring.

On the wall to the right was a large clock with a glass face. A reflection of his stalker came into view, a tall, thin man, with wisps of white hair sticking up everywhere. The man stood still, perhaps listening for Mark to move.

A blur of motion flashed behind the man and Mark felt a sudden bolt of fear strike him. Keeping his eyes focused on the clock, he shouted, "Mel, don't shoot him."

"Wha—?" Mark heard. The man turned and Mark made his move. He stood abruptly taking in the entire scene. The man heard him move and swiveled back. Mel stood in the doorway her rifle aimed. Mark leaped onto the countertop and shoved the barrel of the rifle against the man's ribs. The force of the prod pushed the frail man backward with a grunt.

"Don't move!" Mark shouted, continuing over the island. Mel entered in a rush.

The man, though slow, would not listen. He turned to Mark raising his gun. Mark swept the rifle barrel down across the man's wrist, knocking his hand down and the gun to the floor.

Mel hit the man from behind with an open hand and shoved him forward, bending him over a counter.

"Don't hurt him, Mel."

"You bastards," the old man shouted. "You miserable bastards. Go ahead, rob me blind. Leave an old man to starve and get the hell out."

Mark stooped to collect the gun. "Easy, sir. We're not here to steal from you. We had no idea someone was still alive in here. If we wanted to harm you, Mel would've already shot."

He slid the handgun into his belt and backed away.

"Are you alone here?"

"None of your damn business."

Mark studied the man, then in a loud voice shouted, "If anyone tries to hurt one of us, I'll kill him. So if anyone else is hiding here, it's better to just come out now."

"Why? You're gonna kill me anyway."

"If we wanted you dead, you would be already. We're not killers."

"So you say."

"Are you the doctor?"

The old man rubbed his bruised wrist. "What if I am?" he said defiantly. "I'm not about to help people who break into my house."

"That's okay, we have our own doctor. We were only looking for medical supplies. We will not touch your food supplies."

The man looked at Mark with wary eyes. He was tall and skinny. White stubble, several days old, covered his face; otherwise, he appeared clean.

Mark lowered the rifle.

"Well, go ahead. Get on with it."

"Doc?" Mark shouted.

"Yes?"

"Come on in, please."

Doc stepped into the kitchen, her gun hanging down at her side.

"This is our doctor."

"From doctor to thief. You should be very proud."

Doc's mouth opened slightly, her eyes widened in surprise. "Is there anything in the clinic you no longer need or can do without?"

"Kiss my wrinkly ass."

Mark's lips went tight across his face, then they curled into a smile and he laughed. That seemed to take the man by surprise.

Mark motioned for Mel to lower her gun. She did and backed away from the man.

"Okay, sir, we're sorry we broke in. We'll leave."

The wariness in the elderly doctor's eyes increased. His face scrunched up.

"Are you in need of anything? Water? Food?"

"What's your game? Is this some sort of torture? You make me relax, lower my guard and then you strike?"

Doc spoke up. "No, we're not criminals. If we had known someone lived here, we would never have broken in. We come from a small, but growing community. I use a barn as an operating room. We were going around searching Urgent Cares and clinics for equipment. If you are still seeing patients or have a need for the equipment for yourself, we'll go. But, if you have no need for any of it, we can use it."

The man said nothing. His eyes narrowed as if looking for the trap in Doc's words.

"You are also welcome to join us if you want," Mark added. "Our community is about thirty strong on site, with another thirty in the area at their homes."

Still the man made no reply. He continued to rub his wrist.

"Okay, we're going." Mark moved toward the door. "Sorry for the intrusion."

Mel stepped out.

Doc found a notepad and paper in a tray on the counter. She wrote something and left it there. "If you ever need anything you can find us at that intersection." She gave a quick smile and went outside.

"What about my gun?"

Mark turned and gazed at the man. "I'll leave it out front before we leave."

The three of them walked around the house and toward the truck. Mel and Doc climbed in while Mark kept watch. He slid in and started the truck, then got out and placed the old doctor's gun on the driveway. The old man did not come out.

The front door opened. The old man stood there watching them. With a last glance to make sure the man wasn't about to dart out the door with another gun, Mark climbed into the driver's seat and backed down the driveway.

"Stop!" Doc said.

Mark hit the brakes.

"He's signaling for us to stop," Mel said.

Mark looked. The man was standing on the porch, waving his hands over his head.

Mark glanced at the gun on the driveway and back to the porch, estimating whether the man could get to the gun quick enough to become a threat again.

He reached behind him and slipped his handgun from the belt holster. Giving the gun to Mel, he said, "Keep an eye on him." Then he put the truck in park and stepped out.

"You need something?"

The doctor walked down the front steps. "You're really leaving?"

"Yeah. I told you, we're not thieves."

"And there's really like, uh, a small settlement of people?"

Mark stepped in front of the truck. "Yes. We call it our family. We're all strangers who came together for support and protection. We help each other."

"What would I have to do, I mean, if I wanted to join you?"

Mark smiled and walked closer. "You don't have to do anything. We can take you or you can follow us. You can come anytime you want, either to stay or to visit."

"This isn't some crazy cult, is it?"

Mark laughed. "No, nothing like that. It is sometimes crazy, but it's just a group of people trying to survive."

"And I can come and go as I please?"

"Yep."

They stood in silence while the doctor thought it over.

"I can't deny it'd be nice to have someone to talk to. Let me get a few things. I'll follow you in the beast there."

Mark got back in the truck and waited.

"Should we ask him about the medical equipment?" said Doc.

"Not right now. Let him get comfortable with us first."

"I hate leaving what could be a gold mine here. What if someone breaks in while we're away?"

Mark gave her words some thought. "I still think we wait. We want him on our side. Besides, he's a doctor. We can always use another. It's always nice to have that expertise available. Especially with all the trouble we seem to get into."

They watched as the old man approached the driveway. He stopped next to the truck and bent to pick up his gun. Mark's mind screamed in warning. Shit! They were sitting ducks. Why hadn't he removed the bullets?

Frantic, he reached behind him for his gun and froze as the gun poked through the open window. The Doc let out a gasp and Mel fumbled for the door handle.

"By the way," the doctor said, "I'm Dr. Warren Smahls, and you owe me a new window." He winked, turned, and walked to his car.

A collective gasp blew toward the windshield.

Jesus Christ," Mel said. "I think I peed."

"Me too," Mark said, "but from the other end."

Chapter Twenty-Eight

THEY STOPPED AT ONE MORE CLINIC. THIS ONE A DIALYSIS center located in an old strip mall. The center had a remodeled front. Three of the other four businesses were vacant long before the event. The fourth had been a carryout and had been thoroughly cleaned out.

The dialysis center looked intact.

"This looks promising," said Doc.

"I'll go talk to Dr. Smahls and let him know what we're doing."

They got out of the truck. Mark walked to where Smahls had stopped while Mel and Doc went toward the building. He called after them. "Don't go in the building till I get there."

The doctor had the window down and an elbow on the frame. "Doing more scavenging?"

"Yeah. With so many people to care for, Doc needs more supplies and she doesn't have the equipment she needs for emergencies and surgery."

"Do you have electricity?"

"Yeah. We put in windmills and laid solar panels on the roof."

"I've got a huge gas-powered generator. Living in the country, you have to make sure you always have a source of power. 'Course, I haven't used it much since the world dropped dead."

"We shouldn't be long. You can stay here if you want."

"I think I'll come in and look around. Maybe your doctor there could benefit from an old man's wisdom."

"I don't doubt that a bit, sir."

The two men joined the women on the raised walkway in front of the businesses.

"Mark," Doc said, excitement trembling her voice. "It doesn't look like anyone's been inside."

He nodded but was more cautious with his opinion. "Same drill as before. I'll go first. Wait for me to call you in. Mel—"

"I know. I've got the rear."

Mark tried the door, locked. He didn't want to break the glass door, the noise would alert anyone who might be inside, but he didn't see any other choice. *If we keep doing this, I'll need to find a glass cutter.* He stepped back and smashed the butt of the rifle into the glass. It dented but did not break.

Several attempts later the shatterproof glass separated from its frame but did not break. Using the screwdriver, Mark pried the glass back enough to slip his hand inside. He fumbled for the latch getting a small cut for his efforts.

Unlocked, the door swung inward. Mark crouched and peered in. The room was dark. No sunlight penetrated the heavy curtains. He stepped into the short but wide waiting room. A sliding glass panel showed where the receptionist sat. A door stood next to that. No one had disturbed the space.

Mark walked to the inner door. It opened inward and was also locked. This time he was able to force the screwdriver between the door and the jam and pry it back enough to pop it open.

The large dialysis room held about twenty machines, lined up along the outer walls surrounding a central nurses' station. The room was dim, but a small barred window in the back wall allowed some light to penetrate.

Again, the room looked undisturbed.

Mark called out, "Okay. Come in."

Doc said, "Aw!" as if she had just laid eyes on a massive buried treasure. She walked in and explored the dialysis machines. Mark advanced toward the central nurses' station; two twelve-foot-long sections of countertop sandwiched around a walk-in-work space. The inner section appeared rifled. A few seconds later, Mel said, "Ah, guys, I think you should see this."

The group moved forward. Mel's discovery was a stainless steel table set up behind the nurse's workstation. A bloody sheet lay across it. Blood-soaked towels and bandages lay strewn on the floor. A rolling cart full of medical equipment and supplies stood next to that.

"Looks like somebody performed some surgery here," Smahls said.

Mark squatted and picked up a towel. A red wet spot stained the floor beneath. "And it wasn't too long ago."

He stood and hastened toward the door. "Doc, gather what you need and let's get out of here."

Mark stopped at the front curtains and parted them where they met. The parking lot was as they left it. His senses on alert he thought the truck and car were too far away. He needed to move them up close.

He went back to the inner door. "Doctor Smahls, can you come here, please?"

The elder physician came into the waiting room. "What's up?"

"I think it would be best if we moved the vehicles up close to the front door.

"Okay. I guess that'll save us some steps."

Mark opened the front door just as two pickup trucks drove into the lot, parking on either side of his. "We're too late," he said, more to himself.

The doctor gazed out. "You think they're going to be a problem?"

Six men climbed from the two trucks, each dressed in hunter's camos and carrying a rifle.

"I think we should err on the side of caution. You might want to step back."

The men formed a wide line like flushing prey from the brush. Mark stepped just outside the door. "That's far enough, gentlemen."

The line halted and readied weapons.

One large man, with a bright orange ball cap, took an extra step. "You're on our territory, in our hospital."

"Sorry, we didn't know. If you'll get back in your trucks and drive away, we'll leave." He doubted they would, but he had to try.

The men each glanced up and down their line. The shortest man, standing on the end of the line to the left said, "No, you're trespassing. You gotta pay a fine."

As Mark feared, these men were not the type to walk away. There would be shooting before there was any courtesy. "And what would that be?"

The orange capped man said, "Your trucks, your guns, your possessions."

A tall, bald-headed man with tats covering his skull, said, "And any women you've got in there." The other men laughed. The short man said, "Oh, yeah."

Mark's mind raced for a solution. A little voice kept yelling at him to shoot now and reduce the odds. He might be able to take two of them down if he shot first. But, even knowing this confrontation only ended in a gunfight, he still wasn't able to bring himself to ambush the men. As long as they were still talking there was always hope.

"I don't think so. The price is too high."

"Better than paying with your life," the orange-capped man, who Mark thought might be their leader, said.

"We'd be dead anyway."

"Well, I guess we're at a standoff then," the leader said.

Ever so slowly, the group changed from a negotiation stance to a combative one. Mark saw it unfold before him. As the inevitable became reality, the little voice inside screamed and won out against hope. He pulled the trigger in rapid succession, blowing the orange-capped man off his feet.

He swept the barrel to the left and continued firing as he backed inside. He thought he hit the next man but he didn't go down. The men scattered for cover, the only return shots came from reaction rather than aim, the bullets flying high and wide.

Mark closed and locked the door. Even with the glass pulled back the invaders would have to work to get their bodies through the mesh window. Bullets punched through the large front windows catching in the heavy curtain and billowing it backward. He stood against the short wall between the door and the windows and let the initial barrage wind down. Realizing they had no effect, the shooters would stop and form a plan. Most likely it would consist of one group rushing the building while the remaining men covered them.

Mel duck-walked forward and stopped at the far end of the window. "What we got?"

"I put one down and might've wounded another. So, four or five shooters left, using high-powered rifles."

"Great!"

"Aren't you glad you came now?"

"Guess it wasn't one of my better decisions."

Doc and Smahls stood in the inner doorway. Mark said, "Get back inside. Find some cover." They disappeared.

The shooting ceased suddenly.

"They'll be coming now," he said. "You need to find a hole to shoot through." He flung the screwdriver toward her. "See if you can poke a hole through with that." Mark risked a glance. "You'd better hurry. I think they're preparing to rush us."

Mel drove the blade into the glass repeatedly.

Mark knelt by the door and slid the barrel of his rifle through the opening he had created. No sooner had he done that than the shooting started again. As predicted, two men broke for the large brick pillars that supported the overhanging roof and lined the walkway.

Mark sighted, fired, and dropped one, but he had no clear shot at the second. The man pressed against the brick support to the left of the door. The shooters directed their fire at him as the lone defender. He was forced to duck to the side.

"Mel, hurry."

"I'm trying, but this shit's tough.

The three shooters had spread out even more when Mark looked again. One hid behind the truck to Mark's left, another behind the truck on the right, while the third had moved to the far side of the Marquis. That man worked his way to a place where the pillar to the right blocked Mark's view of him. That meant, within seconds he'd have two men not twenty feet to the left and right of the door.

To make matters worse, a third pickup truck drove into the lot and stopped at the end of the carryout to the far right. Both doors opened, but he couldn't see how many men stepped out. He wasn't in a position to stop them from creeping up along the building front to get within a few feet of the door.

The shooting became sporadic now. Mark envisioned the men signaling their plans to each other while one shooter kept those inside occupied. His mind raced through blurred thoughts. He settled on one and ran to the inner door.

"Hey, if they get past me, put your guns down and tell them you're doctors. You have value, they won't hurt you."

"Screw that," Smahls said. "Those bastards come in here, I'm drilling them."

"Then get away from Doc so they don't shoot her by mistake."

He ran back to his shooting spot and looked out. A shuffling sound came from his right. The men were moving and getting closer. The assault wouldn't be long now. One way or another, the end was coming fast.

Chapter Twenty-Nine

MOVEMENT TO THE RIGHT MADE MARK JERK THE BARREL IN that direction and pull the trigger as a reflex. The man ducked away. Mark kept the rifle facing that way, but his eyes scanned the parking lot. For the moment, no one moved or fired. Perhaps the men by the trucks were afraid of hitting those sliding along the wall.

With his shoulder, he wiped away a trickle of sweat that had dropped into his eye, burning, and blurring it. He slowed his breathing with great effort and attempted to control the adrenaline rush. The gunshot made him jump.

A body tumbled to the ground on the walkway to the left. His first reaction was of confusion, then he realized Mel had found a shooting slot. He glanced at her.

"He was trying to catch you by surprise. Sorry it took so long."

"Do you have an angle at the men to my right?"

She pressed her forehead against the glass. "I can see the first man, but I don't think I can get the barrel turned far enough to hit him. I'll have to widen the hole."

"Can you tell how many there are?"

She looked again. "No, not really. There's at least two."

"Okay, do what you can but if you watch the front, I'll hold these guys off."

He slid out his handgun. It was better suited for an up-close fight. He gave the situation some thought. As long as everything remained motionless he had an idea.

Leaving the rifle barrel protruding through the glass just enough to be seen, he stood next to the door. It swung inward. If he pulled it open, he could stick the handgun out and fire somewhat blind along the wall. He may not hit anyone, but the shots might force them back. Because of the angle and the side they were on, Mark would have to shoot with his left hand or else risk exposing too much of himself to the shooters out front.

Physically, he took several long breaths. Mentally, he pictured what he was attempting, then counted to three.

Slowly, he turned the latch to unlock the door. He gripped the handle, forced courage to his brain and pulled the door. Jamming his left arm out, he pushed the gun far enough past the wall to shoot down the walkway. He pulled the trigger just as the first man in line rushed the door. A startled cry escaped both men. The bullets tore into the man, who danced in front of Mark. He kept pulling the trigger until the body dropped.

The man behind the pillar stepped away from the wall, firing. The rounds ripped into the glass door further destroying its integrity. One bullet creased a deep furrow across Mark's forearm, forcing him to pull back as three more men reached the door.

He backed up and, switching the gun to his right hand, fired at the first man filling the doorway. Another bullet found Mark, this time in the side, striking more meat. He flinched and retreated.

The men out front were firing nonstop into the front window. If they got through the door, Mel would be trapped in the corner with no protection. "Mel, drop back. Hurry!" He continued to fire until his gun was empty, then reached for a fresh magazine, but his injured arm was slow and awkward. He backed up again leaving the rifle still stuck in the glass. His mind whirled. Load the gun. Fire. Back up the invaders. Grab the rifle. Retreat.

A glance in the corner told him Mel was gone. The door pushed open. Two arms snaked through shooting blindly into the room. Forget the plan, he needed to get into the back room – now. His hand fumbled the magazine and it dropped to the floor. Panic rose, burning his throat. Adrenaline threatened to punch his heart through his chest.

In desperation, he ducked to reach the magazine just as a man stepped through the door and leveled a handgun at his head. Avoiding the shot drove Mark back on his bottom, but as the gun fired, he felt no added pain.

A quick look showed the man down. Behind him, Smahls yelled, "Come on, man, don't dawdle."

Leaving the magazine, Mark crawled into the back room while Smahls covered his retreat. He got to his feet and ran for the temporary safety of the desk. Doc lay huddled there, her handgun pointing up, her eyes closed and lips working in a silent prayer.

He reached out and touched her hand. She jumped and cried out. "Easy, Doc, it's just me. Let me have your gun."

She released it to him with obvious relief, her cheeks streaked with tears. He squeezed her arm giving as much reassurance as he could. Smahls was still standing in the middle of the doorway, shooting. *He's gonna get killed if he doesn't move.*

"Doctor, get out of there. I'll cover you." He stood behind the desk and focused on the doorway.

Smahls pulled the trigger again. This time there was no explosion. "Uh-oh." Turning, Smahls moved as fast as his thin legs would go. He reached the side of the desk when shots flew from the outer room. Smahls arched backward and froze for a second, then pitched forward. He went face down to the floor and did not move.

"Shit!" Mark said.

Next to him, Doc screamed but even in her fear and panic, she still moved toward the body.

A head peeked around the corner of the door and ducked back. Voices discussed plans, but Mark could not hear the words. A grunt drew his attention. He looked down to see

Doc, on her knees, tears running, dragging Smahls' body behind the desk.

"Mel, cover the door."

Mark lowered himself, using the desk to cover his torso. He doubted it had been constructed with stopping bullets in mind, but hopefully, his attackers wouldn't think of that. Right now a bullet only had to burrow through the front section of thin plywood.

"Get in here!" he said to Doc in a harsh tone. He pulled her back. Then, Mark reached out, grabbed the doctor under the arms and pulled him inside the workstation. He set the older man down and peeked fast to make sure no one had tried to gain entrance. "How is he?"

"He's still breathing. The bullet entered his lower back. Doesn't look like it came out. I need to work on him now."

Dammit! Guilt washed over him. If the man hadn't come with them, he wouldn't have been shot. On the other hand, if he hadn't, Mark would most certainly be dead.

"Did you find things here you can use to help him?"

"Some, it's obvious somebody did some operating here. If I don't do something he may only have minutes to live."

Mark fought hard for a solution.

"Can you put pressure on the wound?"

"I'm already doing that, but that is only a very temporary help."

"What do you have that can help?"

"IVs and bandages. I also saw some local anesthetic. If I can numb the area, I might be able to extract the bullet. I won't know until I can look."

"I don't know how since we're under fire." He kept thinking while the gunmen were giving him the time. "Where is the stuff you need?"

"Right behind us. On the other side of the desk. I was getting it all together when they attacked."

Mark thought that over. Behind the desk would be better cover than here. A bullet then would have to bore through two thin layers of wood sandwiched around about six feet of open space. Better, but still not good. "Can you work on the floor and by yourself?"

"I can try to get him stable."

"Okay. Crawl behind the desk and get set up. I'll bring the doctor when you say."

She looked at him. A flash of fear displayed in her eyes but faded as fast as it came. "Ready?" She nodded and crawled as fast as she could. Mark rose high enough to give her cover.

No one shot at her. Perhaps no one noticed. He glanced to his right and found Mel had created a barricade behind one of the dialysis machines and lounge chairs. The rifle rested across the arms of the chair. A handgun sat on the seat. The sight of the handgun brought a thought to mind. He snapped his finger until she looked. Pointing at her, he then aimed his fingers at his eyes and toward the door. She nodded. He ducked below the desk and dropped the magazine. He had ten rounds. He wondered if Doc had fired off the others, or if she hadn't loaded it completely.

Cautiously, he raised his head to look at the door. Whatever they were planning, it would happen soon. He stepped toward Smahls and grabbed the man by the armpits. Without waiting for word from Doc, Mark dragged him backward from between the nurses' station to behind it. Doc had laid out what she needed. He placed the unconscious man on the sheet spread out on the floor and rolled him on his stomach. Doc pulled up his shirt. Mark wanted to help but dared not take his eyes from the door for too long. Instead, spying the metal table, he turned it on its side and pressed it against the back of the desk. The table only reached halfway up the height of the desk but it might help keep any rounds from finding Doc while she worked.

Anxiety escalated with each passing minute. He found himself wishing something would happen. No way those men left. They were predators and not the sort to leave with their tails tucked. Maybe they were waiting for reinforcements. If that were the case, time was their enemy. He had to force the action and take the advantage away. But how?

His arm and side were on fire, vying for his attention. With great effort, he relegated them to background nagging.

He looked down where Doc was frantically trying to save Smahls' life. If Mark didn't do something soon, their new friend would die.

Chapter Thirty

MEL COULDN'T STOP HER LEG FROM SHAKING IN A NERVOUS twitch. She was on one knee, behind one of the chairs the dialysis patients used when hooked to the machines. The barrel of the rifle lay across both arms of the chair. Sweat dropped in a steady flow. She wiped at her forehead with her bicep. *Why did I ever volunteer for this mission? I must be nuts.*

All she was trying to do was fit in, to say thanks for helping Tara. She never expected this little drive to turn into a battle.

Mark came through the door. She almost shot him, her nerve endings on fire. She felt she'd explode. Mark disappeared behind the desk. His head poked up, looked her way, and nodded, unaware he had almost died by her hands. She needed to relax. Mel tried to force her breathing to slow, her efforts wasted.

Something moved in the waiting room. The attackers must have entered the building. She tensed even more. Then the old guy came in and got shot. Her stomach threatened to revolt. She didn't want to die here. Not after all she'd been through and especially now that Tara might survive. How ironic would that be. To go through all this to save Tara only to die before she woke.

She kept her eyes on the doorway expecting the attackers to pour through. Mark fired to keep them back, but she had no shot. Then everything went still, setting her already strained nerves on fire.

She risked a glance at Mark. Mel hated that he bossed her around. But then, she'd never much liked anyone giving her orders, especially a man. He wasn't mean about it, or sexist. In fact, he'd treated her fairly, for the most part. But, just like a man, when things got tough, they thought they were the only ones who could make a decision, who had anything of importance to contribute.

He motioned to her now wanting to know how many bullets she had. She wanted to scream "None of your fucking business," but refrained. If she could get out of here, she would. She closed her eyes and forced calmness over her. Then, told him how many. After all, she couldn't get out of there and might need Mark to survive.

But … what? He wants me to do what?

MARK LOOKED AROUND THE ROOM. A HEAVY STEEL DOOR stood in the far right-hand corner of the rear wall, but it was barred and locked to prevent break-ins. He might be able to shoot the lock open, but that would put him in direct line of sight from the waiting room. Where he was now, someone would have to make themselves a target to get a good shot at him.

He looked at the ceiling. Drop tiles. No help or escape there. Even if he could get above the tiles without being shot, they'd never support his weight. Weight? A chord hummed in his head. The wall. Was it a load-bearing wall? He wasn't an expert, but he didn't think so. He tried to find an angle to see the width of the wall. He couldn't, but if the door was flush with the wall, then it wasn't very thick. Would a bullet penetrate?

He held a 9mm. That should bore through, providing he didn't hit any supports. But if they didn't pass through, he would waste valuable bullets. However, a rifle would do the trick for sure.

Mel was looking from the entryway to him. He dropped the magazine and showed it to her, mouthing, "How many?"

Her face scrunched up in a question mark.

He pointed at the magazine again then flashed his fingers from three to four to five and gave a one-armed shrug. She nodded and he reloaded the gun. Mel held up a magazine and showed one finger. Then she pointed at the rifle and held up five fingers. She had a full magazine and five rounds.

Mark moved to the end of the desk and motioned for her to slide him the rifle. Mel gave him a "Whatchu talking about, Willis?" look. He motioned again, more insistent, then mimed shooting through the wall, but wasn't sure she understood. He nodded emphatically.

She frowned. He could see on her face the internal struggle raging within her. She huffed out a breath, pulled the rifle from the armrests and slid it along the floor. It hit the edge of the desk, but Mark snagged the barrel before it could ricochet away.

Keeping below the height of the desk, he moved to a point where he was to the right of the doorway. As he did, a body darted across the opening to the left side. They were readying their attack.

Mark lined up a shot, guessing where the attackers were, then lowering the sight where the larger target of the body might be. Aiming to a spot a little less than five feet from the floor and two feet from the door, he pulled the trigger, moved his aim one foot, and fired again.

Someone cried out in pain. In a flash the man from the opposite side stepped into the doorway, and fired, forcing Mark to duck. Two more rounds whizzed overhead. A third shot came from Mel's area followed by loud crashing.

"Watch out, Mark. One's inside to your left."

She fired again.

Mark slid to the left side of the desk and peeked. One man hid behind a lounge chair. Mel shot and the attacker ducked, then popped up and returned fire. Mark rolled in the open to his stomach, brought up the rifle and aimed. The hurried shot hit the seat back in front of the man's face. He dove behind the chair, but now Mel had a target. She pulled the trigger twice but missed.

Then she shouted again. "Got two inside." Her voice became more anxious. "Mark, he's near you by the front desk." Two more shots.

The man by the chair aimed one shot at Mark then turned to shoot at Mel. He gave Mark too much of a view of his side. This time Mark had time to set the sights. He squeezed the trigger and propelled the shooter sideways into the wall.

More gunfire occurred, but out of sight from where Mark lay. He put down the rifle and pulled out the handgun again. He had no idea where the man by the desk was, but all the hairs on his neck and arms had sprung to life. He fought back the mounting panic, but the urge to flee grew. His throat constricted in response to the rising acid in his stomach.

Mel was busy with a shooter reaching through the door. She couldn't help him. He inched forward on elbows and knees toward the opening at the side of the desk. Only the thin layer of plywood making up the front counter separated him from the second gunman. Focusing all his senses on the desk he listened, looked, and smelled for any hint of the enemy's location.

He paused at the edge of the opening, his nerve endings alive with rapid-fire warnings. Where was the shooter? He wanted to yell to ask Mel, but that would give him away. Mark wanted to peek, but the man could be waiting for him to do just that. A gun could be inches from his face. Paralysis spread through him, afraid to move in any direction.

Something fell to the floor inside the workstation. His prey was either leaning or climbing on something that held papers. Shelves, or the desk itself. Like a bolt of striking lightning, Mark knew what was going to happen: the man was inside the workstation. Pushing forward into the opening between the two workstation walls, and landing on his side, Mark pulled the trigger in quick succession at the man who had just climbed onto the desk.

The bullets struck him as he drew a bead on the top of Doc's head. The wounded man rolled sideways and draped across the top wall of the workstation, shot back at Mark. The hurried shots had the desired effect, forcing Mark back undercover.

Someone screamed. Fear for Doc's life spurred him back into action. He rolled across the opening, bringing the gun to bear. However, his target clutched at a spurting wound to his neck. Mark rolled in the other direction. On the rear side of the workstation wall stood Doc, a bloody scalpel in her hand.

Gripping his ruined neck, the man slowly slid down the desk, collapsing to the floor as his life drained away.

Mark risked a quick look at Doc. Her face, contorted into an agonized yet furious, almost unrecognizable mask, she looked at Mark, blood streaming down her face. Her harsh, rapid breaths blasted through gritted teeth. Then her features softened and she dropped from sight.

Fearing the worst, Mark scrambled around the back of the desk. Doc inserted an IV into Smahls as if nothing else was going on around her or had happened. He took a quick breath and hurried to the opposite end of the workstation to see how Mel was doing.

She caught the movement and looked his way. "No one else has tried to come in."

Mark crawled to the front of the desk and looked at the space beyond. Mel had added another body to the collection there. He waited and listened. Taking a gamble. He darted to the wall three feet from the door. He pressed his ear against the barrier but couldn't hear anything. Of course, that didn't mean someone wasn't out there.

Inching to the door, he steeled himself then dashed across the opening. No shots tracked him. He peeked out. A body lay to the right. The outside door was in view. No one lurked there.

Taking a large, quick step, he entered the waiting room and spun to his left, gun up. Empty. Four long strides took him to the window where Mel had made her shooting hole. He pulled the curtain back and took a long scan of the parking lot. If anyone was still out there, they were well hidden.

A moan drew his attention to the man on the floor, just past the door. Mark went to him, removed the gun from reach and bent to examine him. A bullet had passed through his chest. He tried to speak but wheezed instead. The bullet had passed through the lung.

"Help ..." he managed, arched his back, groaned, and re-laxed, dead.

Mark frowned. It didn't have to be this way. He couldn't understand why, in these strange times, people didn't want to work together. To help and support each other. The violence and killing made no sense. Enough of the world had died. It was time to rebuild. To come together in peace.

He stood as Mel came to the door. "You all right?"

Mark just nodded his head.

Chapter Thirty-One

HE HANDED BACK HER RIFLE AND LEFT MEL TO WATCH THE parking lot. In the back room, Mark said, "Can you help him?"

"I don't know," Doc said. "The bullet's still in there. It could be lodged against his spine. I don't know. Without an X-ray, I'd be going in blind and may do more damage than good." She looked up, frustration etching extra worry lines. "This is really beyond my capabilities."

"For sure he's gonna die if you do nothing, Doc."

She sighed. "He needs blood. Whatever they might have here is bad."

Smahls opened his eyes and looked at them through pained, watery eyes. He tried to speak.

Mark bent lower. "What was that, doctor?"

He spoke again, then coughed. A splattering of blood flew from his lips.

"I think he said X-ray," said Doc. "I know," she said to him in a louder voice, as if he were deaf.

"X-ray?" Mark said. "Do you have an X-ray machine at your place? Is that what you're trying to say?"

The old man gave a feeble nod.

"What about blood?" Doc asked.

A nod.

"Refrigerated?"

Again he nodded.

"That settles it," Mark said.

Doc said, "But, he'll never make the trip. He might die along the way."

"He'll die if we don't take him. Plus, it's not safe here. More men could show up at any time. We have to go."

"We have to keep him flat. And the truck will bounce him around too much."

"We can lift him onto the table and carry that outside. We'll put him in the backseat of his car. It's big enough and will offer more cushioning."

Doc looked around.

"Doc, I know it's a risk, but we have to do this, and now."

She nodded and raised a hand. Mark took it and helped her to her feet. Grabbing a pile of folded white cotton sheets she spread them out on the floor while Mark pulled the keys from Smahls' pocket. He walked to the door. "We still okay out there, Mel?"

"Yeah, for the moment."

"I need you to move the vehicles up to the door." He handed her both sets of keys. She looked at them, then at him and went out the door.

He went back to help Doc. They lifted the wounded man to the sheets. Doc placed the IV bag on his abdomen. Grabbing two corners each they hoisted Smahls to the stainless-steel table. He moaned. His feet hung over the edge.

"This will be heavy. Can you handle it?"

"I'll do the best I can."

"If you have to stop, say so. Ready?"

She nodded and they heaved up. Doc grunted but maintained the lift. Mark walked backward. By the time they reached the door, Doc needed a break. They set the table down, waited a moment and squeezed through the doorway. At the outer door, they stopped again. Doc checked to make sure her patient was still breathing.

Mel had parked the truck and was on her way back with the Marquis. They waited until she parked and got out.

"Mel, help Doc with her end. We're gonna put him in the back of the car."

Mel slid past the table, set her rifle on a chair, and grabbed a corner. Only one of them could squeeze through the door, so Doc let go. The stockier woman had no problem handling the table. Outside, Doc went ahead, opened both rear doors and climbed inside on the far side.

Mark and Mel slid the doctor off the table. Once they had him inside the car, Mark said, "Doc's gonna have to stay in the back to hold him still. You'll have to drive. Follow me. We're going back to his clinic."

"Hope he makes it. He's not looking too good."

"Yeah, let's get moving."

They caravanned as fast as Mark thought safe for the old man, all the while keeping a constant lookout for any pursuit. They arrived at the clinic and Mel used Smahls' keys to open the clinic door. She tried the light switch and to their surprise the lights went on. Must have stored, charged batteries.

They carried Smahls to a room set up for operating and placed him face down. Doc wheeled in a portable X-ray machine. Mark left her to set up and went outside to find the generator.

He found it in a small shed attached to the west side of the building. The machine was massive. Wires ran through an entire professional system that ended in a stack of batteries, similar to what he and Jarrod had created at the farmhouse. Mark checked the fuel level, looked through the electrical panel, got familiar with the setup and fired it up. The big unit rumbled to life and purred, smooth and quiet.

Back inside he found Doc working with feverish intensity. "I'm gonna need help."

"Do you want me to run back and get Lynn?"

"Oh heck, I don't know. She would certainly be a big help. How long would it take?"

"I might be able to make it in forty minutes. Once in range, I'll use the radio so she's ready when I get there."

"Okay, go. Mel, I'm going to need you to help me until they get back."

Mark stopped her. In a quiet voice, he said, "Make sure you keep checking the area." She nodded.

Mark flew down the long country roads. At the Airport Highway, the main road, he floored the pedal, not worrying about who might see him. Closer to home he called ahead and explained the situation. "Lynn, just in case, have someone who can handle a gun with you."

Silence greeted him, but to her credit Lynn didn't waste time asking why.

Screeching around the corner and racing up the driveway, Mark found Lynn, Caryn and Zac waiting for him. They piled in and the truck was in motion before anyone was settled.

"So, what's the story?" Lynn asked.

"We found an elderly man who's a doctor. He was following us here. We made a stop to check a clinic and a large group of men attacked us. The doctor got shot. We took him back to his place where he has the equipment to handle the surgery. Doc needed someone with more experience than any of us had."

Mark glanced in the mirror at Zac and Caryn. The boy could handle a gun but was only seventeen. "So, uh, was Lincoln or Bobby busy?"

She hesitated.

Her lack of reply ignited new worries. "Lynn?"

"We got an emergency call from the Richardsons. Their son and daughter are missing. Lincoln organized a search party.

Mark let that filter in. They lived southwest of the farmhouse, the furthest of any of the families. Could the disappearance be related to the attack? No, they couldn't have reacted and found the Richardsons that fast. This had to be something separate. But, if so, was it another element of the same group which attacked them, or someone altogether different? Damn! Crises never ended.

He drove on at high speed, his eyes focused ahead, but his mind far beyond that.

Chapter Thirty-Two

AS THEY NEARED THEIR DESTINATION, LYNN SAID, "SOME better news, the wounded woman woke up."

"That's good. How's she doing?"

"As long as there aren't any complications from infection or internal bleeding, she should recover."

"That's great." He wished he could be happier about the news, but too much was happening right then.

He rounded a corner, pulled up a driveway and slammed on the brakes. Everyone was thrown forward, but at the speed Mark was traveling, everyone had been smart enough to buckle up.

They piled out from the truck. "Zac, stay here and watch the streets." Mark led the others inside. Doc was dressed for surgery and studying an X-ray. Mel stood by the surgery table pressing on the wound and watching a beeping monitor.

Lynn went straight to Doc. They discussed the situation in quick low tones. Caryn stood back and listened. Mark stood next to Mel.

"How's he doing?"

Mel shook her head. "Not good. His pressure is dropping fast. She gave him some sort of gas to put him out, but he's not going to last long."

Doc came to the table while Caryn and Lynn slipped into scrubs and washed their hands. Mel and Mark backed away to let the professionals work.

"Doc, is there anything we can do?" Mark said.

"No. If the three of us can't handle this, extra hands won't matter."

Mel touched his arm. "I need to borrow the truck if that's all right. While I was standing here, I remembered I left my rifle at the clinic."

Mark curled his lip as he thought. "I'll go with you. There's a lot of stuff we can use there. Plus, it might not be safe." To the women, he said, "We'll be back in a minute. Don't go outside or open the door." No one responded. Their hands busy and minds occupied.

Outside he gave instructions to Zac. "Zac, get inside but keep your eyes on the roads. If you see anyone, do not let them in. Shoot if you need to. The ladies are counting on you to protect them. We'll be back as fast as we can."

The young boy swallowed hard. "Okay. You can count on me."

Mark and Mel went out the door. Mark pushed in the lock on the knob, shut it, and checked that the door was secure. He trotted to the truck. Worry about the three women's safety nagged at him. "Let's make this as quick as possible. I hate leaving them unprotected."

"They've got that boy."

"Yeah, but he's barely seventeen."

"I could've gone alone. I can handle myself."

"I'm not questioning that, Mel. You've proved you can. If another group of men attacks, you might not be able to hold them all off. Especially if they catch you in the open."

Mel didn't respond.

"This will give us a chance to strip the bodies and search the trucks for anything useful. Plus, Doc had a pile of stuff she wanted."

"What if we took one of their trucks? It will give us an extra vehicle."

"That's a good idea."

Mark crept to a stop within view of the clinic. They sat for several minutes watching for signs of life. "You go inside when we get there, get your rifle and search the bodies. I'll check the vehicles and the bodies outside."

He parked close to the building. Mel reached for the door, but Mark grabbed her arm. "Be quick." She nodded.

Mark checked the bodies near the door, tossing any weapons into the truck bed. On one, he found keys attached to a large Swiss Army knife. Mel came out with her arms loaded with weapons. Mark glanced at the trucks, his gaze passing over the stainless-steel table. An idea struck him.

He hopped into the bed, handing down the guns. "Mel, I want to move the guns into the cab. We're going to take the table."

"What about all the stuff inside Doc wanted?" Mel asked.

Mark thought. He hated taking the extra time, but the important items might not be there if they ever returned. "Yeah, let's grab it all now while we're here."

They spent the next fifteen minutes gathering and hauling. Not sure exactly what Doc wanted they took everything to let her decide later. With the truck full, Mark drove between the attacker's two trucks. One was a Dodge Ram the other a GMC Sierra. Both were newer, bigger and in better shape than his.

Mark tried the keys. They belonged to the maroon Sierra. He started the engine and drove close to the table. Mark dropped the tailgate and they slid the table in upside down. He handed the keys to Mel. Her eyes lit up with the exchange. Mark laughed.

"What?" She said, a flush of embarrassment touching her cheeks.

"Kid with a new toy."

"Oh, yeah!"

Mark led. Much equipment remained, but he was loath to spend the time. If it was there when they returned so be it, but for now, he wanted to get back to the clinic. Driving from the parking lot with caution Mark picked up speed once he hit the street. The return trip took much longer. He didn't want to bounce and damage any of the equipment.

He rounded the corner of the street where Smahls' home office sat. Fear hit him so hard he couldn't breathe.

The front doors of both the house and the clinic hung from their hinges.

Chapter Thirty-Three

MARK PULLED HIS HANDGUN AND GRABBED ANOTHER FROM the pile behind the seat without looking. Jumping from the cab, he ran for the office door. He pressed his body to the side of the opening. Mel came running and he motioned for her to go in the front door of the house.

He peered into the waiting room. Nothing moved. No sound came from within. A crash behind him sent him spinning, pointing both guns, but it was only Mel stepping over the ruined door to the house.

Swallowing hard, Mark stepped inside, both guns leveled like some TV western cowboy. The door to the examination room was no longer there. It lay in large, splintered sections on the floor, as if someone had taken an ax to the wood. Tension tightened like a band across his chest. The body of a man lay sprawled on the floor.

Quick long strides took him to the doorway. He knew caution should be the rule, but his fear for the three women's safety, for Lynn's safety, was too great, he stepped through and swept the room from left to right. He stopped halfway on his sweep, turning back to the surgery table.

Smahls lay face down, one arm limp, hanging over the side, a bullet hole dotted the back of his head. Zac lay in a heap on the floor, his face a bloody ruin.

Mark's legs went rubbery and he struggled to stay erect. His breathing labored, his eyes welled, and he felt faint. An unsteady step brought him to the wall in time to keep from falling. *Oh God! Lynn!*

Noise from behind cleared his mind, but too slowly. In stepped Mel. Had it been an intruder, he'd be dead.

"Oh shit!" Mel said. "The others?"

Mark shook his head. "I don't know."

"I'll check the other rooms."

She left leaving Mark struggling to regain control of his body and mind. He wiped at his eyes. His thoughts returned to another time when Lynn had been captured. The abuse she'd endured at the hands of those monsters took a long time to bury. No! He refused to allow those thoughts to enter his mind. He had to find her, and the others, before it was too late. But who had them?

Mel came back in. "Nothing. Whoever took them had no interest in the medical supplies or equipment.

"How long were we gone?"

Mel considered. "An hour? No more than that."

Mark focused hard. Even if the abductors had been watching and attacked as soon as they left, figuring maybe ten minutes to get in, corral the women and load them up, they had perhaps a fifty-minute head start. If Zac had delayed the attackers at all, and from the dead man, that looked to be the case, that lead might be a lot less.

"Well, at least we know they're not dead."

Mark buried his emotions and drew a veil over his mind. Angry, he pushed away from the wall and looked from Smahls to Zac. In a cold hard voice, he said, "There're worse things than death." Mel shuddered. Brushing past her he stood outside. He looked up and down the roads. Was it friends of the men they'd killed, the group that attacked Mel's group, or maybe a new gang altogether? Which direction should he search?

He closed his eyes and pictured their flight from the clinic to here carrying Smahls. He was sure no one had followed them. He'd checked his mirrors constantly. The streets were mostly long, straight country blocks. If anyone had been following, he would've seen them.

So, someone else stumbled across them, either by accident or they'd been watching. Too many possibilities. Four roads leading away. Eliminating the road they'd arrived on still gave them south, east, and west. An impossible task but standing still wasn't helping. They had to move.

He ran to his truck and retrieved his rifle. He snatched the binoculars, a back-up rifle and extra ammo and went to the Sierra.

"Keys," he said in a demanding tone.

Mel tossed them to Mark and then climbed into the passenger side. He reversed, screeched to a stop and threw the truck into drive. The tires spun and caught, shooting them forward to the west.

He had only one known entity. That was where they would start. They might never find Lynn and the others if it was a traveling band of unknowns. He'd start with the known entity and either find the women there or eliminate the possibility. In which case, he'd have no idea where else to look. He prayed he made the right choice and doubled up on the prayers that he wasn't too late.

"Can you get me to that compound you and your friends ran across?"

"Yeah, I think so."

"Well, take a moment and know so. We don't have time for mistakes," unable to prevent himself from snapping at her.

"Keep going. I'll tell you when to turn."

"It's all my fault." He slammed the steering wheel. "God, it's all my fault. I should've stayed with them. If anything happens to her ... them," he choked, "I'll never forgive myself."

"We'll find them, Mark. And when we do, they'll pay."

He wiped the blur from his eyes. The thoughts and images assaulting his mind weren't as easy to clear. He swallowed hard, then again. He fought to control his breathing. He had to focus. Emotion was as big an enemy as those he planned on punishing.

"Mel," he said, when he could, "try the radio. See if you can raise anyone. We're going to need lots of help."

She did. Repeatedly. But either no one was monitoring their radios or they were too far out of range. They flew in pursuit of an unknown foe, in a direction that was pure guesswork. The odds of success were slim.

"Turn left here."

At the speed they traveled, he couldn't hold the road. The truck threatened to flip. He managed to straighten the wheels in time, but they side-swiped a tree, careened into and through a ditch, coming to a stop in an open field.

His façade crumbled. Mark banged his head on the wheel and cried. "Oh, God, not again. Please."

Mel reached across and put a hand on his back. "Mark. Mark! I know how you feel, but this isn't helping get them back. Get yourself under control or you can't help them. Getting us killed won't either. I'm worried too. I know what those cocksucking assholes will do to them. I can't let myself think about that or I'll be unable to function. We're wasting precious time. You can go all emotional when we find them. Then we'll kill the shit out of them, but we have to find them first."

He lifted his head and looked at her. Two deep breaths later, control restored, Mark pulled forward and turned the truck around. The truck climbed back onto the road and shot forward.

Chapter Thirty-Four

TWENTY MINUTES LATER, AFTER SEVERAL WRONG
TURNS, they found the right road.

"I think that's it down there."

"You think?"

"We went past them on the other side. We were avoiding
the roads. We came out of some trees and found this huge
fenced area. We didn't know it was inhabited until these
large gates swung open. They probably have a way in from
both sides."

Mark nodded as he studied the area through the glasses.
At first, he saw nothing. Trees blocked the view on the left.
Open field ran the length of the land to the right until it
came to a large farmhouse. He let the truck crawl forward.
Four truck lengths gave him a better angle. As he sighted
on the fence, he stopped. The fenced yard was indeed
large. He inched forward revealing more. The ten-foot-high
metal fence stretched for a long way back from the road.
He estimated the area must be some ten acres. Because of
the height of the fence he was unable to see anything inside. However, he did notice a few heads moving above the
fence. That told him there must be a walkway on the inside, like a rampart, which enabled them to see out.

Heavy metal slats ran through the chain links blocking
the interior. They had little information to go on and no
proof Lynn, Caryn, and Doc were inside. He lowered the
glasses and stared, lost in thought.

"What are we going to do?"

"I don't know." He backed the truck off the road to be
less conspicuous. "Short of going up and knocking on the

door and asking if they have our friends, I have no idea what to do. Somehow, we need to see inside that camp.

"Look!" Mel pointed.

Switching his gaze, Mark saw a pickup pull up to the front gate. The driver honked twice and waited. Mark focused the glasses again. A few moments later someone manually opened the gates, one section at a time. Above the gate to each side, an armed man looked down. A burly man carrying a hunting rifle came out and had an animated discussion with the driver. He pointed inside the gate, then, threw his head back laughing.

Seconds later the man waved and the truck passed through the gates. The big man pushed the gates back in place. The heads above the fence disappeared.

"They must have a lot of people in there," Mel said.

"How many did you think you saw?"

"I'd guess maybe thirty or forty, but that's only what we saw. They had wrecked cars lined up all over. I couldn't see past them. You can see the buildings, though. There are three. Two looked like businesses and that one," she pointed, "is obviously a two-story house.

"I need to see inside."

"Okay. How you gonna do that?"

He scanned the area stopping at the farmhouse across the road from the gate. It sat back off the road about twenty yards. An attic window looked out on the street. If they could get up there, he'd have a great position to see the entire interior of the compound.

"That should work. We have to find a way there without being seen."

The ground from there to the farmhouse was all open field, offering no cover. Too long a distance to go without discovery. He had to find another way.

The field ran a long way behind the farmhouse, ending at a small copse of trees, perhaps a hundred and fifty yards back.

"We need to approach from behind the house, keeping it between us and the compound. Even still, we'll be in the open for a long time." He looked around. "What about on the far side of the fence? Is there anything high enough to see inside?"

"Just trees. I suppose, if you climbed one, that would work."

"Let's try the house first."

They retraced their route. At the first intersection he turned left, stopping halfway down the block. Mark pulled off the road on a dirt track and parked behind an old wooden barn that looked like it was waiting for that final gust of wind to push it over.

Grabbing weapons and equipment, they took off at a trot across a smaller field to the long stretch of trees that ran parallel to the street. Once through the wooded area to the other side, Mark stopped and used the glasses again. Open space spread out before him, as wide as it was long. Whatever crop had once grown there had been harvested long ago and plowed under. Only weeds grew now. To the far right, a long line of trees ran from the street perpendicular to those they hid in. If they approached staying to the woods they'd be shielded from view, but getting to the house placed them in view from the fence for a good fifty yards. This way was faster and hopefully, safer.

Keeping in line with the farmhouse, they ran along the long furrows. The ground alternated between soft dirt and hard clumps, making running difficult without looking where you stepped.

The sun had long begun its descent. They had an hour or so of daylight to gather information. A small flock of black birds took flight in front of them. Mark motioned down with his hand and dropped to the ground. "Keep your head down. Don't look up and don't move until I tell you."

For long agonizing moments, they lay perfectly still. The dirt stuck to the sweat on his arms. With slow, compact movements, he set the glasses on the ground in front of his head. Lifting his chin from the ground, he pressed his eyes to the glass. A head looked out in their direction from over the stockade. From what Mark could see, the man wasn't using binoculars.

The watcher turned his head, sweeping his gaze across the field, left to right and back. He stopped and seemed to be looking right at Mark. The thought kindled new fear. He felt his sweat level increase.

Time dragged and Mark grew restless. They couldn't afford this delay. A good five minutes later the man moved on. Still Mark waited. He was glad he did. Not a minute later, the man returned and studied them again. Mark could only hope the distance was too great for the guard to make out clearly what he was looking at.

Lifting his head inch by inch, he glanced above the glasses. The head staring back at them was a small dot, barely recognizable as such.

The sun set further, robbing them of precious light. They might have to wait until dark to move, but would he be able to make out anything inside then? His thoughts went to Lynn and the condition he found her in when he rescued her from Buster and the Horde. She was a basket case for a long time and forever changed. Could she survive another ordeal like that? Giving his mind a mental shake of the head, he tossed the images aside. Stay focused.

The floating head vanished again. They had to move. "Crawl," he said, moving along the ground like an alligator. They hadn't gone ten feet when his heart skipped a beat. "Stop!" He focused the glasses, confirming his fears. Damn! One side of the gate swung inward and the burly man stepped out.

Chapter Thirty-Five

THE GUARD STOOD FOR A MOMENT. MARK HELD OUT SOME hope he would not come nearer, but those hopes were dashed when the man cradled the rifle under his arm and advanced toward them.

"Mel, we've got company. Stay down. Very slowly pull out your handgun and keep it under you." He couldn't see her, but assumed she followed his instructions. He slid his hand down and withdrew his knife from its sheath. "If he keeps coming, don't shoot unless you have no choice. Let me take him out."

The man crossed the road and advanced past the farmhouse. He stopped about two hundred yards away and raised his rifle. "Shit! Keep your head down and don't move."

Mark pushed the glasses into the ground to hide them then attempted to do the same with his body without wiggling. He held his breath and said a silent prayer. The shot kicked up dirt into his face. Every nerve in his body screamed in advance from the potential pain to come. He wanted to jump up and run. His mind begged to take flight, but he held on and waited out the shooter.

The wait was agonizing. Not knowing when the next shot might come or if it would strike was driving him crazy. He thought he heard Mel whimper. Lord knows he wanted to as well. What was happening? He desperately wanted to look but was afraid the man was watching through his scope. But if he was coming closer how would he know without at least peeking? The closer he got, the better the chance of him hitting his target.

He inched his rifle to a shooting position. Opening one eye a slit, he tilted his head to the side and tried to find the hunter. The angle of his head didn't allow him a view of the stalker. He had to know where the man was. Mark moved his head a little more, then more again, until he caught sight of the man. He was coming closer.

The sky had darkened, but not nearly enough. Plenty of light still existed for a good shot. As he watched the man approach, he readied the rifle for a snap shot. The rifleman stopped and sighted the rifle again. Mark closed his eyes and froze. This was it. His mind whirled in mortal combat with itself, between shooting first, running and staying.

Flies landed on him. To the side he faced, birds touched down in the field pecking on the ground for some unseen morsel. Perhaps they would help sell the idea they were dead. Minutes passed like hours. The sun crept ever lower. Still, nothing happened. Mark forced his clenched eyelid open a fraction. Then wider, until he found his antagonist. Relief flooded through him, relaxing his taut muscles to the point his bladder almost emptied.

He couldn't believe his eyes. The back of the man grew smaller as he walked away from them. Evidently, he was convinced they were dead. Despite their great fortune, they could not risk moving until the sunlight faded. "He's gone," he said. Now, he was sure he heard Mel whimper.

Mark raised his head and used the glasses. The guard had entered and was closing the gate. He scanned to the left and right of the opening and found no one else watching.

"Quick, crawl forward until I say."

He got to hands and knees and scurried forward. He counted in his mind the seconds he thought it would take the man to shut and lock the gate and climb to his perch above the fence. He reached ten and dropped. "Stop!"

His breaths were short and quick, as if he had just sprinted a hundred-meter dash. He didn't move, anticipating the guard would take one more look at them before relegating them to unimportant. Again he counted, this time to one hundred, before risking a look. No one looked back.

Sunlight was now a slit on the horizon. They had to get to that house in the next fifteen minutes or be unable to see inside the camp. The horrid thoughts returned. Lynn, Caryn, and Doc had been gone for too long. Only bad things could be happening by now. Things he refused to think about. But the one main question remained. Were they in there, or had they wasted all this time for nothing? If he'd made the wrong guess, he might never find them again. The idea was too much to bear. He covered his head with his arms as if the act prevented the thoughts from entering his mind.

Forcing himself to wait two more minutes, he checked the fence line again, then rose to his feet. "Let's go," he said and sprinted toward the farmhouse as fast as his legs could carry him.

By the time they reached the house, dusk was heavy in the sky. Mark ran up the back steps and tried the rear door. Locked. He couldn't afford to break out the glass. The sound might carry too far. Using the knife, Mark sliced through the putty of the nearest of six small panes of glass in the door.

The blade made quick work of the hardened glaze. He was able to insert the blade along the edge of glass and pry out the window. Reaching through the opening, he flipped the deadbolt and turned the handle, releasing the push-button doorknob lock. He shoved the door and scanning in a hurry, made his way to the stairs and raced up.

The house was dark. Little of the remaining sunset penetrated the interior. Threatening shadows danced in every corner, but Mark ignored them, taking the stairs two at a time. No stairs went up to the third floor, however.

"Check the closets in each room. See if there are stairs leading up."

He tried the first room on the left, nothing. On his way to the next room, Mel said, "Found it."

Mark changed direction and entered the first room on the right. Mel was already ascending. The stairs were in a closet. The attic was walkable. Each step kicked up dust that made him sneeze. At the window, he fumbled the glasses anxiously to his face. He gasped.

"What?"

"There's a lot more people in there than I thought." In the dimming light, he scanned the yard. Bodies moved all over the grounds, dodging between parked junkyard vehicles. They all appeared to be moving toward a long flat building in the middle of the compound.

Cars had been lined up all around the interior perimeter of the fence. The guards used them as ramparts, walking along them to see above the fence. A light on top of long poles shone at each corner of the fence. Other lights attached to the walls lit the house in the distance and the main building behind. The third structure, to the right near the western fence, was dark. The camp had electricity from some source, perhaps generators. Mark saw no evidence of solar panels or windmills.

Streams of smoke rose from half a dozen fires in the yard, used either for light or cooking, most likely both. Shadows moved in and out of the light cast by the flames.

Mark moved his focus back to the main building. A flat roof covered the fifty-by-eighty-foot yellow brick building. It appeared to be a gathering place for the residents. Maybe a mess hall or meeting room. With the people spread out so far and blocked from sight at different points by the cars or buildings, Mark could only guess at the number of people inside. He put the total at eighty to a hundred, including women and children. Every man carried a gun of some sort; most were rifles.

A loud roar filled the night, emanating from the main structure. As he watched, more men streamed inside. Something was going on and he doubted it was bingo. Movement caught his eye to the right. A knot of men appeared from the smaller, darkened building near the fence. Two men led the way and six followed, two either side of a woman.

As they passed from darkness to the flickering light of a fire, the faces became less shrouded. He sucked in a quick breath and held it. Lynn, Caryn, and Doc. The flash of relief he felt was only momentary. They were alive, for the moment anyway. But death could be physical or mental. He might be able to rescue them physically, but he had no way of stopping whatever they might endure, killing them mentally.

Chapter Thirty-Six

"I FOUND THEM," HE SAID. HE WATCHED UNTIL THE WOMEN were led inside the main building and out of sight.

"They're alive?"

"For now. They look unhurt, but that might change. The whole camp seems to be in that main building." He checked the fence again. Four guards still patrolled, one on each side. That left a lot of ground for them to cover. His mind formulated a plan. The lights in the corners only went so far. He might be able to scale the fence in the center of one side unseen. But once inside, what then? How to get the women away and over the fence without drawing attention? Getting in might be easy enough, but he could see no way to get out. As eager as he was to rescue the women, it was impossible to battle the entire compound to accomplish it.

The women were obviously important to the men inside. They might not kill them, but no way would they keep him alive.

"Okay, listen," he said. "Right now, we know they're alive."

"Alive is one thing, raped and abused is another."

Mark closed his eyes against the words. With a violent shake of his head he tossed off the images. It was time to be strong. He opened his eyes and started again. "Please, just listen. Can you find your way back to our house?"

"Ah, I think so, but I'm not ..."

Mark raised a hand to cut her off. "Mel," he hissed. "Just. Listen. Do what I say. We need help. It's dark. Can you find your way in the dark?"

She blew out the breath she had been holding. "Yeah, I think so."

"There is no way the two of us can get them out of there. Get back to the house. Use the radio when you get closer and get people moving. Tell Caleb to contact the General at the Air National Guard base and tell him what's happened. Tell Caleb to remind the General of how we went to his rescue. It's time for him to return the favor."

He paused to collect his thoughts. "Have someone call the other families. Gather everyone. Tell Lincoln to organize the community. I need you to lead them back, but don't delay. If things are moving too slowly, take whoever's ready. Park in the same place and meet back here. Any questions?"

"What are you going to do?"

"I'm going to find a way inside."

"Mark, you can't do it alone."

"That's why I'm sending you for help. Now, hurry." He pressed the keys into her hand, but she didn't move. "Mel, please, those women don't have much time and we don't have any other choice. I'll leave the binoculars here."

Without another word, Mel turned and ran down the stairs. Alone now, Mark searched for a way in. He couldn't afford to wait for help to arrive. Even alone, he had to do what he could to get them out. While everyone was still inside that building it was be a good time to sneak in, but without knowing where the women might be moved, he wasn't sure of the best place to get in.

Slowly he took in the area one section at a time. Rows of cars lined the grounds. Some were crushed and placed in stacks of three or four cars high; others were arranged in long aisles, like a mobile home park. Mark wondered if some of the vehicles were indeed used for homes, if only for beds.

The main building stood in the front third of the grounds. The darkened structure to the right was closer to the fence and in the second third. If that's where the women were being held, that might be the best place to enter. But, would they return them there after whatever was going on inside the main building was over?

The house stood closer to the rear gate on the back third of the land. It favored the left side of the yard, but only slightly. Along the back right-hand corner was a line of port-a-potties.

He organized his thoughts. If he came over the fence behind the dark building he had good cover, but he wouldn't be able to see where Lynn and the others were taken. If they split them up, he'd have a lot of ground to cover to rescue them all. What if they never left the central building? Maybe the entire area had cots or mattresses spread out like a shelter house. The way they did after a disaster, like a hurricane or tornado.

This wasn't helping. He had no way of knowing what they used the space for unless he went down and found out. Once inside he could adjust to whatever happened. About to implement his decision, a loud roar exploded from the main building. What had happened? It sounded like someone just scored a touchdown for the home team. He focused the glasses on the front door. Less than a minute later, four men left the building and walked toward the front gate. Between them, they led a woman. Her hands were bound in front and her head hung low.

Adrenaline rushed through him like a stampede of horses. He pressed the binoculars hard to the glass trying to get a look at the face. While they walked, one of the men reached down and grabbed the woman's hair. He yanked backward, elevating the face. It was Doc. The man leaned forward and licked her cheek. She tried to pull away, dropping to the ground, but the men laughed and hauled her forward, dragging her for a while. Then they stopped and one of the men kicked her. That must have accompanied an order to stand because she did. The men laughed again and continued to walk.

Mark tried to figure out where they were taking her. The only things along their path were cars. Their intent was obvious. Doc was about to be gang-raped. Mark tightened his grip on the rifle. If they tried, smart or not, no way would he stand by and watch another woman be abused.

His mind called up an image of Summer, his ex-neighbor, as Buster and his men took her in her own family room. He had been powerless then. Or had it been cowardice? He didn't like to think about it, but he was still haunted by the scene and his failure to act.

Shoot or move? The question burned into him more with each passing second. In another half dozen steps the group would be out of sight from this angle, and behind the fence. He sighted the rifle scope back to the building, but none of the other women were in view, yet. Mark decided to move. Glancing back down, he was already too late. He no longer saw Doc.

He ran from the attic, pounding down the stairs. He burst from the bedroom, dashed toward the stairs to the main floor, spun around the balustrade, hit the first step, and froze. What the …?

He backed up and looked through the large window in the hallway with a view of the street. Confused, he watched with a mix of excitement and angst as the four men and their new toy exited the gate and moved to the street.

Chapter Thirty-Seven

MEL REACHED THE TRUCK WITHOUT INCIDENT. HER MIND whirled with possibilities. Frustrated at being ordered away by King Macho, she had reached a decision. Upon arriving at the farmhouse, she would give directions and see them off. After they were gone, she would collect Tara and leave. They'd have to steal the truck, of course. She would feel guilty, especially after all they'd done for Tara, but it couldn't be helped.

As she drove, other thoughts invaded her mind. What about Caryn? If she was rescued, she'd be happier staying with the community. That left Tara and her better able to survive and move more easily. But, she couldn't leave her without knowing she had done everything possible to give her the best chance to survive. Mel picked up the radio.

"Can anyone hear me? This is Mel. You know, one of the three new people. Is anyone there?"

A female voice answered, "Mel, this is Becca, what's going on?"

Mel filled her in and told her she was on the way. "My ETA, I think, is about ten minutes."

"Okay, we'll be ready."

She put down the radio and thought about what to say when she got there. Sooner than expected, a familiar corner appeared. She paused to be sure then turned left. A country block later the farmhouse came into view in the headlights. She made the turn up the driveway. To her amazement, eight vehicles were loaded and ready to move. Becca ran to the truck, opened the passenger side, and jumped in.

"Okay," Becca said, "lead us."

Mel stumbled for words to make an excuse to see Tara. Becca misunderstood.

"Hey, it's okay. We have a lot of support here. This is what families do."

Before Mel could speak, the young woman added. "Oh, by the way, I just left your friend, Tara. She wanted me to tell you she's all right and will see you when you get back. She's nice. I like her."

Mel swallowed. It tasted like guilt. Mumbling "Thanks," she backed down the driveway and led the caravan like a cavalry charge to the rescue.

HIS MIND WHIRLED. ADVANTAGE? DISADVANTAGE? HE FLEW through each option. The gate closed behind them. Definite advantage. He didn't have to go inside; another advantage. However, there were four of them. If they stayed in a group their attention would be occupied by Doc, giving him a chance to get behind them unseen. Mark was sure he could drop two with his handgun before they moved, wound the third and, what? Go from there. He shrugged. That was better than taking on the whole army.

Of course, the gun shots would alert the camp. He'd have to finish the fight fast. He and Doc would then disappear into the darkness behind the farmhouse. Perhaps veer off toward the woods to the west of the house. It could work.

He refocused on the group. Wait! They were coming toward the house. That wasn't good. He couldn't afford to get trapped here. Exits were limited, as were shooting lines. Getting up close might be impossible, especially if the old house's floorboards creaked. He tried to remember, but he had entered in such a hurry, any noises were lost.

The group reached the porch. Loud voices lifted upward. The men were in a party mood. That might be his only chance of getting a jump on them. But how did he get to all four? He'd have to wait and see how things developed. Which might be too late for Doc.

The pressure built in his chest and head as the stress and unresolved solution intensified. The front door opened, the voices louder. Backtracking, Mark stepped with slow movements to the room with the attic stairs. He stopped in the doorway and listened.

A husky voice said, "So, how you want to do this?"

Another man said, "I don't care. Everyone's gonna get a chance. It's just a matter of who goes first."

"What should we do," a third man said, "draw straws?"

Doc's frightened voice cut through, "Please," she pleaded, "don't hurt me."

Silence filled the room for a second, then a boom of laughter covered her sobs. The husky voice said, "Well, that all depends on you, honey. The more you fight, the more you get hurt."

More laughter. The second man said, "So, back to the question of who goes first?"

Mark listened, hoping for a clue to help him form a plan. If they brought Doc upstairs to utilize one of the beds, he stood a chance. If they stayed below, Mark would have to go down, guns-a-blazing. That was the worst option.

As he listened to the men argue, another thought came to mind. If he couldn't get them all, he could do what he did with Summer. He shuddered but continued with the idea. *If I take out as many as possible and then Doc, I might be able to escape.*

He let the possibility sit in his head for a moment. Mark vowed that if all else failed, Doc's death was the best last option. Pushing all emotion from his body, he steeled himself for that very real possibility.

In the back of his mind an unnerving voice, raised the question, But what about Lynn and Caryn? If Doc's fate was in his hands, who would be there to help them?

Another blast of laughter brought his attention back to the men.

Husky voice, bellowed above the din, "We can always arm wrestle for first place."

"Screw that," someone said.

Another voice answered, "Save that for her."

"Whatever we decide, let's stop wasting time and get to it."

"How 'bout highest card?"

"That'll work."

"Fine by me."

"Here's the deck."

The men were quiet for a moment. Mark slid the knife free and looked around the hallway for anything of use or information that might help with whatever he had to do. It dawned on him then that there were four men and four bedrooms. If this was their residence, maybe each man had a room. That might be beneficial for his attack. He had a one in four chance the man brought Doc here. If only the others remained downstairs.

"A four. A fucking four."

The others jeered. A gasping sob drifted upward. Doc's face floated before Mark's mind's eye. His eyes blurred. *No, can't afford that.* He wiped them with vigor and snarled.

"Six."

The others made fun of him.

"Laugh all you want, but right now I'm first."

Their good time and continued laughter fueled Mark's rage. He dragged the fine edge of the blade along the door frame, peeling off a six-inch splinter that curled and fell to the floor.

"Ha! Ten. Read it and stroke yourself, boys."

Those who had already drawn chanted at the fourth man. "Two. Two. Two."

Someone began a drum roll.

"King."

A collective "Aw!" escaped the losers.

"That's right, 'cause I am the king. That's me."

"Bastard."

"Don't hate me because I'm first."

"What are we worried about? He'll be done in ten seconds and I'm next."

The moment of decision and possible action had arrived. Mark listened with focused intent, gripping the knife in a death grip. The handgun hung from his right hand. He took a tentative step into the hallway, ready to spring if the sounds below dictated.

"Come on, pretty lady. Let's go have some fun."

That sounded as optimistic as the situation allowed.

"No, no, please," Doc cried.

The man's voice grew firm and threatening. "You remember how you begged us not to hurt you. You dragging your body behind me is a good way to feel pain. One way or another, you're going up those steps. Whether you're bleeding or not is up to you."

It was all Mark could do to rein in his fury and keep from running down the stairs and gutting the man now. With great effort he drew in calming breaths. They no longer worked. The fire behind his eyes increased, the room took on a red haze. Hold on, he insisted. A few moments longer. For Doc.

Doc cried with a steady sob, perhaps accepting her fate. No more threats were made.

The three losers continued to throw insults at the winner, but to Mark's great relief only one heavy set of steps climbed the stairs. He slunk back in the darkness of the closet and waited.

Chapter Thirty-Eight

MARK STRAINED TO HEAR THE MAN APPROACH. HE LEANED his head forward, just out of the frame, to pick up clues.

"This way, my love."

Doc squealed. The man must have done something to her.

They came closer. Mark's heart rate increased again. He bent at the knees, ready to launch.

The creak of a door. Mark relaxed. The door to this room was open already. His heart sank. He had to go to them. The door slammed shut. Close. He guessed the room across the hall was the intended bridal suite.

He crept from the closet and listened at the doorway. Across the hall the man's voice ordered. "Either take them off yourself or I'll rip them off."

Doc cried harder.

Mark tiptoed across the hall listening with one ear to the chatter below, his split attention on the door. When was the best time to move? Should he go now or wait until they hit the bed? He cringed at the thought of waiting. The rape might have already begun but that was the best time to make a move.

"Yeah, thatta girl. You look good."

"Please."

A slap. A cry of pain. More crying.

Mark put a hand on the knob and twisted slowly.

"Get on your knees. You know what to do. Oh, and just in case you have any bad thoughts, if I feel teeth, I'll cut off your left breast."

Mark pushed the door with steady pressure, resisting the urge to fling it open and pounce, for fear of making too much noise, thus alerting the men below. The old door held its voice. The space inside was revealed with agonizing yet necessary slowness.

A Coleman lantern lit the room giving off a faint odor. The large back of a naked man stood in front of him. Mark could barely see Doc kneeling before the brute. The size of his target made his task more difficult. He had to end him quick and with no sound. He couldn't afford for the brute to cry out or hit the floor too hard.

"Enough with the hand, open your mouth. Do it."

The space widened enough for Mark to slide in. Where the door had held its tongue, the floor had no such intent. Mark froze at the creak, but the sound was lost in a moan and the words, "Thatta girl. That feels just right."

Anger and revulsion flared within Mark at the forced act. Two strides and a leap and Mark was on the man's back.

"What ...?"

Mark wrapped his arm around the large forehead, yanked back and cut deeply into the throat making sure to sever the vocal chords. The huge man staggered backward clutching at his ruined neck. Gurgling and gagging sounds erupted from him, as did a gout of blood.

As the man backed up, Mark planted his feet against the wall and pushed. The force propelled the two of them toward the bed. The naked Doc scrambled out of the way just in time to avoid being crushed. The big man hit the bed knee high and toppled face first.

Mark pushed his face into the mattress as hard as he could to muffle any sound and hasten the end. The man kicked and rolled, but Mark held tight. He held on for a long minute after the body stopped moving.

Rolling off the bed, he stood gasping for air. Doc stood and threw herself into his arms, sobbing violently. He put an arm around her but couldn't return the fierceness of the hug for lack of breath. He let her go for a moment if only to gather enough air to speak. Then, gripping her arms, he gently pried her from his body.

"Doc, Doc, listen." He put a hand under her chin and held her face, forcing her to make eye contact. "Doc, hush and listen." As she quieted, he said, "Are you hurt?"

She shook her head. "He-he ..."

"Sh-sh, it's all right. It's over. You have to focus. We're not out of here yet. I'm going to need your help, but I have to know you can function. Can you run?"

"Yes." She nodded and wiped at her face.

"Okay, get dressed."

Doc picked up her clothes. Just then, a voice shouted from the hallway. "How's it going in there?"

Mark grabbed her arm and put a finger to his lips. Doc froze.

"Hey, we got a bet going on how long you last. You still going or you spent already?"

Footsteps put the speaker outside the door, most likely with his ear planted against the wood.

Mark placed his mouth by Doc's ear. "Moan like you're having sex." She nodded and complied. Mark sat on the edge of the bed and pushed up and down to create bed spring sounds. He grunted in a deep voice, "Just getting started."

"Yeah, right." Steps moved away from the door, but not down the stairs. "He says he's still going. I think he's lying."

Distant laughter answered.

"Don't worry. I'll stay right here until he's done. I'm sure it won't take long. I'm gonna win this bet."

If the man stayed outside the door, escaping through a window wasn't possible. Mark had to get rid of him. He glanced from the door to Doc and got an idea. Mark kept moving but motioned Doc toward him. She had some of her clothes pressed to her breasts but hadn't had a chance to dress yet.

"Doc, I need your help to get rid of this guy."

"Wh-what do I have to do?"

She sounded on the verge of a breakdown.

"I know it will be hard, but I want you to go into the hall naked."

She stiffened and tried to pull away.

"Wait. Listen to me. He's not going to touch you. I swear. Trust me. I need you to lure him past the door where I can reach him. Right now he's too far away and can alert the others. I won't be able to deal with all of them at once. If they beat me, they'll have you again. And no one will stop them then."

"Why can't you just shoot them?" she whispered, her voice vibrating with desperation.

"If I have to I will, but the gunshots will bring others from the camp. If that happens, we'll never get away. This is the best way. Doc, can you do this?"

"I-I don't know. Mark, I'm so scared."

"I know. Truth is, so am I. But you know what that man was going to do to you. If you don't help me, that will still happen. We don't have time to debate this. This same scene might be playing out for Lynn and Caryn too. I'm not trying to scare you even more, but, if I fail, this will happen every night. You're the best bait I have to even up the odds."

"We have to do this now."

She looked at the body. "What he was going to do. What he made me ..." She stopped. Mark felt her shiver through his hand. She stiffened again, but this time with resolve. "What do you want me to do?"

Chapter Thirty-Nine

"GO OUT THE DOOR. FACE HIM SO HE GETS A GOOD LOOK AT you and motion him forward with a finger, as if you're inviting him for his turn. As he comes closer, back up down the hall beyond this door so I can get at him from behind."

She sucked in a deep breath and stood. Without speaking she walked to the door, paused, and looked back at Mark. He stood still and nodded. Doc pressed her forehead to the door as if drawing strength from the wood, then opened the door and stepped out.

Mark went quickly to the door and pushed it closed, leaving enough gap to see and hear. For the moment, he could not see Doc. A voice said, "Whoa!" Then, "I'm not next. I sure wish I was. You've got a great body."

"No, I want you next," Doc said, her voice trembling. "Come on. Take me now." She backed into view, her long-legged, slender body moving past the door, her face alluring. Her finger crooked and motioning.

One heavier footstep, then, "But, I'm third. It wouldn't be right."

Doc drew her tongue around her lips to seal the deal.

"Oh, hell, he'll get over it." Hurried steps rushed past the door. A long-haired man in a beat-up cowboy hat flashed past and engulfed Doc. She gasped and tried to push away, panic now replacing her lustful look of moments before.

Mark was out the door and behind the man as he buried his face between Doc's breasts. Mark shoved his left hand between skin and mouth, clamped down and pulled back.

Before the man could speak Mark drove the blade up under the rib cage, in the direction of the heart. He hugged the would-be lover to his body and shoved the knife deeper. Legs kicked against the floor. Doc went for the legs and wrapped them in her arms to stop the flailing.

Mark dragged the body into the room where the first man lay. The scraping sound made more noise than anticipated.

A voice boomed from below. "Hey, what's going on up there? You bastard! You're skipping line aren't you?" Running footsteps pounded up the stairs. Mark released the body, letting it hit the floor, the time for stealth gone. He leaped over the body, pushed Doc in front of the door where she'd be seen and pressed against the wall far enough from the door to avoid being hit by it.

Someone pounded on the door vibrating the wood in its frame. "Open up, you bastard. It don't matter if you're both doing her, it's still my turn."

The door flung open, striking the wall, and bouncing back. Mark flinched and ducked reflexively. The new lover caught the door before it shut and pushed it open. Mark caught a glimpse of the man through the crack between the door and frame. He tensed, ready to spring. The man's eyes ran up and down Doc's pale skin, before doing a double-take and stopping at the body. "What'd you do, bitch?" He rushed in and Mark pounced, aware of more movement outside the door.

The first man in, sensing Mark, spun around, but he was too slow. The blade tore through his neck like a spear thrust. The man screamed and clutched at Mark's hand. Mark drove him back until he hit the wall then turned his head to the door. The last man stood in the doorway, paralyzed for the moment. He took a step forward, but when Mark withdrew the blade, thought better of entering and fled.

This man could not escape. Mark made for the door but stumbled over the second body and went down on hands and knees. He cursed and bounced to his feet, afraid that each precious second lost might be the one that ended his life.

Ahead, his prey bounded down the stairs. Without thought or hesitation, Mark gripped the balustrade and vaulted over the top. He free fell, landing on the step behind his opponent, falling into, rather than tackling him. The two tangled and rolled down the remaining steps. They sprawled on the main floor and separated, Mark rolled further, slamming into the wall. Stunned, he lay there for a moment while the last man stood and wound up a violent kick at his ribs.

Mark dodged most of the blow, taking the brunt on his right arm. Numbness crept upward, the knife clattered away. Before his assailant wound up for another kick, Mark dove for the man's legs, wrapping his left arm around both, as if taking down a running back.

Unable to move without falling, the other man pounded on Mark's head. Attempting to get to his knees, and unable to protect himself, the blows were having a cumulative effect.

A sudden shriek filled the room like the arrival of the Valkyrie, and the man toppled over with Doc clinging to and clawing at his face. They hit the floor with a solid thud. Doc rebounded off the floor and lay still. By then, Mark had regained his feet, but his opponent had found the knife and swung a vicious backhand slice at Mark's midsection.

Unable to dodge the entire cut, fire lit Mark's stomach as a fine line of red appeared like an artist's stroke.

The man stood, ready to strike. Mark backed and circled away from where the inert body of Doc lay. He wanted distance from her and any further action. The man feinted a thrust, then again, before attempting another deadly slash. Mark was running out of space. There was only one way to end this confrontation. He reached behind him and pulled out his gun. Pointing it, the man, froze. The expectant victorious look on his face melted away.

"Put the knife down."

The knife wielder considered that for a moment. "If you shoot, the entire camp will be here in seconds. They'll cut you into little pieces, cook you, and feed you to the slaves."

"Yeah, but you'll still be dead." He cocked the hammer and leveled the gun.

The man's eyes widened, realizing he had miscalculated. The knife hit the floor a second later. Hands in the air, he backed away. "Okay, don't shoot." His feet struck Doc's body and he went down over the top of her. He hit the ground and rolled.

Mark stepped forward, an involuntary action to protect Doc from harm. But, in so doing, lowered his gun and stretched out his hand. Before he realized his mistake, the fallen man produced a gun from somewhere and had an arm around Doc's throat.

From a sitting position he pulled the pliable body in front of him as a shield. The gun aimed at her head. "Now, you drop the gun or I'll kill her."

Mark tried to buy some time. His gun trained on Doc's body, he said, "And once you shoot her, I'll kill you."

"You're bluffing. You didn't go through all this to let this woman die. Drop the gun."

Mark shrugged. "She's just a woman. Not worth my life. I can always find another. In fact, I'll shoot right through her to get you. Without her trailing behind me, slowing me down, it will be easy for me to escape before your friends get here."

Doc's eyes fluttered open, unfocused. A few rapid blinks later awareness returned. She took in her situation in an instant and locked on Mark. She had taken the time to put on her panties but was otherwise still naked. Her remaining clothes lay strewn around the floor.

"Your choice. It's time for me to go."

"Well, then go. If the woman isn't that important to you, why stay?" The man must have felt some tension in Doc's body and realized she was awake. He pulled her tight and squeezed hard. "Stay still."

Mark shifted his aim a hair. He had a slight opening to the side of Doc's right ear, but it wasn't much. He narrowed his gaze to the future dead man's right eye. However, the man must have noticed and understood his intent. He moved his head behind Doc, enough to eliminate the shot.

Mark glanced down as Doc moved her hand along the floor. She found the discarded knife.

A moment of panic assailed Mark. Whatever she planned to do with the knife would be too slow and result in her death. But how to warn her? Mark's pulse quickened. The other man must have noticed a change. His eyes widened, his nostrils flaring, ready to shoot.

Mark shouted, "No!"

Chapter Forty

DOC TWISTED AND PUNCHED THE KNIFE INTO HER CAPTOR'S shin. Two shots went off simultaneously. Mark wasn't sure where the other man's bullet went, but his penetrated the man's eye, taking out the back of his head.

Doc fell limp to the floor. Mark dove for her, scooping her up to check the damage. A deep gash ran along the side of her head. So much blood flowed he couldn't tell if the bullet had punctured her skull or just grazed it. Regardless, he had to move.

He checked her pulse and her breathing. Both were still in operation. Taking off his t-shirt, he pressed it to the wound and tied it as tight as he could. He placed her head gently on the floor and went to the window. In the dim light from the corner post, Mark saw the guard had stopped patrolling, and now looked at the house.

He had to do something or the curious guard would raise the alarm. Taking the stairs two at a time, he found the cowboy hat and scooped it up. He jumped halfway down the steps in one bound then repeated the process landing on the floor. In the dark perhaps no one would notice.

He stepped out onto the front porch. They were a good fifty yards apart and in the dark. He thought he had a good chance of pulling off the deception. Keeping most of his body and a part of his face behind the stone support pillar, he waved the cowboy hat. "Sorry, got a little excited."

The guard watched, leaning over the fence to see better. Mark placed the hat on his head and stepped out a little more.

"Is that you, Billy?" the guard said.

"Yep. Someone was just upset 'cause they drew last." Mark shouted across the street hoping he had the voice and pitch correct. "Won't happen again. See ya in the morning." He turned and went back inside. Shutting the door behind him, Mark went to the front window and peered out. The guard was still in the same position, staring at the house.

"Come on. Move on," Mark said. The wait continued. He was about to throw Doc over his shoulder and make a run for it, when the guard straightened and continued his patrol, away from the house. Perhaps his ruse had worked. But his efforts had bought some time.

Doc groaned. He had to get her ready to move. They couldn't stay here. Someone would come eventually. He gathered her clothes and dressed her as best he could, abandoning the bra. Done, he tried to rouse her. Mark needed information from her about Lynn and Caryn. "Doc. Doc. Wake up. Can you hear me?'

She moaned again.

He let her be and went to explore the house. In one corner of the kitchen he found cases of water stacked. He tore two bottles out. He drank the first one in one long draw, then opened the second. Kneeling next to Doc, he poured some in his hand and sprinkled it on her face. She flinched, but her eyes remained closed. He tried again, with no response. He tipped the bottle and trickled a small steady stream over her head. This time her eyes opened, but she seemed unfocused. She didn't blink, nor did her eyes move from the spot where she looked.

"Doc, I need your help. Doc, can you hear me?" He patted her face. Placing the water bottle to her lips he tried to pour some down her throat, making her cough, but had the desired effect. She leaned forward on her own to expel the fluid.

"Doc, you okay?"

Her eyes filled with tears. She hugged him, but not with much strength.

"You've been shot. You've lost some blood. Can you hear me? Do you understand what I'm saying?"

"Yes," she croaked, coughing some more.

"Do you want some water?"

She nodded and screwed up her face. Her hand went to her head and she winced from the touch.

"Sit up a bit." He helped her. She swallowed noisily several times before coughing some more.

"Doc, where are Lynn and Caryn?"

She struggled to speak. Closing her eyes seemed to help. "They were going to auction them off."

"Is that what they did to you?"

"No. They just gave me to those men because they were the ones who captured us."

"Were they both," he swallowed, "unharmed."

Doc hesitated. "No. They hit Lynn a few times because she fought them."

"I have to get in there to help them. Do you have any suggestions?"

"There are too many of them. You'll never survive." Her voice faded. "My head hurts bad."

"I'll see if I can find anything for the pain." Mark scrounged around in the kitchen cabinets finding a half-full bottle of ibuprofen. He brought the bottle over and gave three to Doc. Though coughing, she managed to swallow them.

"Rest for a moment while I check things out."

MARK WENT BACK TO the attic window after collecting the rifle and binoculars. Judging by all the activity around the main building, the meeting, or auction was still going on. He hoped that was a good thing, for Lynn and Caryn's sake.

Once more he swept the grounds looking for the best way inside. Movement near the front gate drew his attention. The guard had his back to Mark, leaning to the inside of the yard. He had to be talking to someone because he kept pointing back at the house. He wasn't sure what the outcome of the discussion would be, but he felt it was time to move. He couldn't save anyone if they found him there.

He trotted down the attic stairs and looked around the room. He found an old discarded book bag that could be slung over one or both shoulders. Taking it downstairs, he filled it with bottles of water, a package of cookies, the ibuprofen and a box of Band-Aids. He slung the bag over one shoulder, his rifle over the other and went to the front room.

"Doc, we have to go. Can you walk?"

"I think so."

He helped her to her feet, but she nearly collapsed. Mark saw an obvious wave of nausea pass through her before she doubled over and vomited on the dead man. Done, Mark let her rest while he checked at the window.

His breath was pulled from his lungs. The gate was opening. Ready or not, they had to go. Now!

Chapter Forty-One

"DOC, WE HAVE TO GO. MORE MEN ARE COMING." HE REACHED over and set the deadbolt, then looked at Doc.

She wiped her mouth, her eyes had the faraway look of confusion. The shock was too much for her. In two fast strides, he stood over her. Bending, he grabbed under her arms and lifted until she stood upright. He gripped her chin, moved his face close to hers, forcing her to make eye contact, and said, "Doc, we have to go."

Tears fell, but she nodded. "Okay."

Mark took her hand and led her to the back door. Her gait was awkward, but she moved. They ran down the steps and straight back, keeping the house between them and the pursuers. With luck, the men checking the house would take a few minutes to get in and several more to search the house, before looking out back. By then, Mark hoped to be lost in the darkness.

Once away from the house he veered toward the woods on the left. Doc struggled but kept her feet moving. The dim moon and starlight felt like a spotlight that followed their every move. In his mind, Mark tried to count down the time before the alarm sounded. He pushed harder, his legs lifting and falling over the ridges of the plowed land. The dark mass of the trees loomed in front of them, a distance that never seemed to diminish.

Behind them, Mark thought he heard a door crash open. Imagination or not, he didn't want to risk discovery. "Get down." He pulled Doc to the ground next to him. Lifting the rifle he found the house through the scope. He had enough light to see a man standing on the back porch looking out over the open field.

Another man joined him and they had an animated discussion. A minute later, both men entered the house.

"Hurry. Run."

Resuming their flight, the two pounded ever closer to the safety of the woods. What seemed like an hour later, they reached the tree line and plunged into blackness. Mark latched onto Doc's arm and pulled her close.

"They're going to come after us in a large group. They'll probably split up, sending one group straight back and one to each side. I want you to head in that direction," he pointed, "keeping inside the cover of the trees. There's a road back there. Once you reach it, stay there. Mel went to get help and when she returns, she'll be on that road. Wait for her. Tell her where I am."

"Where will that be?"

"Here. I'm gonna try to pull all pursuit to me so they won't follow you."

"But Mark, there's too many of them. You'll never get away."

"I'll be fine. I'm going to lead them away from you then disappear deeper into the woods. Once I lose them, I'll go around to the back of the camp. Tell Mel to meet me there. If enough of them are out here searching for us, we might be able to get inside and rescue Lynn and Caryn."

"Mark, I ..."

"Doc, this isn't open for discussion. I can't do this if I have to worry about you. Go now." Taking one bottle of water from the bag he handed it to her. She took it, then he held out the handgun. "Take this just in case."

She took the gun, hesitating as if ready to voice an objection, then turned and slid quietly from sight.

Mark moved in the opposite direction about twenty feet before taking up position behind a small fallen tree. Placing the barrel of the rifle across the trunk, he drew a bead on the house. Sweeping left to right and back, Mark kept watch waiting for the inevitable posse to assemble. His wait was shorter than he hoped. They must have sent word to the camp. The men swarmed around the house like stampeding cattle.

They stopped in the backyard, a good twenty strong, all armed with a rifle of some sort and flashlights. After a brief discussion, one man appeared to take charge, assigning duties. He pointed to the field behind the house, then toward the trees where Mark hid.

Despite knowing the search would encompass his position, an involuntary shudder swept through him. Taking a deep breath, he readied for what he had to do.

A large group of men spread out through the field and moved forward as one, in the classical hunting tradition of flushing prey. Six men headed toward the trees.

Mark weighed his options. He thought about waiting until the six reached the trees then try to eliminate as many as possible through stealth. However, taking them out in that fashion would take time. The main line of searchers might get too close to Doc.

He thought about leaving then, finding his way to the camp and trying to rescue Lynn and Caryn while the odds were more in his favor. However, he had no idea how many men remained inside the compound, nor did he have any notion as to where to find the women.

A picture of Lynn formed and faded in an instant. As much as he was driven to find her, Mark couldn't throw Doc's safety away for his personal concerns. He studied the men approaching.

If he left them alone they might not find Doc. Maybe Mel would arrive before they did. If Doc stayed hidden and undetected in the dark and Mel and company showed up when the hunting party was at that end of the field, they would be ambushed, without standing a chance. No, too many ifs and maybes. He had to draw them all to him first. It was the only way to keep everyone else safe.

Mark let them get closer. With each second that passed they became a greater threat, but the longer he waited, the farther the larger group drew away. It would take them more time to get to him and be more difficult to pick up his trail. He had enough ammo to deal with the smaller group, but having given up his handgun, his backup weapon now was his knife. He'd have to let one of them get close enough to take his weapon.

The line of men stretched from north to south, with Mark lined up with the fifth man from the south. He chose to take out numbers five and six, the closest men, then try to pick off the others. He wouldn't get them all.

He lined up the first shot and waited. The group was twenty-five yards away. He glanced to the left. The line moving away from him comprised small black shapes that appeared to glide over the ground.

Mark rehearsed his movements, sliding the barrel from left to right then back. If these men were untrained, they'd freeze for an instant after the first shot, giving him time to change targets and fire. Trained soldiers would hit the ground immediately leaving him searching for a shot.

Twenty yards. He couldn't wait much longer. Mark inhaled and released a breath, increasing pressure on the trigger. A gentle squeeze and the rifle barked. The target in front of him dropped from sight. Pivoting the barrel he found number six's head had turned, staring where his buddy had just been. His knees buckled, looking for the safety of the ground, changing the target the scope had set on his chest. Mark's shot hit high ripping off the top of the hunter's head. Two down.

Without looking for the other four men, Mark peeled off to the right and ran. Shots tore through the area where he had been. The shooters fired nonstop, but Mark was no longer a target. He set up in a hurry ten yards to the south. His scope found one shooter who had risen to one knee to shoot. He put a shot under his left arm where the heart would be. Three down. As another man turned toward him, Mark pulled the trigger again. This time he didn't see any results of his work. The remaining men switched lines of sight and poured rounds in his direction.

A quick look through the scope showed many darkened forms heading his way. He swept toward the tree line. More than one man had entered the woods to the north. He had little time. He fired two hasty shots at the oncoming men, dropping one and forcing the others to slow their approach.

Switching out magazines, he shot twice more at the nearest men, unsure if either shot struck home. It was time to move again. He ran south toward the street, then turned west and tore through the undergrowth. In a shorter distance than he'd hoped, the trees ended. Ahead of him stretched another wide and open field. South, they would know he was near the camp. West, they could see him for a long way. His only choice was north, toward Doc, but he had to slip past his pursuers.

He ran outside the western tree line for about ten yards. That allowed him to move faster and quieter for the moment. Mark ducked and stepped into the first row of trees and brush. There he waited and listened.

Voices filled the woods coming from many directions, leaving him unsure where the nearest man was. With extreme caution, he slid forward then headed north. He stopped, moved, and stopped and moved. Bodies stepped through the undergrowth to his right. They made no attempt to hide their presence, perhaps figuring there was safety in numbers. He pressed to the ground and waited.

Much of the noise moved away from him. But how many more were still in the trees, searching? He listened intently.

"Make a line and spread out. Make sure you can see the people next to you." An authoritative voice boomed.

A flurry of voices followed as they formed their line. Then, everything went silent. The eeriness of the sudden change embraced Mark like an arctic wind.

Chapter Forty-Two

"ALL RIGHT, MOVE OUT. CALL OUT IF YOU SEE ANYTHING."

Mark froze, his heart in his throat. They were systematic in their search. But where did the line start? To the north, they'd find him for sure. He had to find the end of the line.

Crawling back to the edge of the trees, Mark peered at ground level left and right. He couldn't see anyone. However, that didn't mean someone wasn't there watching. He alligator-crawled to the north, dropping flat and staying still every five feet. He went as far as he dared in the open before ducking back inside the relative safety of the trees. There he put all energy into his ears.

Far to the right, movement gave him pause. The search line was moving away from him. He relaxed, expelling a breath he had not known he held. Then, as easy as that breath had left, the intake was cut short. A stealthy step fell somewhere very near to his left. Against all desire to see where the person was, Mark buried his face in the ground. Digging his fingers into the soft earth, he pulled up dirt and wiped it over his sweaty face. Only then did he risk a peek.

A sound came again. Someone who had stalked prey before was moving through the area with only the merest of noise. The slight crunch of a dry leaf. The soft scrape of a slim branch dragging across cloth. Mark's heart seemed to stop beating, as if afraid its normal function would be heard.

With great care, Mark slid his hand down his body, stopping at the handle of the knife. He eased the blade from the leather sheath one inch at a time. Another disturbance, this one seemingly a foot from his head. That had to be a false read by his angst-filled brain, or the man would have seen him.

Inching his head sideways to see upward, Mark watched, expecting a bullet or cry of alarm at any second. The sound ceased. Yet nothing was in view. Then, a change of darkness flashed like a phantom not five feet away. The shadow stopped as if alerted to his presence. The darkened shape of its head swept side to side.

Mark's brain screamed "run" as the head turned in his direction. The knife wasn't completely out yet. He'd been afraid to move the blade further. Basically unarmed, the rifle pointing forward away from the hunter, Mark fought the urge to jump up. He wanted to scream, lying there with no defense or chance to survive if discovered.

Another crunch. The man moved on. Little by little, second by agonizing second, the sounds of his passing became fainter. No longer able to see the shadow, Mark though anxious to move, was afraid to do so. Anyone that attuned to his surroundings would hear him, even at a distance. He waited. Minutes passed, the natural sounds of the woods resumed as if calling out an all-clear.

Mark slid a knee under him and levered his torso from the ground. He pivoted his head in a long scan of the entire area, a panoramic camera taking in a vista. The almost total darkness within the trees made finding his pursuer next to impossible. Instead, he relied on his hearing. Satisfied he was alone, he stood. With a last glance behind he started forward. Three steps later he ran head first into a startled man. Both men gasped audibly.

Instead of grappling or using the rifle as a club the frightened man attempted to bring his rifle down between them to shoot. He stepped back to gain room. Mark was quicker with the knife. He lunged forward impaling the man, but unable to stop the cries of pain. He pressed in closer, body to body, and tried to cover the man's mouth. At the same time, he pushed the blade in deeper and lifted through the soft flesh of the man's large stomach.

The gun exploded past Mark's head, the sound deafening. He flinched but continued to drive the man backward until they hit a tree. The shooter's body slammed hard and twisted to the right, then fell. Mark landed on top, the gun went off again. Releasing his hold on the man's mouth, Mark found the rifle barrel and ripped it from the weakening grip.

The man continued to cry out in pain. Mark had no choice, but to pull the knife free and plunge it into the man's throat. The shouts turned to gurgling, then to silence.

Mark turned his head and listened. Crashing. At high speed. From multiple directions. Quickly he rummaged through the man's pockets finding some loose rounds. He couldn't grip them all, and some fell to the ground, but he didn't have the luxury of time to search for them. He sheathed the knife, snatched up both rifles and fled north.

With no chance to use stealth, Mark had to hope the noise made by his pursuers partially concealed his. Voices shouted out directions. They were closing in. Perhaps they already had him pinched. He had to think, to find a way out, but panic overruled thought. He ran on, desperate for distance and safety.

A sound to his right told him neither was possible.

Swerving to his left, he hit a root, tripped, and went down. Scrambling, he hid behind a tree and fought to control his breathing while extending his hearing. His breathing was too loud in his ears to hear anything.

Lifting the rifle, he sighted and swept the scope. A shadow. He fired. Everything seemed to stop at once. The shot was too fast. He doubted he made contact. Now they knew where he was. The longer he waited, the easier it would be to surround him. About to move, the woods suddenly lit up with gunfire. The flashes looked like a swarm of lightning bugs.

Mark ducked, curling his knees to his chest, to wait out the barrage. Bullets smacked trees and ripped through leaves all around him. The shooters had the basic direction but hadn't pinpointed the spot. Still, moving would be difficult. Any sound would redirect their aim, and even a lucky shot killed.

His brain worked feverishly to find a way out. He aimed toward the open field to the west. If they hadn't thought of it yet, men would soon come that way to cut him off and come up behind him. If he broke free, he could run north, but they'd hear him. Sliding backward, he might reach the field undetected, but the open field ran a long way.

Regardless, he had to do something. Staying was certain death. The rate of fire decreased. Mark assumed men were moving into better shooting positions. It was decision time. Gathering his courage, Mark slid backward, keeping a tree between him and the shooters. He prayed this was the right decision, knowing it was the only one he had.

Chapter Forty-Three

WITH THE HAIR ON THE BACK OF HIS NECK STANDING AT constant attention, Mark reached the tree line, waiting for the bullets to tear into him at any second. Keeping his head near the ground, he looked right then left. Right was clear. Two men approached at a jog from the left.

He looked straight out, the open field both inviting and dangerous. If he took these men down the others would know where he was. How far could he run into the open space before someone saw him, drew a bead, and took him down? If he got out far enough and hit the dirt, he might be able to burrow in deep enough to cover himself, at least until dawn.

That was his best option. Sliding the rifle forward, Mark took aim at the first man and squeezed the trigger. The man acted as if he'd hit a wall. He straightened, staggered back, and dropped. The second man skidded to a stop, but instead of dropping for cover, ran for the woods. Mark tracked him and put him down.

He didn't watch to make sure either man stayed down. He scrambled to his feet and ran as hard as he could in a northern direction. He did a mental countdown, figuring at most he had ten seconds before someone discovered his flight and sent bullets in pursuit.

At nine, he dove for the ground, landing with an *oof* he could not contain. Scurrying, he turned to face the woods and dug ferociously at the dirt, like a squirrel burying his find. All the while he worked, Mark kept his eyes on the trees. They might be able to see him, but unless they came out of the woods, he wouldn't be able to see them.

Knowing he was pressing his luck timewise, Mark pressed his body to the ground wiggling his torso to create a more concealing hole. He set both rifles on the ground in front of him and scooped dirt into a six-inch mound in front of him. Placing a rifle on each end of the pile Mark put his chin into the dirt and sighted through the scope on the right side.

He panned the tree line, but nothing moved. Had he gone unseen? If so, he couldn't believe his luck. Maybe they still thought he was in the woods. He tried to recall the action, like a sports reporter doing a recap of a game. He had estimated a starting number of twenty. Kills he was sure of totaled six, maybe seven, leaving two to three unknowns. The odds were still bad but getting better.

He waited. His body relaxed, exhausted, drained from exertion and the mental strain. His eyes burned. With a sleeve he wiped the sweat from his eyes and forehead, momentarily blurring his vision. He tried to blink them clear but had to wipe them again. His focus better, Mark saw men had emerged from the trees. This surprised him, increasing his angst. He scanned around him for fear his laxity had allowed them to get behind him.

Nothing.

He sighted on the men. Three of them stood just in sight, all of them held rifles to their eyes. They were doing the same thing he was. He moved further behind the mound keeping only his right eye clear.

One hunter stopped, his scope pointing directly at Mark, giving him the feeling the man could see right through his lens. Despite the low light, Mark angled the rifle down to deflect any reflection off the lens.

A shot rang out. The bullet struck the mound. Mark flinched and hid his face. He waited. Nothing happened. Were they approaching, or waiting for him to move? Another shot. This round struck near his rifle. He wanted to pull it back but was afraid to move anything. If they were shooting to draw him out, it wasn't going to work. A third shot, same result.

Were they fishing, unsure if he was there, or was one man shooting to keep him pinned down while the others advanced toward him? He had to look. He had no choice. They could be on him before he knew it, even if his movement gave him away.

Mark righted the rifle and looked. Other than separate, the men still stood by the trees. Now, however, they were joined by three others, with two or more rifles aimed in his direction. They were obviously unsure of what they were seeing or a full-scale assault would be underway.

They were in as much danger coming across the open ground as he was fleeing. He understood their anxiety. Until they flanked him, he could hold out here for a while. Of course, time was not on his side. As soon as the sun came up, he'd be an easy target. If he intended to make a break for safety, he had to do it when dark. In the hands of a good shot, the rifles certainly had the range to take him down while he fled.

He rolled onto his back and looked out beyond into the darkness, imagining the path of his escape. Running a zigzag pattern was a must but would eat up precious time. The darkness swallowed the horizon. He only had his memory to use as a guide for how far he had to run. All he knew for sure was it was a long way to anything re-motely resembling cover.

If he drew them out, they'd be in the same situation: no cover. He had as much chance of picking them off as they did him. The downside was he had no one in reserve.

At a loss, Mark looked toward the street, seventy-five long yards away. Across the street stood a narrow copse of trees that ran parallel to the western side of the com-pound. He couldn't tell from there how far back from the road it went, but the sight offered him an alternate plan. The move was dangerous, but no more so than staying there or running off into the distance. This was a shorter dash, although, moving across the shooters' sight lines, offering himself as a target all the way. If even one of them had tracked and put down a deer before, the shot would be easy. Running away from the shooters, he diminished as a target with each step.

But, if he reached the trees across the street, the positions would be reversed. He'd be in cover and the hunters in the open. He liked that thought. Getting there alive was the problem.

Turning his attention back to his pursuers, he saw two men had moved closer. One on the right, one the left. Time to choose.

Chapter Forty-Four

MARK ACQUIRED THE FIRST TARGET, THE MAN ON THE RIGHT and fired. Without waiting to see the result he switched to the second man, who was already dropping to the ground. Mark had no real shot but loosed one anyway.

As soon as he pulled the trigger, he was up and running. Return fire whizzed behind him like a swarm of angry bees taking up the chase. Afraid to stop lest they make the appropriate adjustment and begin leading their shots, Mark raced on. The words from an old Marine instructor played through his head, *It takes skill to hit a moving target.* Then the second part of that lecture came through, *and sometimes luck.* He kept running.

The shot that changed his mind whipped past his nose, close enough to wipe it. He dove for the ground. He hit and rolled to a position facing his pursuers. Three men had taken up the chase. Others were stationary and firing.

Bullets plunked into the dirt around his head. At any second the next shot could finish him. He aimed at one of the runners and squeezed off a round. His lead was perfect, spinning the man like a drunken ballerina. He stumbled and fell. The others ducked.

He rolled one complete revolution to make the shooters adjust. Then, sighting as fast as he could, fired off a bullet in the direction of each standing shooter. The intent was not so much to hit, as to disrupt their aim and rhythm. As the last shot left the barrel, Mark was on his feet again.

Reacquiring him didn't take as long as he'd hoped. Shots passed close enough to feel them. One shot hit the stock of the rifle, tearing it from his grip, surprising him, taking him off stride and down. Pain shot through his knee. At first, he thought he'd been wounded until he touched the injured area and found it blood-free. A strain was all, as he twisted to the ground.

Using the second rifle, Mark fired off two quick shots and took to his feet running. He hobbled as fast as possible, pushing aside the sharpness of the pain. Mark went another ten yards until once more the bullets zeroed in. Dropping, he absorbed the impact on his hands and arms to save his injured knee. The landing was far from graceful.

Mark scanned in a hurry. The road was still a good twenty yards away. The hunting party had gained. Two men pulled up level with him, near the trees. Reaching the safety of the trees across the road was doubtful.

He thought about Doc. He had given her the chance to escape but Lynn's fate was different. A lump formed in his throat. Frustration at the situation and anger at his failure flared. He pulled the trigger twice for no reason.

No!

He could not quit. If he was going to die anyway, he'd go down fighting.

Mark rose to his knees. A spike of pain shot through him. Aiming in the direction of the two nearest men, he fired once and broke for the road again. The distance shortened. Ten yards. He should drop for cover. Mark continued. The shots flew past. How much longer would his luck hold?

Five yards. A bullet grazed his shin; another his left arm. Still he ran on. A depression, just before the street tripped him up and perhaps saved his life. Face planting, he came up spitting dirt. He rolled and pressed against the slope. He surmised his new position was a drainage ditch. Slapping the barrel down on the rise he sighted and fired. A shrill scream pierced the night. The man fell but continued his cries. Everything else fell quiet.

Mark's targets had all taken to the ground, no longer visible. He dropped the mag and thumbed in loose rounds. Full, he slapped it back in place with one bullet left in his pocket.

The voices started again and his heart pounded so loudly, he missed most of what was said. The gist was "flank him, we'll cover you." The road behind him looked foreboding. The hard flat surface offered no cover. If he made it to the far side there was safety, if only temporarily.

Bullets pounded the earth around him, pinning him down. He knew others would be moving. He crawled to the left about ten feet and came up ready. Acquiring a target he fired twice. The man staggered two more steps and went down.

Mark ducked and crawled to his right about fifteen feet. Now, when he bolted, they had to readjust again, giving him precious seconds. He was about to make his move when someone jumped into the ditch forty feet further to his right.

Startled, Mark shot in a hurry, missing.

A bullet struck the ground near his feet. It had come from behind him. He was too late. They had him trapped. Returning one shot in each direction, he rose to make his dash, knowing it was the better of two chances, though the outcome was still inevitable.

He froze at the sound of an approaching vehicle. Now he was truly trapped. Defeat was an even drier dirt in his mouth. As the headlights exploded the darkness away, a pickup truck braked in front of him, blocking any chance of escape. He swallowed hard, determined to use every bullet before they took him down.

Bodies jumped from the truck and his last thought was I'm sorry, Lynn. Forgive me.

Mark readied to meet them. They came out in a swarm firing. He found his first target squeezed the trigger and heard, "Mark! Come on."

Shocked at hearing his name, he jerked the barrel, the shot flying high.

"Mark," the voice repeated. It was Lincoln. "Hurry."

Indescribable relief filled him and with tears in his eyes, he scrambled up the ditch to the road. Once there, it was like a car's tires finding traction. He accelerated, reached the truck and clambered over the side wall.

With bullets chasing them, his rescuers piled in and the truck lurched backward. A few seconds later, making a hard one-eighty turn, the truck fled. Lying on his back, breathing hard and staring up at the night sky, Mark wanted to weep.

Someone dropped next to him. "Dad," Bobby said, "Are you all right?"

Mark gulped, cleared his throat, swallowed again and said, "Yes, son, I'm fine. I'm more than fine." He latched on to the boy, pulling him down and hugging him. He didn't let go until the truck stopped two turns later.

Everyone climbed out and closed around Mark. Lincoln, Mel, Bobby, Caleb all tried to speak at once. "Okay, okay," Lincoln said, stepping into the middle with his hands up. "Give the man a chance to breathe."

"God, it is so good to see you," Mark said. "How did you find me?"

"Please," said Bobby, "we just listened for gunfire and knew you had to be involved."

"Wait, what are you saying?" he laughed.

"Seriously?" Lincoln said. "Wherever there's gunfire, you're always in the middle of it."

"Oh, really?"

Everyone said, "Yeah," at the same time.

"Well, maybe." He smiled as they laughed. "Did you find Doc?"

"Yeah," said Mel. "She's safe, with the others."

Mark's smile faded slowly as he remembered Lynn and Caryn. "Well, I'm afraid the gunfight has only begun. I wasn't able to rescue Lynn or Caryn. They're inside the compound."

Silence enveloped the group.

Lincoln said, "Yeah, we know. Everyone's waiting for us down the road a bit. These bastards also took the Donnollys. They killed Ian and took his wife and son."

Chapter Forty-Five

THE NEWS ROCKED MARK. HE TOOK A STEP BACK AS IF someone had punched him in the chest. Ian and his family were new to the community. So much so, he couldn't recall what the wife and son looked like. Tension mounting, and mentally upset, he couldn't remember their names, Mark pressed his temples between his thumb and middle finger and rubbed. With a jolt, a memory returned.

"Wait! What about the Richardson kids? Lynn said they were missing."

"They're okay. They were up in a tree picking cherries and left their radio on the ground."

"Oh, thank God." Mark covered his face with his hands. A hand landed lightly on his shoulder. Mark looked up to meet Lincoln's eyes.

"Let's get them back and make the bastards pay."

Mark's jaw tightened. He nodded. "Let's."

In two minutes they reached a line of vehicles parked along the side of the road. They joined a large group led by Jarrod. The big, burly farmer, with the wild mop of curly black hair covering his face and head looked more imposing in the dark.

"Well, here we go again," he said.

"Yeah," Mark said. "What've we got?"

Before he could respond Becca came running from the woods and threw herself into Mark's arms.

"Daddy, I'm so glad to see you." She held him tight. Then, just as suddenly, released him and stared at her hand. "Oh, my God, Dad, you've been hurt." She showed the red smear on her hand.

"I'm all right, Becca."

"Bullshit!" She moved around him searching his body. "God, Daddy, are these all bullet wounds?"

Mark turned, grabbed his daughter by the shoulders and held her at arm's length. "Becca, I'm fine."

"Bullshit!" she reiterated. "You need a doctor."

"Lynn, Caryn, and the Donnollys need our help right now. I'll worry about my wounds later."

She opened her mouth to say something else. "Becca." His tone harsh and final.

She moved away muttering, "Bullshit" and "Stubborn old fool."

Jarrod laughed. "I wonder whose kid that is?"

Mark frowned at him, "Yeah, real nice. Now, what've we got?"

"The junkyard these dogs are using for their home base is directly through those trees."

Mark glanced in the direction Jarrod pointed. A long line of trees blocked the view from the road.

"They're about ten yards wide, then we got problems. The space to the fence is about fifty yards. Other than a tree stump or so, there's nothing to use for cover. We got about twenty-five people against who knows how many inside. Bottom line, it's not gonna be easy."

"We have to try. Lynn and the others are counting on us."

The group gathered around. Mark let his eyes slide from one face to another. "You know what we have to do and you know what might happen. But that's what communities do. They stand together and help each other. It could be any of us inside and our one hope would be the rest of us will come and get us.

"We've got four of our family members in there. We have to get them out. I hope you feel the same and will stand with me."

Lincoln said, "You don't have to make speeches, Mark. We all came knowing what had to be done. Let's just figure how."

"All right. First, I need Bobby, Caleb and, uh, Mel, to go to the front of the camp. Take up positions in the house across the street from the front gate."

"No, Dad, I want to ..."

Mark stopped him with a raised hand. "Listen to me," the words barked, loudly, and as a command. "We have to control the front or they'll be able to get out and circle us. You three are good shots. Drive right up the driveway and park behind the house. The backdoor is open. Do it fast and control the ground. In one of the closets you'll find stairs leading to the attic. That window will give you a good view of the compound. Mel knows. She'll show you. One of you should be on each floor.

"Your presence will hopefully draw their attention to the front, giving us a better chance of getting inside before we're detected.

"Myron, you go with them and watch the back of the house. Make sure no one gets behind them. Oh, and give me your rifle and any extra ammo. All you'll need inside is a handgun." He looked at the selected four. "Go now." They started moving. "And take a radio."

As they drove off, Mark went toward the woods. "I need to see what we're up against. Jarrod and Lincoln, come with me. Everyone else, stay put."

They entered the trees moving from dark to darker. It only took a few steps to reach the other side. He sighted through the scope of the rifle but saw nothing but a blur. *Christ, this kid must be near blind.* He made some adjustments and the camp came into view.

The sight was the same as the other side. The fence stretched a long way on either side of the gate. Above the gate was a metal header that connected to both sides and once held the name of the junkyard.

To the left of the base, a long line of trees – the ones he had been trying to reach – ran from the street the full length of the fence and connected in an L-shape with the woods where they now hid. Those trees were only twenty yards from the fence. That offered the best place to get into the camp.

Two men patrolled the makeshift rampart. As in the front, two lights, stationed in the corners lit the area. Unlike the front, another, smaller light shone above the sign. The insufficient light failed to cover the entire open ground, but the cone extended for twenty yards. Approaching unseen would be difficult. Their only hope for success was surprise.

Without taking his eyes from the scope, he said, "Lincoln, take six people and make your way through the woods to the left until you're midway down the fence. Wait for my signal. We'll try to create a diversion for you to get inside the camp. Ah, you better choose people who can climb that fence and aren't afraid of using a knife up close."

Lincoln hesitated. Mark turned his attention to the large man who was studying the area. He met Mark's eyes. "I don't think getting in will be the problem."

Mark understood. "I don't want to sacrifice one group to save another. If you don't think it can be done, hold off."

"I think we can get in but moving around unseen will be a problem."

Mark gave that some thought. "What if, instead of trying to find the others, you open the gate instead?"

"That will work. If we can get everyone inside, we all stand a better chance."

Jarrod sighed. Mark and Lincoln turned his way. The man didn't speak.

"Well, go on, Jarrod. I've never known you to hold your peace."

He released another long breath. "You both have to know we're gonna take some hits here. There's no way we're not gonna have casualties."

Mark nodded. "A very real possibility. Ideas?"

"What if we just kinda laid siege to the place and tried negotiating a less deadly solution?"

Mark gave that some thought. Lincoln was the one to respond. "I agree with your assessment, but if we do that, we lose time and surprise. This may not be the safest way, but it might be the best way."

Mark turned and sat, his back against a tree. They were both right. Someone was going to die. Did he have the right to decide? His personal interest aside, what were acceptable losses? But they'd already taken losses. Zac, Ian Donnolly, and although they'd only just met, Dr. Smahls, too. He thought of Lynn, remembering the tortured look she carried for months after her last ordeal. The memory brought pain and he saw red and then a watery blur.

"Maybe I'm not the best person to make this decision for the group. My interest is too personal."

"Man, we don't doubt your integrity on the decision," Lincoln said. "We all know what has to be done. We're just pointing out the reality of the situation."

Jarrod said, "One way or another, we've got to get those people out. If we let this slide, they will only come again. The question isn't whether we do this, it's how best to proceed."

Mark rubbed his face as if the wrong choice could be wiped away, leaving the winning answer. "Let's get into position and go from there. Lincoln, make sure you take a radio."

The big man said, "I'll let you know when we're ready." With that, he slid away and out of sight.

Mark turned back to the junkyard fortress. "Jarrod, bring everyone up, quietly."

"You got it, boss." The farmer also melted into the dark.

Mark panned the scope from left to right along the fence line. As he watched, the guards turned toward the front of the compound, then, to his surprise, went running along the fence. Their heads rose and dropped as they ran from hood to trunk like human Bop-a-Moles. Bobby and company must have made their appearance.

"No one's watching the back," he said to himself. Excitement coursed through him. He looked around, but as yet, no one had joined him. They had to move now, before the defenders realized their mistake.

Gunshots rang out in the distance. Mark said a silent prayer for Bobby and his comrades. A rustling sound announced the arrival of his invaders. He stood and met them. "No one is watching the back. We need to move now. I need six of the best shooters to stay here and cover our approach and retreat. The rest will come with me. I'll climb over and open the gate when we get to the fence."

"What if it's locked?" Jarrod said.

"I'll either have to shoot it open, or I'll signal for others to climb. If you can't climb, stay outside and wait to cover us. We have to go now. Spread out and run hard but keep quiet. No one fire unless someone sees us and shoots."

Mark didn't wait for any more comments or questions. He burst from the trees and raced hard. All the while he ran he scanned the top of the fence for signs of heads. He reached the edge of the cone the lights cast and ran harder. The amount and volume of the gunfight increased as he drew closer.

He reached the fence and pushed his fingers through the chain links. Pushing aside the thick metal slats inserted the entire length and height of the fence, Mark peered inside. Cars, both crushed and intact, blocked much of his vision. He did not see any people.

He slung the rifle and jammed his shoe in a link as others reached the fence. As fast as he could scale without making noise, Mark reached the top. Grabbing the top bar he pulled up high enough to see into the grounds. Although he could hear voices and shouts, no one came into view.

Lifting a leg to the cross bar, Mark balanced for a fraction, then vaulted over, landing with a solid thud on the roof of a car. He squatted, sliding the rifle into his hands. So far he had gone unnoticed. Sliding down the windshield, he crossed the hood and jumped to the ground. A sharp pain shot through his knee, as though someone had driven a nail into him. He gave an audible gasp and froze for a moment.

No one came to investigate, so he moved to the gate. The two large sections were chained together, held by a lock. Damn! He should have known getting in wasn't going to be that easy. With a gentle push, he checked the give. The fence didn't budge. He looked closer. A small center rod attached to the center pole and running into the ground held the gate in place. Yanking up on the handle, the rod slid free from the hole that housed it. Mark tried again. The gate moved, but nowhere near enough for a person to squeeze between.

"Jarrod," he whispered.

"Yeah," the response came seconds later.

"The gate's locked. Send those who can't climb back beyond the light so they have some cover. Tell the rest to be ready to climb if they hear shooting."

"What are you going to do?"

"I'm going to try to locate where they're holding our people."

Jarrod didn't respond. Mark knew there was nothing to say. He was on his own. Again.

Chapter Forty-Six

MARK TOOK IN THE CAMP AROUND HIM. NOW THAT HE WAS closer he realized the stacks of crushed cars were used to divide living spaces, much like campsites, or rentals at a flea market. Between each pile of crushed autos were parked cars. Apparently, those were used for living quarters. They created a twenty-by-twenty, U-shaped area. Some had metal roofs over the top, while others just had tarps spread out as awnings. Some of the residences were lit with candles or camping lanterns.

There didn't seem to be any pattern overall, but the living spaces were bunched together in groups, anywhere from three to six in number. Several had a front wall, constructed of paneling or plywood. Those all had a door. Of the open and lit spaces, Mark noticed shadowy movement in two. He moved toward the nearest one.

Mark held little hope he'd be lucky enough to find Lynn or the others in one of these spaces, but, he might get information as to their whereabouts. Of course, by showing himself, he was announcing to the camp an intruder was inside. He had no choice. Success depended on how fast he found the captives and made his escape. Looking from makeshift house to makeshift house would take time.

With a long look around the immediate space, Mark slid along the car being used as the outer wall and rounded the front bumper. His sudden appearance startled the resident, a woman, whose age was difficult to discern. A bedraggled female child stood behind her.

The woman let out a cry and pulled the girl into her body, a protective gesture. Mark leveled the rifle and shushed her. "I'm not here to hurt you. Tell me where my friends are and I'll leave you alone."

Even in the dim light, Mark could see the wide-eyed fear on the woman's face. She rocked the child, to comfort her and soothe her whimpers. She didn't speak but kept staring at him. Can she speak? He wondered how she had come to be here. Had she been captured like Lynn? If so, maybe she would help willingly.

He opened his mouth to speak, then noticed something change in her eyes. Fear disappeared and defiance replaced it. The woman sucked in a large amount of air, ready to scream. Mark stepped inside the shelter and pointed the gun at the girl. The fear returned and the air exploded from the woman's lungs in a gush.

She clasped the girl tighter trying to position her body between the gun and her child. "Don't make me hurt you. I just want to get my friends out." What should he do now? If he left them, they'd sound the alarm. Did he have the time to bind and gag them?

He tried again, "Please, help me."

The woman tensed, her eyes darting behind Mark. The hairs on the back of his neck stood up. He spun just as a shape barreled at him. The man collided with Mark and blasted him backward. He hit Mark with enough force to drive the air from his lungs and the rifle from his hands. The impact with the ground further deflated Mark, his body convulsed with new pain.

His attacker straddled him, lifted a fist, and drove it downward. Mark moved his head, dodging the blow. The fist grazed his head and struck the ground; the man winced and grunted.

Mark twisted and drove an elbow into the man's side. The man had too much meat there for that attack to work. Latching on to Mark's arm, the man pinned him down and launched another punch. This one landed on the side of his head with a smack. His head recoiled, striking the ground.

Mark brought up his knees, alternating them like riding a bike, and pounded them into his assailant's back. The strikes were barely an annoyance. Another punch landed. A black cloud encircled his vision. He twisted hard in the opposite direction, thrusting upward with his free hand. He struck at the eyes, but the man was far enough away to easily dodge the attempt. He swatted Mark's hand aside and lifted his fist again.

But Mark's effort had slackened the hold on his other hand. He bucked once trying to dislodge his rider. The man lifted and leaned forward, as Mark broke loose of the grip. Before the man could land another blow, Mark snapped his fingers upward and into the right eye.

The man screamed, clutched at his eye, and leaned away. Mark didn't hesitate. He sat up and rolled, swatting the man with an open hand on the side of the head. The combined actions dislodged the combatant. In one motion, Mark, grabbed the man by the neck, pushed him hard to the ground and slid his knife from its sheath.

He lay on the man and drove the blade deep into his gut. Releasing the hold on his neck, Mark slapped his hand over the man's mouth and pressed his full weight on the thrust. The man kicked and screamed, but Mark held fast and muffled the sound as best possible. Sliding the knife out, he jammed it in again, higher this time, toward the heart.

His victim continued to squirm, gave a sudden gasp and his eyes turned up, then stilled, as the life drained from him. Immediately, Mark leaped from the body and scanned the area. No one was coming yet. He searched for the rifle but couldn't find it. His gaze rose to the woman. She stood there, rifle in hand, pointed straight at him.

The woman didn't flinch. She had him and Mark knew it. Why was she delaying? In a tremulous voice, she said, "I'll help you, on one condition. You take us with you."

Mark didn't have much choice. The answer came quick and easy. "Of course. Where are my friends?"

"It's not that easy. In the meeting, they were bid on. Someone owns them now, just as he once owned me." She jabbed the barrel toward the dead man. "Are you alone?"

Mark nodded.

"The people you seek will be in different places. You won't be able to get to them all." A strange look covered her face. Mark recognized it. She was reconsidering her position. In a fast step, Mark grabbed the barrel and ripped it from her hands. The woman slunk backward, defeated and once again afraid.

"Okay, here's the deal. I don't have much time. Tell me where one of them is. You can go wait by the back fence." She shook her head. "Tell me, and when I get them, I'll come back this way. You can decide then if you want to go with us."

She thought about that.

"Hurry. Decide."

She nodded. "You see the main building?" She didn't wait for an answer. "The building to the left has one of the women. The house has the woman and the child. I don't know where the other one is."

The Donnollys. Again he struggled to recall their names. "Is there anyone inside guarding them?"

"I don't know. If not, they will be tied up and locked in a room."

"What else can you tell me?"

"Nothing. He told me to stay here and not to move when the shooting started."

Mark grabbed the body and dragged it across the living space to next door. He stripped him of a pistol and stuck it in his belt. The shooting at the front of the yard had slackened. He didn't know what that meant but feared time was shorter than he hoped. "Be there or I will have to go without you." Giving the woman one last look, he sprinted for the back of the long central building.

There, he pressed against the wall and studied the living quarters he passed along the way. If anyone saw him, no one cried out. Sliding to the corner nearest the side building, Mark peered around. Forty yards away, a line of shooters had taken to the ramparts. Everyone faced forward. He looked at the distance he needed to cover to reach safety. Twenty feet to the first cover. Maybe thirty yards to the dark structure. Didn't seem like much unless you were dodging bullets.

He dashed for the first line of cars. Reaching an old Cadillac Seville, he continued to the trunk and ducked. From there, he duck-walked from vehicle to vehicle, until the building was the only thing left to attain. Darting for the side wall away from the shooters, Mark stopped and caught his breath, hoping it also calmed the heavy thumping of his heart.

A loud pounding sounded near the fence ten yards further on, as if someone knocked on a metal door. Almost too late he recognized the sound and understood the meaning. He ducked low and hugged the wood wall as an armed man ran along the tops of the cars used as ramparts. He passed Mark, his eyes focused on the gunfight ahead. Swallowing away the dryness, Mark slid under a window. On tiptoes, he peered through the dirty glass. No light shone within and no images came to focus. He had to go in blind.

The window was an old style, wood frame, with an upper and lower pane. Mark withdrew the knife and grabbed onto the windowsill. He pulled upward, pressing an elbow along the ledge to keep him balanced. With his free hand he slid the blade into the space between the two window frames. The blade struck metal and stopped. Withdrawing the knife, he turned the blade around so the spine hit the latch. He pressed hard, but the lock would not budge.

Dammit!

His arm strained to hold him. Mark was forced to drop to the ground. He didn't want to break the window if possible. About to try the latch again, Mark heard footsteps.

Chapter Forty-Seven

THE GUNFIGHT HAD BEEN STEADY AND INTENSE SINCE arriving at the house. Her fear barely contained, Mel sighted and pulled the trigger again. The opposing forces had attempted to rush the house twice, but both times had been driven back. Several bodies dotted the road between the two sides.

Right now they were in a lull, with only occasional shots fired. Bobby had yelled down for them to stop shooting. "Save your bullets for if they try to attack again," he said.

She was getting used to taking orders. She had to concede, Bobby was better than she was with a rifle. She had almost insisted on taking the top spot with the better angle into the camp. Now she was glad she hadn't. He was so accurate and so fast, both attacks stalled before they'd really begun. Had the enemy force been able to get across the street things might have gone differently. The battle now had settled into a sniping contest.

She dropped the magazine again as if the number had magically multiplied since the last time. Four shots remained and one more full mag. How much longer were they going to stay? She knew what was at stake but didn't want to die here.

And, what if they did run out of bullets? How would they escape? They certainly couldn't drive out the way they came. Too many guns were trained on them now. They'd have to go cross country. She took a quick look through the now glassless second-story window. How much longer before the sun comes up? Would daylight help or hurt them? It sure wouldn't help any escape attempts.

God, what had she gotten herself into? Mel had to admit she was scared. Dealing with one or two attackers was one thing, but this, this was like being in a war. She wanted it to be over, for them to stop shooting at her. She sat down next to the window. She understood why they had gone to the community's farmhouse. Tara needed a doctor. She was doing better now. Isn't that what Becca said? Maybe if she sneaked out now while it was still dark and made her way back to the farmhouse, her and Tara could head out.

Then a stab of guilt pierced her heart. But what about Caryn? Was she willing to turn her back on her? She thought about how the woman had found her courage and tried to protect Tara. Then, at the house she'd fought hard against a lot of men before they broke inside. Caryn had come a long way in the past few days. She deserved better for her efforts.

And, what of these people? They had taken them in as if they were family. No questions asked. If Bobby and his sister hadn't come to their rescue, all of them might be in there now. And, most likely, Tara would be dead. These were good, safe people. Lord knows they hadn't found many of them along the way. In fact, she could count only two, Tara and Caryn. No, despite the fear that refused to release her, she couldn't abandon them.

A bullet whizzed through the broken window, embedding in the wall down the hall. Mel shuddered, deciding then to keep her options open. Someone had a good line on the window. She decided it was time to move.

Crawling from the hallway to the bedroom on her left, she moved the curtains with the rifle barrel. To her surprise, this window still had a full pane of glass. Placing the rifle down, she unlocked and slid the window up. She didn't want to break the glass, announcing where she was. That gave her first shots the advantage of not being under fire.

As she watched from her new perch, Mel thought about Caryn again and what she must be going through. Although no longer sure she believed, she said a silent prayer for Caryn and one for herself. Then she expanded the coverage to include everyone in the new community they were now a part of, if only for the moment.

MARK SLOWED HIS BREATHING. THE FOOTSTEPS CAME CLOSER and stopped. He squatted, knife in hand, ready to spring. His body leaned toward the front of the building anticipating his attack. The wait was intense, making him jumpy. Then he heard the jingling sound of keys. His heart skipped with added adrenaline. Could he be so lucky? But, how many were entering the building? He had to know.

Quicker than he liked to ensure stealth, he slid toward the front corner, staying crouched. A door creaked. Mark risked a peek. The leg of a man disappeared through the opening, the door closing behind him. He was too late. Moving to the door, Mark listened for a lock to engage. He couldn't be sure.

A muffled scream penetrated the wall. One of the women was inside. A red haze descended like a veil over his eyes. He pictured Lynn about to be abused. All the willpower he possessed barely held him back from crashing through the door, locked or not. He forced his hand to steady and tried the knob. Pushing it open, he stepped inside ignoring the creak.

He stood in a small hallway that ran to the back of the building. Each wood-paneled side wall held two doors. All were closed. He stood and listened.

A slap reverberated through the interior, rebounding like a racket ball, amplified by his brain and the rage that flamed within. A cry of pain followed. Then a male voice issued commands in words Mark's pulsing heart drowned out. He shut the door with his foot, the click of the latch audible.

Footsteps, to the left; second door. He stepped forward.

The man was interrogating whoever was inside. "Who's out there?" the voice boomed.

The doorknob turned. Mark tensed. The door swung inward revealing a short, thin man, his bib-overall straps hanging loosely. His arm was raised, ready to deliver another strike. I said, "Who's out ..." He stopped and turned to see who entered.

Mark didn't as much thrust the knife, as punch the blade through the man's eye. The scream was abrupt and died with the man. The force of the blow drove the body back into the room. Mark kept moving until the dead man hit the wall. He wouldn't let the body fall. He growled his hatred and shook violently.

"M-Mark?"

The voice filtered through his consciousness. Like being brought out of hypnosis, he shook his head clear. Arms wrapped around him from the side. He jumped and yanked the blade free then realized the crying female was not attacking him. He returned Caryn's hug, allowing the contact to drain away his rage.

He let her be for a moment, if only to control his disappointment that it wasn't Lynn. Prying himself free, he said, "Are you all right?"

She nodded and wiped her face. A red welt marked her cheek. "Did they hurt you, or ...?" He let the question hang in the air.

"No, not really. This was the first time any of them struck me, or ... or ... anything. I think something might have happened earlier, but a disturbance drew them away. Was that you?"

"Yes. Caryn, where's Lynn."

"I don't know … after they bid for us … they sold us like slaves, Mark." Her words started the tears anew. "My God, we've become animals."

"Caryn," Mark urged her back on track.

"After he and his friends bought me, they brought me here and locked me in. I didn't see what happened to Lynn. The lady doctor was taken out before me. Maybe Lynn's still in the big building. I hadn't been here long before the commotion started."

Mark pictured the main building in relationship to where he was. He had to find a way in through the back, because the front was in clear view of those on the fence. He remembered the light over the front door. He'd be seen for sure. No, he had to find another way in.

"We have to go, now."

He took her arm, heading for the door. She pulled away. "Don't grab me like that. I'm not some pet or possession that you can order around. Do you understand?" Her voice shrill, shock initiating hysterics. "I'm a human being. A person. I deserve to be treated with respect," she ranted, her voice escalating.

Mark held up his hands. "Whoa! Whoa! Stop. I'm sorry. I'm concerned about Lynn. I apologize, but we really do need to go. Okay?"

Her eyes though watery, were hard, her jaw set. Her face drooped a bit as she relaxed and nodded. Mark went back to the body and took the man's handgun. He handed it to Caryn. "Take your anger out on those who have hurt you. But not unless we have no other choice. Right now, no one knows we're here."

Mark was angry too. Lynn was all that mattered now. He turned and left the room leaving her to follow if she chose.

Chapter Forty-Eight

PEERING OUT THE DOOR, THE WAY WAS CLEAR. HE FELT Caryn's presence. "I'll walk as casually as possible to the back of that building." He didn't tell her what to do.

"Sh-should I follow?"

"It's up to you, but it would be better if you walked with me, as though we belonged here." Without waiting for a reply, Mark exited the building. It took great effort to remain calm and not hurry or look at the manned fence. Movement to his left attracted his attention. His heart rate raced. By the time he reached the back wall of the main building, it was pounding to a marching cadence.

Stopping to calm his nerves, Caryn pressed in next to him. Their eyes met. Her lips trembled, her breathing sounded asthmatic. "Stay calm," he said, hoping she didn't take offense.

He walked along the back wall. At the far end, he spied a door. Now, if only it's not locked. Before he could find out, the door swung open and two men exited in a heated discussion. All four of them stopped in surprise.

Mark reacted first, flashing his knife and lunging. Both men backed away and reached for weapons as sounds of alarm escaped their mouths. Mark kicked the first man in the knee, who dropped to the ground with a scream. In one continuous motion, he thrust at the second man, who blocked the attack with an arm. Continuing his momentum, Mark rammed the opponent against the door jarring them both. Mark slashed, the blade biting deep into a forearm.

His opponent cried out. Mark had to end the fight fast. He shot his elbow up under the man's chin snapping his teeth together. He followed with a punch to the gut, doubling the man over and finishing with the knife driven into the man's neck.

As quick as he could, Mark withdrew the blade and spun on the other man, already knowing it was too late. The gunshots were testament. The man fell. Caryn sobbed, the gun shaking in her hands.

The camp came to life. Voices shouted, running footsteps sounded. They had to go, but he had to see if Lynn was inside. "Cover me," he said and stepped inside the door. The large space was dimly lit and wide open. A quick look told him the room was empty. Disappointment shrouded his heart. He ran out and grabbed Caryn's arm. Not caring if she didn't like it, he led her away from the building. She offered no resistance or angry retorts this time. He released her and she ran with him.

Their path took them past the woman and child standing in front of their shelter, the mother's arms wrapped protectively around the child. Mark didn't slow, but said, "If you're coming, follow us." He didn't look to see if they did. He pulled the gun from his belt.

He ran toward the rear fence. A voice behind him shouted, "There! Hey, they're over here." The fence was still a long way off.

With twenty yards to go, the first bullet chased them. A man suddenly appeared from the right side. The look of surprise on his face evaporated when Mark's bullet tore through his chest. Mark turned and fired at the pursuit while Caryn, the woman and child ran past. He covered them until they reached the fence.

Loud pounding sounds drew his attention, both left and right. Men ran along the tops of the cars that bordered the fence. He spun and fired two shots in both directions and the gun was empty. Dropping it, he ran, drawing the 9mm from its holster. The rifle still bounced on his back but was not much help up close.

Caryn stopped at the closed gate as if puzzled what to do next. "Climb!" Mark yelled. "On the car."

She scampered up the hood. Bullets pelted the ground around Mark. The woman lifted her child onto the car. Mark reached her as she attempted to ascend. He grabbed her by the hips, lifted and pushed. She fell to her knees on the hood. Mark clambered up after her.

"Caryn, climb the fence. Don't wait. Run for the woods when you get over." Mark squatted and lined up a shot. He knocked one man off the cars to the right, but too many were converging on them. They were easy targets on the car and in the light.

Caryn disappeared over the fence with a scream. The woman helped her child. Mark fired twice more, holstered the gun, and scrambled up the fence. At the top he swung one leg over, straddling the bar and reached down, snagging the child's hand. He pulled and the girl's feet came free of the links so she dangled from his hand. He lifted her up and over the crossbar, lowered her as far as he could and let go. He didn't watch her land. The woman had only just begun to climb.

"Hurry." He pulled the handgun out again and shot rapid fire in different directions, more to limit return fire than to hit a target. He reached down for the woman as a new round of shots ripped past them. She cried out and lost her grip, falling to the roof on her back. Her hands reached for Mark. "Please, save my daughter. Go. Please." Her eyes closed.

Frustrated at yet another failure but knowing there was nothing he could do for her, he swung his leg over and jumped. Caryn was nowhere around, but the girl stood there crying. Mark had no time to find out if she was hurt or give her instructions. In one motion he scooped her up and sprinted for the trees. He didn't have to wait long before the bullets flew around him.

If he could just reach the far edges of the light, he'd have a chance. However, the bullets hit closer and closer. The heat of some rounds touched the sides of his head. Any second now he expected one to end his life.

Then, like phantoms from the depths of hell, figures appeared in front of him, their gunfire sparking like flashing Christmas lights. His legs pumped harder and his heart threatened to explode in his chest. He reached the trees and fell. The girl went rolling away and Mark lay panting for air as if it was in short supply. Then darkness surrounded him and blocked out anything else.

Chapter Forty-Nine

MARK SAT UP FAST AND GRABBED THE ARM SHAKING HIM violently, his other hand in motion before his vision cleared. Jarrod caught the punch with a meaty hand and held tight. "Whoa, there, tiger. Settle down now before someone gets hurt. That someone most likely me."

"Oh, God, Jarrod, I'm sorry. What happened? Was I out?"

"Just a little exhausted, I think. Leastways, I don't see any perforations."

Jarrod helped Mark to his feet. His legs did not want to hold him. He wobbled and Jarrod steadied him. "You gonna be all right?"

"Yeah, just give me a minute."

As his strength returned, Mark noticed others had gathered around. His eyes stopped on Becca. Concern shone out. He smiled to reassure her. She came forward and put an arm around him. He did the same and gave a quick squeeze.

"How long was I down?"

Jarrod shook his head. "We just got here, but not long. Maybe a coupla minutes."

"What's the situation?"

"Well, right now, we've got them bottled up. Bobby's group has control of the front. Lincoln and his people stopped a few of them trying to climb the fence that way. We've got them here, although I did send a few shooters to the east to make sure no one can get out that way. Right now, I'd say, we control the play."

Mark stepped forward, did some trunk twists and some stretches and groaned. He ached all over. "How's Caryn?"

Becca said, "Shaken, as you can imagine, but she's tougher than I gave her credit for. She says she shot someone. Is that true?"

Mark nodded. "Probably saved us both." He walked toward the tree line. Everyone followed as though he was a prophet about to give words of wisdom.

"Well, I think it was her first time because that seems to have bothered her more than whatever else they did to her."

"Did she mention anything about that?"

Becca shook her head. "No, but I get the feeling nothing happened. At least, not yet."

Mark nodded. His thoughts were of Lynn. Has she been as lucky, so far? A lump climbed his throat. An image of her face drifted past his eyes. A touch on his arm broke his spell. "She'll be all right, Daddy. We'll get her back."

He smiled with more confidence than he felt. "I know, honey." The words almost stuck. He cleared his throat. "Let's see what we've got. Who has my rifle?"

Jarrod handed the gun to him. He focused and scanned the walls like a usurping lord laying siege. A score of heads stuck up over the fence. From where he stood he could make out another half dozen or so on each side. The house and main building blocked his view of the front fence, making it difficult to discern numbers. He guessed at another ten to twelve.

The numbers didn't bother him. Their fortified position and higher vantage point did. An assault would be suicide. Too much open ground stood between them and the fence on all sides. The west section was the closest. Putting shooters in the trees was a big threat, but if the men inside had any skills at all, the snipers were easy targets. Still, that strategy was worth considering.

Bobby and his people had a good vantage point to shoot into the camp. If the defenders at the front kept their heads down, perhaps they could thin out the men on the back ramparts. That wasn't too far a shot. He could make it. The solution might be to whittle them down until they either surrendered, or an attack was more feasible, meaning less suicidal.

He lowered the rifle. The defenders weren't doing themselves any favors keeping the lights on. They were much better targets right now than his people were. Of course, that changed when the sun came up. He glanced toward the east. The sky was just a bit lighter. They might have the advantage of darkness for another hour. No more.

He turned to Jarrod, the general speaking to his lieutenant. "Do all sides have a radio?"

"Not to the east. I think there's one more in the truck."

"Make sure they get it fast."

Jarrod spoke to someone, passing the command down the line.

Mark continued to study the scene before him as if an answer would suddenly spring from the ground.

"I take it you want this, then." Jarrod handed the walkie-talkie unit to him. "It's set on Bobby's frequency."

"Bobby, come in."

Static. He repeated the call. "Yeah, here. Dad? Is that you?"

"Yes. Are you secure there?"

"Yeah. So far. They made two runs at us but when the bodies piled up, they stopped. Now we're just trading shots."

"Are you getting good shots?"

"Not really. I mean, we can see them, but usually just the head and only for a second. They pop up to shoot then disappear."

"Okay, don't waste bullets. Do you have a good line of sight to the back fence?"

Pause. "Not great. The house and that big building in the middle block most of it."

"Can you see anyone?"

"Yeah. I can see one full body and one partial."

"Can you make that shot?"

"Yeah."

His confidence came through the radio. "Take him down."

"Now?"

"Yes. Then line up on the partial in case he exposes himself more."

"Roger that."

Mark handed the radio back to Jarrod. "Find Lincoln for me." Then, he put the scope to his eye and waited. Perhaps five seconds later the shot came. A man to the right of the metal banner over the gate, straightened, bounced off the fence, and disappeared backward. A second shot echoed across the grounds, but if it struck home Mark didn't see.

A crackle came from the radio. Static and distorted sound. Jarrod handed the radio back.

"Lincoln?"

"Yeah, Mark. What's up?"

"Can you get someone into a tree without making them a target?"

"Ah, I guess so. You thinking of using them as a sniper or lookout?"

"Both."

"Okay, let me see what I can find. I'll get back to you."

"Jarrod, can you get Bobby back for me?"

"Sure, but I ain't sitting on your lap for shorthand."

Mark gave the man a confused look.

Jarrod said, "Never mind."

He handed back the radio.

"Bobby, this is just for you. Anytime you can take a sure shot, do it. Tell the others not to fire unless they're attacked. Got it?"

"Yep. No problem. We're kinda short on bullets anyway."

Mark held onto the radio this time. He scratched at his chin with the antenna while he considered options. The image of Lynn tried to impose itself on his thoughts, but he blocked it. He couldn't afford to be sidetracked or to react with emotion. He had to believe she'd be all right.

"I know you're forming a plan, right?" Jarrod asked. "I mean, other than standing out here watching."

"I need to even the odds a bit and keep them pinned down. I want them on edge. They have the better position and more men, but we have the advantage. They can't get out."

"But that advantage is only good over an extended period. Meanwhile, our people are in there having who knows what done to them."

Anger flashed through Mark. Like a shot, he whirled on the big man with an uncontrolled desire to trash something. "I know what's at stake. Better than most. You don't have to tell me what might be happening, right now, as we stand here."

Spittle flew from his mouth. His fists clenched ready to pommel. "If you have a better way of saving them, aside from a suicidal storming of the gates, feel free to divulge that plan."

"Hey, hey, settle down and back off."

"Dad!"

The anger dissipated with a heavy throbbing at his temples. His knees felt rubbery. He clutched at his head, rubbing the sides between his fingers while trying to steady his balance. He winced, touching a long crusty furrow. He'd forgotten what caused it. "I'm sorry, Jarrod."

No one spoke for a long moment.

"Dad," Becca said, "we all know the situation. We all want to rescue Lynn, Martha and Matthew."

Mark had to think for a second who Martha and Matthew were.

"I, we, know how hard this is for you, but we're just trying to help, by talking things through. What we do here should not rest just on your shoulders. We came here as a family to save family members. We should all have input, especially since our lives are at stake."

"Well said, youngster," Jarrod said.

"I know. I know. I'm sorry, Jarrod. I didn't mean to snap."

"The question I have now is, are you too emotional to be making decisions?"

Mark closed his eyes and exhaled. "I'm okay. If you have any ideas, any of you, now's the time to discuss them."

"My point was," said Jarrod, "whether we had the time to take the slow approach, or if something more aggressive had to be done?"

The radio came to life.

"Mark! Come in, Mark."

"Yeah, Lincoln, go ahead."

"I've got two shooters in trees. They've got eyes inside."

"Can they get an approximate head count?"

Silence. The time dragged.

"One says they guess forty. The other says upwards of fifty on the ground and the walls. That's total potential threats, not counting women and children."

"What about shots?"

"They both say they've got 'em. You want 'em to take the shots?"

"Yes, but listen. I don't want them to shoot if they can't put the tree trunk between them and return fire. You understand? If they're too exposed, either get them in better spots or tell them no."

"Okay.

The wait was agonizing. No response came until the shot. A second followed. After a brief pause two more blasted. Mark couldn't tell if anyone was hit. Then the camp came alive. A furious barrage aimed up at the trees filled the air. It continued for almost a full minute.

What sounded like a branch breaking came from Lincoln's location. Something plummeted. Then, all went silent again.

"Lincoln! Lincoln, come in. What happened?"

The static was not enough to cover the emotion. "Oh, damn, man. Eddie's dead. It had to be a lucky shot, but they got him. They killed him. Aw, fuck."

Grief crawled over Mark. He bore the responsibility for his death. "Lincoln, tell the other person not to shoot anymore. Just have him keep you posted about what's going on inside."

"Yeah, okay," his voice robotic.

Then, to make matters worse, someone finally figured out the disadvantage of having the lights on and the camp pitched into darkness. Now Mark and company were at the disadvantage.

Chapter Fifty

"WHAT NOW, MARK?" JARROD SAID.

Mark wished he had a good answer.

Becca said, "Well, we can't see them as well now, but they also can't see us. We can get closer perhaps. Maybe rush the fence, get inside."

Mark said, "But if we get caught in the open we'll be massacred."

"What if we get someone inside to open the gate," Adam Brandford said.

Mark shook his head. "This isn't like storming a castle in medieval times. We still have a lot of open ground to cross."

One-by-one, options were presented to Mark, only to have them shot down for safety or feasibility reasons. One thought stayed with him. "Jarrod, send someone to the base. Update the General on our current situation and ask for whatever help he can send – but tell him we need it now."

"After everything we did to help them, it's about time they returned the favor," said Jarrod. "I'll take care of it."

Just then, the lights flared back to life. All along the fence men had rifles aimed and ready. The plan was obvious. They'd hoped to set up a killing ground, catching Mark's group in the open. If they had tried using the dark to sneak up on the compound, they'd have been massacred.

Becca placed a hand on his shoulder. "Good call, Daddy." She walked away.

Pressure built behind his eyes. Mark wanted to massage his temples but didn't want the others to see the strain he was feeling. The longer they waited, the greater the chances for Lynn and Martha to be abused, repeatedly. His fists clenched and the throbbing intensified. He forced himself to take in a deep breath and release it in a long exhale. His muscles relaxed, but not much. He wouldn't risk anyone else's life, but that didn't mean he was beyond trying something stupid, like a one-man assault on the compound.

Mark lifted the radio. "Lincoln!'

"Here, Mark."

"Is it possible to get to the fence unseen?"

"Ah, man, I don't know. I guess, it is, but if they see you, there's no place to hide. Why?"

"Your position is closest to the fence. If it can be done, that's the best place."

"I'm not comfortable telling these people to try for the fence. A lot of them won't make it. I'd just be throwing their lives away."

"I'm not asking you to send anybody, Lincoln. I just wanted to know, if, say, one person can make it?"

"Yeah. One person who knows how to move with stealth. But even if they got there unseen, then what? They can't get over the fence without making noise."

"Okay, thanks." His mind whirled around the thought. He tried to picture the scenario and what had to happen. Could he cut his way in? He knew Jarrod probably had something in his truck to do the job. But snipping the links would make noise. Slipping through the breech would not be easy. Cars were in the way. How did he get past them?

Whatever obstacle he put in the way Mark continued to give the plan attention. Was it something he planned on doing or was the foolish idea just something to fill his mind because he was desperate to rescue Lynn and didn't have anything better?

"Daddy, I know what you're thinking. I'm not going to let you go in there alone."

Mark looked at his daughter, surprised she read his thoughts.

"You can't do it by yourself. It's stupid to try it at all, but if you insist, I'm going too."

"Becca, I ..."

"I don't want to hear it, Daddy. I know your mind's in turmoil over Lynn, but how will she feel if you throw your life away to save hers?"

Jarrod interrupted. "You ready for a real plan?"

"More than ready."

"We load some of us up in vehicles. We drive a truck right through that gate. We pull up other cars broadside to the fence here and to the east, to keep the shooters busy. There won't be anyone inside the truck, because, well, that'd just be suicide, but while we keep them occupied on those two sides, a small force can cut their way through the fence to the west.

"A coupla good shots with handguns can take care of the guards there. Meanwhile, Bobby's snipers can keep the front pinned down. We still may lose a few, but overall it'd be a lot safer than a frontal assault."

Everyone stared at the big man.

"What? I didn't belch or anything. Did I say something stupid?"

"No, actually, that's a really good plan.

"Huh, well, of course it is. That's why I said it."

Mark gave orders in a hurry. For the plan to work best, they needed to implement it while they still had some darkness left. "I need three vehicles on this side, two on the east. Only two people in each. Whoever drives the truck will have to fix the wheel so it drives true, and bail. The follow-up vehicles will turn sideways. Shoot, but don't go trigger happy, otherwise, you'll be out of bullets too quick. The truck driver can crawl for cover behind the cars while we cover him.

"Everyone else can fire from the woods. Jarrod, call the east side. Becca," he handed her his radio, "call your brother. Tell him what we'll need. No one goes or fires until I say."

He turned to go deeper into the trees.

"Where you going?" she asked.

"I'm going to get the fence cutters and join Lincoln's group. Hurry everyone. I want to go before it gets too light."

Chapter Fifty-One

FIFTEEN MINUTES LATER THEY WERE READY. THE EASTERN sky had lightened enough to make the assault more dangerous. Jarrod volunteered to drive the truck since it was his truck. The teams were picked from volunteers. After Mark left to join Lincoln, Becca followed. She refused any orders, no matter how forcefully delivered, to stay behind. "I'm going with you and there's nothing you can say to change that. So stop wasting your breath and our time."

Mark gave in. "But once we get there, you listen to me and do what I tell you. Understand?"

"Of course, Daddy." Innocent sweetness dripped from her words like a Girl Scout trying to sell cookies.

"Lincoln, see if you can find two more volunteers to get in the trees. With everyone directing fire at the camp, the defenders won't be able to consolidate shots toward any one target."

"I'm going with you," Lincoln said.

"Okay. I'll cut away a section of the fence big enough to squeeze through. There'll be a car in front of us. We can use that for cover. You take anyone to the left, I'll take those to the right."

"And I'll kill anyone in front of us," his daughter said with a smile.

Mark frowned. "Look, when we get there, you have to keep an eye upward. If they see us, we'll be easy targets. Keep their heads down and give me time to cut through."

Mark checked by radio to make sure all was set. Then, before he could give the word, Jarrod called. "Mark, I think you should come over here and see this. Uh-oh. Come a-running."

Something in Jarrod's tone chilled Mark's blood. He handed the radio and cutter to Lincoln and ran. On reaching the group at the south end, he said, "What's going on?"

Jarrod pointed.

Mark looked at the compound.

The lights on the south side had flared to life. In the glow of the light over the gate, two men hoisted a woman to the cross bar. He recognized her instantly. The mother who had helped him stood gagged, hands bound behind her, a rope around her neck. The other end had been tied around the metal sign that hung over the gate.

Her shirt and pants had been stripped away. She wore dingy panties and nothing else. A bloody bandage covered her right shoulder.

Mark's chest tightened like a vise, making breaths difficult to draw. "Oh, God. They wouldn't."

"Hey, out there." A large man, with a ball cap covering a mass of brown hair, stood to the woman's side. One hand held the noose over the woman's head. The other had a rifle.

"You watching this?" He wiggled the noose. The mother's legs turned soft and she almost collapsed. The two men held her up. "She wanted to go with you. Here, we're gonna give her to you."

The two men lifted the woman. She kicked hard, throwing her body backward. Muffled screams filtered over the field. Mark started forward, fear and revulsion erupting in his stomach. Bile, like lava, crept upward, burning his throat. Hands grabbed at him, pulling him back.

The woman's legs seemed to defy gravity for a second dangling over the fence. Then, she plummeted until the rope jerked her to a stop. The crossbar holding the sign between the gate posts sagged from the impact. The body swung, but she did not fight for air.

"Ahhh!" Mark cried out, dropping to his knees.

Jarrod said, "Those bastards!"

Somewhere behind them a girl screamed, "Momma!"

Mark shouted for someone to take the child away.

Jarrod said, "Her neck must have snapped instantly. A blessing at least, for that."

Mark watched the body swing. Anger so fierce he no longer had vision, took over his body like an alien entity. Snarling, spittle flying from his mouth, he vowed the man would die as horribly as he could make it. He had never hated anyone as much as he hated that man right then.

On the other side of the gate, two more men climbed to the rampart. Between them they held another bound figure. This one a boy.

From behind, someone cried out, "Oh, God, no, it's Matthew."

They watched in horror as the boy was lifted high and held.

The large man pointed at Matthew Donnolly from his perch. "This is what will happen to anyone who tries to come in here. We will kill you all."

Inside the compound, a woman's voice pierced the air. "No! Matthew! Please!"

The man looked down, then back toward the woods. "We still have two more to hang. If you're not gone from here in two minutes, the boy dies. Then we'll move to the women. You hear me? Two minutes."

Mark stepped back and fell against a tree. He tore at the collar of his shirt as if it were shrinking around his neck threatening to strangle him. The air was suddenly too hot to inhale, burning his throat and his eyes.

All around him people cried, prayed, or swore. His eyes met Jarrod's, the question "What are we gonna do?" etched across his pupils.

"Pull, pull everyone back, out of sight," he ordered.

Jarrod stood staring.

"Do it, Jarrod."

Jarrod gave the command to the group, then repeated the order over the radio.

Mark covered his face with his hands. The image of the dangling woman burned in his memory. He choked for air as she must have. This was his fault. Then, as the fury returned, he said, "No. It was theirs. And so help me, they are going to pay."

Chapter Fifty-Two

HE STOOD, STRETCHED, THEN FLEXED HIS ARMS FEELING LIKE the Hulk. His body shook from the effort, tossing off some of the pain and the anger. Done, he said, "Jarrod, get everyone ready to move."

"What," the big farmer said, "we're backing down? We're just gonna let them win?"

"No, we're going in. This ends now." He snatched the radio from Jarrod's hand. "Bobby?"

"Yeah, Dad."

"If you get any shot at anyone on the back fence, take it. I'm especially interested in the gate area. If you can't see it move to where you can."

"Roger that."

He switched channels. "Lincoln!'

"Yeah. What's going on there?"

"They hung a woman who helped me and are threatening to hang our people if we don't leave. They've got a noose around the Donnolly boy's neck right now."

"Them rotten fuckers. What are we doing?"

"Tell your people in the trees if they have any shots at the rear fence to take them."

"You got it."

Mark handed the radio back to Jarrod without looking, then took his rifle. He stepped forward, placed the barrel over a short branch and sighted. With great effort, he controlled his breathing. For what he planned on trying he needed to be relaxed and focused.

Behind him, the sound of engines drew his attention. Someone guided the assault cars through the trees like the man at the car wash when he helped to line up your car.

"Your time is up," the man shouted. "I can still see you. I warned you. This is on you."

Motioning across the gate, the two men lifted the frightened boy. Mark blew out and fired. The bullet blasted the man on the left off the rampart. Matthew dropped, but inside the fence and on something solid. Not far enough to take up the slack in the rope. The other man gaped in shock, then dove for cover.

With no target, Mark swept to his left to find another victim. The scope passed over the woman's still swinging body. Something caught in his throat, but he quickly swallowed it away.

He waited. Soon, the bottoms of two shoes appeared over the crossbar to the right of the gate. Someone was attempting to lift Matthew over the fence without showing themselves. Mark held on a spot to the left of the boy.

His legs arced up and hung over. A hand pushed under his back to lift him further. Apprehension threatened to erode Mark's confidence. Shoved forward again, only Matthew's torso remained inside the fence. Desperate to find something to hit, Mark shifted to the right side. An arm, then a shoulder and finally the side of a head appeared. Mark squeezed the trigger. The head jerked from sight in a geyser of red. Matthew disappeared though his legs still hung over the crossbar.

Mark's breath caught as Matthew came flying over the fence feet first. Behind Mark people gasped, screamed, and wailed. Mark pushed it all aside and focused on the path of the rope. The world slowed down. He pulled the trigger. Missed. Matthew fell further. The next shot missed as well. The target was too small and moving too fast. Mark squeezed the trigger again. Not having the benefit of time, and knowing any hit at this point, would be sheer luck. The third shot, as the rope began to straighten, missed. Fourth as the rope grew taut.

The boy's legs swung out to the side, his head lifted backward. The fifth shot. The rope jumped like it had hit a snag. A partial tear, but the rope held. Matthew's head was wrenched back and up, his body seemed to bounce, then, he went flying, his head free of the noose, landing on his back.

Mark lifted his eye from the scope. Whether from a lucky shot or the boy's head just slipped from the noose didn't matter, he was on the ground. The world exploded back to life. All around him people cheered, cried out, and released held breaths. Then everyone went silent. He watched the ground in anticipation. Had he been too late? He cringed at the thought. His failure was Matthew's end. Then, someone gasped and pointed. "Look!"

Movement in the dirt at the base of the fence drew his attention. Matthew rolled to a sitting position. "Stay down, boy," Mark said to himself. "Just lie there. Play dead." The gathered community grew vociferous. Mark spun and shushed them. "Quiet! If they know he's still alive, they'll shoot him." A tense hush descended over the wooded area.

Mark found the boy in his scope. His tear-streaked face contorted in pain and fear. He rocked to his feet and stood up. Mark wanted to shout "Stay down."

Matthew wobbled on his feet, saw the woods, and took off running. His strides were unsteady. He tripped, fell, and rose again, running.

Mark scanned the fence line. Heads popped up. "Everyone, focus on the top of the fence. Don't let them get a shot off," Mark said. Guns began barking. He pulled the trigger. Nothing happened. Damn! He pulled the magazine – empty. He patted his pockets. One bullet. He pushed the round in. "Anyone have any ammo?" Someone dropped bullets into his palm. He examined them. They would fit. Sliding them home he snapped the magazine back into place. Chambered, sighted, and fired.

Matthew was halfway to the woods now and taking fire. Before Mark could get off another shot, the boy arched his back, face tilting skyward. A plume of red sprayed from his chest and he fell, face first.

Mark pressed his forehead to a tree too numb to think.

Within the trees, anguish turned to silence, then to quiet tears. Angry comments followed.

"Son-of-a-bitch."

"Bastards."

"That poor boy."

Then, "Oh, dear God, no."

Mark looked up. Standing on the ramparts trussed like Matthew stood his mother, Martha. Then his heart fell with a painful thud. Lynn. Both women struggled, receiving slaps for their efforts. The skin-on-skin contact reverberated across the open space.

Clenching his fists, Mark stepped forward. *These men are going to die.* The entire battlefield had gone red before him. As he watched, the two prisoners' shirts were ripped open, exposing them to the waist.

Hands grabbed him, hauling him back. His arms swung with vicious blows. Several landed, but more hands wrapped him up and dragged him back. Jarrod got in his face. "Mark, think. You can't help them if you're dead. They're counting on just this reaction. They either want you to give up or do something rash. They're desperate. It's their only play."

"Let me go."

"No, not till you calm down. Maybe we can deal with them. Let's go talk to them."

"Time for talk is gone. Or haven't you been watching?"

"It's not too late. They still have two of our people. It's time to get them back, one way or another. But we can't make this work if you go running out there and get killed. Lynn and Martha are counting on you."

The fury and strength behind the big man's words had the desired effect on Mark. Some of the rage dissipated, but the anger still fueled the flame within.

"Okay, let's do this. Let me go."

Jarrod nodded to whoever was behind.

A shrill voice pierced his soul. "Matthew! Oh, God, no!" Martha had seen the body of her son sprawled on the ground. The scream helped clear his mind and spark him into motion.

"I need something white. Jarrod, is everyone ready to go?"

"Yep. Just waiting to see what you wanted to do."

Mark looked to the eastern sky. Dawn crested the horizon. There would be no cover of darkness to help them. Someone peeled off a white t-shirt and handed it to him. Pushing a finger into the farmer's massive chest, Mark said, "I want everyone ready to move. Everyone who is not in the attack should have a rifle pointed at that top cross bar. As soon as I give the word, they open fire. They have to keep their heads down."

Mark gave his rifle to a woman he only vaguely saw. "Make your shots count." Pulling the handgun, he checked his shots. "Anyone have an extra 9mm mag?"

A man stepped forward and handed him two. Mark nodded his thanks, tested both to make sure they fit, then pocketed the ammo and slid the gun behind his back. Wrapping the white shirt around his hand once he stalked out of the trees. He stopped and waved his white flag. Jarrod came to stand next to him while they waited for a response.

Marks eyes sighted on Lynn. He imagined she was staring at him. He nodded as if sending the message, "I'm coming for you." The image of her in his head nodded back.

"So, is there more to this plan, or is it hope and a prayer time again?"

In a hard voice, he replied, "The only hope is if they let Lynn and Martha go. The prayers will be for their dead if they don't."

Someone above the gate waved white back. A truce was underway. Mark stepped forward. Jarrod stayed with him.

"I take it you've got someone driving your truck."

"Yep. It's been all taken care of."

"If something goes wrong. I need you to cover me. Don't follow. Just wait for the cars to arrive."

"And the chances of something going wrong?"

"About the same as the sun rising and setting."

"That low, huh?"

Mark grunted.

Chapter Fifty-Three

THEY STOPPED ABOUT MIDWAY ACROSS THE FIELD. TO HIS left lay Matthew Donnolly's body. A pang of grief and guilt struck him. Silently, he apologized and vowed revenge, and that he would do all he could to save his mother.

The gates parted in the middle and two men walked out. One was the man who had issued the warning; Mark noted he was nearly as tall as Jarrod. The second man wore a ball cap backward over long thick brown hair. He was clean-shaven, thick-necked, and larger than the first man. The leader carried a hunting rifle, the taller man, a shotgun.

They stopped ten feet away. Too far.

"The way I see it," the leader said, "you're out of choices. You need to leave or the women die. Simple as that."

Mark stared hard at the man, grinding his teeth from side-to-side. He took a casual step forward and said, "All we want is our people back. Then we'll leave."

"You're not hearing me. The only way they get to live is if you leave."

"That's not going to happen. You took our friends. We want them back." He took another step. Jarrod stayed put.

"I guess we got nothing further to talk about, then."

They backed away. Mark took two fast steps and the taller man, shotgun leveled, said, "That's close enough."

The leader came closer, perhaps feeling bolder with the shotgun now in play. "Before I came out here, I left orders to toss the bitches over the fence if anything happened to me."

"That would be your last mistake. Those women are the only things keeping you alive."

"And yet, he holds the shotgun."

"But you have four snipers aimed directly at you." Mark stepped closer. "Go ahead, give the order. You'll die before the women will."

Mark saw the momentary flicker of doubt and with it the first flash of fear. It faded fast and the bravado returned.

"Then I guess we'll die here together," the leader said.

Mark stared so hard his eyes burned. His opponent matched his glare.

Jarrod said, "How 'bout a compromise?"

The leader flinched. His eyes looked sideways. Mark used the distraction to slide inches closer.

"What kind of compromise?"

"Give us one of the women and keep the other. Both sides win."

Mark couldn't believe what he was hearing. He wanted to shout, "No," but didn't want to break his eye lock. He waited to see where Jarrod's idea went.

"So, let me get this right?" the leader said. "If we give you one of the women, you'll leave and not come back for the other?"

"Makes sense, doesn't it?" Jarrod said. "We both get something and no one dies."

The leader moved his gaze back to Mark's. "And you'd be okay with this, hardcore?"

"If that's the deal."

"Hmm! But which one to give you?" He glanced back at the compound. The two women stood on either side of the gate. "They both got nice tits. Be a shame not to sample them both first." He paused to let that sink in.

"Well, since I bought the one up there on the right, I'm not willing to part with her." He meant Lynn. The leader displayed a wicked smile. "I tell you what. I'll go back and talk to the guy who owns the other one. If he says it's all right, we got a deal. 'Course, he's gonna want to use her a bit first. You can understand that."

Something in Mark's face must have given the man pause. He had tried not to react when the leader said he was keeping Lynn but failed. "Wait, you want the other one, don't you?" The leader closed on Mark. "You want my woman, huh? Why's that? She yours? Is that what this is all about? I took your girl?"

Mark held his tongue, but the fury blazed inside.

"Tell me, is she good?"

Mark kept his mouth shut. His fingers opened and clenched.

"Soon as I get back inside, I'm going to find out. I'm going to take her and pound her. I'm going to ride her over and over until she can't walk anymore. Maybe when I'm done and tired of her, I'll give her back."

Mark breathed out slowly and let a smile play across his face. He took a step forward and to the right, closing the distance. The barrel tracked him.

"You think that's funny, eh? Why's that?" the leader asked.

"First of all, you're not man enough to ride her."

"No?"

"No!"

"And ...?"

Mark turned right a quarter turn. His hand drifted down his leg. The taller man's shotgun was now aimed at his left side. "She'll kill you before you can pull your little pecker out." He leaned toward the leader as he spoke, to cover his slide step forward.

"Oh, you think so."

"There's only one thing that can stop her from killing you." He leaned away yet inched his foot forward, keeping his eyes locked on his opponent's.

"Oh, I'm real curious, now. What's that?" Visibly angry, the leader leaned toward Mark.

"If I kill you first."

The confidence in the man's eyes turned to anger, then fear as Mark drove at him, pushing him toward his partner and shoving the shotgun to the side as it exploded. A few pellets tore through Mark's side, twisting him, but the wound was not sufficient to stop the violence of his attack. The unsheathed knife cut deep but had to penetrate a lot of muscle and fat. The taller man howled in pain and tried to step back far enough to put the shotgun between them. His left hand pushed at Mark's chest, but Mark wrapped his free arm around his foe's neck and pulled tighter.

Mark ignored the leader. Since making his play, he had to hope Jarrod could handle him. He went face-to-face with his foe, foreheads touching. The tall man grunted, trying to separate from Mark. He lifted the shotgun and tried to club Mark, but the blows fell across his shoulders, for the most part unnoticed in his rage.

Two shots sounded and the leader fell. Mark shouted, "Now!" He couldn't see if Jarrod gave the signal. Mark continued his struggle with the taller man, heaving upward on the knife with all his might. The blade climbed with slow steady progress through the soft flesh and hard muscle, like lifting a dumbbell that was too heavy for him. Panicked sounds escaped the desperate man. A fine mist of blood filled the air with each breath.

He dropped the gun. While one large hand fought to keep Mark's hand from lifting the knife higher, he slid his left hand under Mark's chin. Pushing with considerable strength, he managed to bend Mark backward.

Feeling his advantage wane, Mark pulled the knife free. His opponent gasped. Then, as fast and hard as he could, Mark drove the point into the side of the man's neck. His enemy screeched and released Mark, his hands flying to the wound.

Letting go of the man, Mark tripped him and let him fall. The large body hit the ground hard. The bill of his cap, trapped under his head, flipped it away, spilling his long hair over the ground. Desperate hands grabbed the knife and tried to pull the blade free.

Mark leaped on the thrashing body as bullets peppered the ground around him. He slapped at the large hands wrapped around the hilt, driving the knife in deeper. The man's legs kicked wildly, his body squirmed in all directions at once.

Mark glanced up. Martha Donnolly, stood in view. He punched the wide-eyed man in the face once and looked up again. Lynn was up now too. He forgot about the wounded man and sprinted for the fence. Guns blasted from everywhere. Mark paid them no notice. He focused hard on Lynn and ran for all he was worth.

As he closed the gap, his heart raced. Fear fueled his every step, as Lynn was lifted in the air, her feet crossing the point of no return.

Chapter Fifty-Four

VAGUELY AWARE OF RACING MOTORS SOMEWHERE
BEHIND him, Mark pressed on. Twenty yards. Bullets
flew in both directions. His eyes stayed fixed on
Lynn. He had to reach her before the rope drew
tight. She would not survive the jerk on her neck.
Once she reached full extension, Lynn would be
dead in an instant. He pushed harder.

Lynn kicked at the air, searching for footing. Arching
her back, she lifted both legs in the air which lowered her
butt enough to catch on the top bar. She fell from view.

A scream drew his attention to the other side of the
fence where Martha was lifted over the fence. Mark
slowed, not sure what to do. Lynn was no longer in immediate danger. She was more capable of fending off her
assailants than was Martha. The decision should have
been easy, but he hesitated.

He looked right: Lynn was nowhere to be seen. Left,
Martha's feet cleared the fence. He pulled his gun and
veered. Past the gate, he aimed a shot but with Martha
struggling, he couldn't pull the trigger.

With a big push the two men heaved Martha clear. She
fell fast. Mark fired twice on the run, dropped the gun,
and reached out. He caught Martha knee high. His momentum caused her body to bend over his shoulder, her
upper body still moving down. Though he held much of
her weight, the noose tightened around her throat. Martha
gagged.

Twisting, Mark sliced the bloody knife across the thick
rope. Grunting, he lifted to relieve the pressure on Martha's throat. Choking sounds emerged from her mouth.

Her face turned red. Mark sawed violently. Someone leaned over the fence and fired down at him. The bullet struck between his feet.

Someone, maybe Jarrod, loosed a barrage driving the shooter back. Mark increased the speed of his cuts and the rope severed. Martha's weight carried her with a thump to the ground. He dragged her to the fence and tore the rope from her neck. Martha gasped with relief as the air rushed into her lungs.

Rolling her onto her stomach Mark sliced through her bonds.

"Martha, stay here. You understand me? Don't move, okay?"

Sobbing between gulps of air, she nodded and rubbed her throat.

Mark looked up. No one was watching. His gun lay ten feet away. Across the open field the vehicles had lined up broadside, as planned, but the battering ram truck had come to a stop for some reason.

"No!"

He looked up. Lynn was in sight and dangling. Pushing to his feet, Mark raced to catch her knowing he was already too late. His heart power drummed. If he missed Lynn, his heart might as well burst.

Lynn fell. Mark choked on the pleading prayer that came to his lips. With all his strength he ran, stretching as far as he could. His only hope, though slim, was to get underneath her before the rope grew taut. A sickening snap sounded in his brain, anticipating the end. Pain ripped up his leg. He tripped and fell with a scream panic. He landed, crawled, and waited, but nothing happened.

Rolling, he looked up. Lynn had managed to catch her arms across the top fence post. She dangled there, her bound arms rising painfully behind her back. Two men pried at her hands. Frantic, Mark looked around for something to use to help her. The gun was too far away.

Behind him, the roar of a truck made him turn. Speeding, the truck bounced over the uneven ground. The distance closed in a hurry. Bullets punched through the windshield. Jarrod ducked but drove on, aiming the large vehicle at the gate. At the last second, before crashing into the gate, he spun the wheel hard, pulling up broadside next to the fence.

Mark understood in an instant. Clambering over the sidewall of the truck, he reached up just as Lynn fell. He caught her, the free fall weight driving him to his knees. The fine edge of the knife made quick work of the rope. As soon as she was loose, Mark shouted, "Go! Go!" He covered Lynn with his body as the big man sped away.

Two cars had driven onto the open field and stopped bumper to bumper midway between the compound and the trees. Jarrod pulled up broadside behind the two cars. Mark slid over the side and helped Lynn down. She wrapped her arms around his neck and squeezed him breathless. He held just as tight but released her in a hurry. "Lynn, I have to go back."

"What! Why? I'm free. There's no reason to go back. It's too dangerous."

He grabbed and held her hands. "I left Martha back there. I have to get her."

Lynn spun, hands pressed to her face. "Oh, God. I was so scared, I forgot about Martha."

"Jarrod, you okay?"

Mark noticed blood streaming down the big man's face. Jarrod wiped at it, red smearing his hand. Using his sleeve, he blotted the wound. "Don't know if it was glass or a bullet. Something nicked me, though."

Lynn stepped forward and on tiptoe examined the area. "I'd say, bullet. You've got a furrow carved from front to back."

"Jarrod, can you drive?"

"Hell, yeah. What d'ya have in mind?"

"I want to go back to the original plan. We have to get Martha." A thought came to him then. He looked at Matthew's body. "And they have to pay for killing Matthew."

"Mark, can't we just get Martha and leave?" Lynn asked.

He studied her face. "If we don't deal with them now, they'll always be a threat to us." Turning to Jarrod, he said, "Let's do this. I need a gun."

"What? Again? Maybe we should tie a string around this one so you don't lose it."

"Don't worry. This one isn't leaving my hand until this fight is done."

"Or you get us both killed." Jarrod turned toward the truck.

Someone handed Mark a gun. "Everyone shoot to keep them from shooting us," he said to the remaining fighters. He climbed on the bed.

Jarrod slid the rear window open. "Ready? It's gonna be bumpy, back there."

"I'll try to keep them from shooting at us."

"Sounds good to me." He put the truck in gear. Through the window, he said, "Into the valley of death rode the old farmer and his crazy ass friend."

Chapter Fifty-Five

As one, Mel, Bobby, and Caleb opened up on the men standing on the cars at the south side of the camp. One man fell, another spun as if stung by a bee; a huge metallic bee. After that, no one dared cross that section of fence.

The shooters on the north side made continuous shooting difficult. They could only shoot once or twice before being forced to duck.

Bobby called down from his attack perch. "Caleb, you keep focused on the rear gate. Mel, you and I are going to switch to the west side. We need to keep them ducking so they don't see Lincoln and his people trying to get in."

"You got it," she said and adjusted her scope.

"You take the first two, I'll take the last two."

"Okay."

Mel knew what he meant. The men along the west ramparts were almost in a direct line with the house making them easy targets. However, after some initial success, several detached car hoods had been propped up along the route for protection. Even though Mel could no longer see the defenders, placing shots into the hoods, or ringing the bell, as Bobby called it, had the desired effect of keeping their heads down.

She placed a shot into each hood, then her breath caught. Movement from the woods announced the assault had begun. Shoot dummy! Mel chastised herself. A surge of adrenaline made her shots erratic. She blew out her breath to relax and forced her eyes away from the attackers. Her job was to protect their approach, not watch them like a spectator in the cheap seats. She fired until empty, slapped in her last loaded magazine and lined up her next shot.

The small band reached the fence. Mel said a silent prayer for their safety and squeezed off another round.

THE FOUR-PERSON ASSAULT GROUP STOPPED INCHES SHORT OF the fence having been told not to make contact with the links. Becca squatted next to Lincoln. While he went to work snipping the chain links, the others aimed upward to protect him.

The mixed gunfire and shouts were thunderous this close to the action. Becca tried to squeeze her ears shut. A head poked over the side, spotting them. Before she got off a shot, one of the snipers in the trees took him out.

"Shit!" Lincoln muttered. "My hand's getting tired." He had cut nearly three feet high.

"Let me," Becca said, reaching for the cutters. Lincoln handed them over. Becca had to put her gun down and use both hands to snip the metal links. She didn't want to go too much higher or someone inside might notice. She worked laterally. After a foot, she started cutting downward. Lincoln was right, it was hard work.

Unbidden, Lincoln took the snips from her hand and finished the task. He pulled the section away. Facing them was the rear car door of an older model Mercury. Lincoln leaned forward and glanced up and around. He pulled back and pointed left, then right, indicating the approximate spot where two shooters stood. Pointing at the car he shook his head. No one was in front of them.

Lincoln reached for the door latch. The door opened, but did not swing wide enough to get through. Squeezing his arm through the gap, he found the old style crank for the window.

Halfway open, the descent taking far too long for the impatient Becca, she leaned forward and said, "Hold my legs."

Lincoln furrowed his brows in confusion.

Becca tugged his arm back and Lincoln withdrew it from the window. Becca tucked the gun into her pants and placed both hands on the window. "Hold my legs." She lifted one leg toward Lincoln. He frowned but took her leg. Reaching down, he grabbed the other one, holding her as kids used to play wheelbarrow.

Standing behind her, Lincoln guided Becca through the half-open window. Becca crawled inside. Lincoln followed her progress delivering her feet all the way to the interior before releasing her.

From inside the spacious car, Becca lowered the window fully. A minute later, Lincoln joined her. The roof sagged inward, the result of weight from above. Becca slid across the seat keeping below the height of the glass. There, she peered out into the compound. Little moved, but stacks of crushed cars blocked her vision.

Turning to Lincoln, she said, "Ready."

He nodded and said, "You should let me go first."

"Yeah, that's gonna happen."

"If you get shot, your father's gonna kill me."

"Guess you'd better watch my back real well then, huh?"

Pushing the handle down, Becca shouldered the door open and stepped out, gun leveled, searching for her first target.

Chapter Fifty-Six

THE TRUCK HIT THE GATE, BUT IT DID NOT BLOW OPEN AS expected. Instead, the truck hit with a crash that exploded the air bag. The rear end lifted into the air, pitching Mark upward and against the cab. He slammed back to the bed and lay stunned.

"Son-of-a-bitch," Jarrod said. "The bastards put a truck behind the gate."

The words filtered through a haze, as though spoken from a long distance. A man leaned over the fence and fired down at Mark. The bullet striking the bed next to his face snapped him from his fugue. Lifting his arm, he triggered a three-shot burst, forcing the man back to cover.

Jarrod reversed, muttering every obscenity he'd ever learned, and creating a few new ones. Shoving the stick into neutral, he gunned the engine and slammed the tranny into drive. Bullets pelted the body from all directions, the truck jumped, like a hunting dog being released for retrieval.

Even braced for impact, Mark was thrown like a corpse, with no control over where he landed. The truck plowed forward, moving the obstacle enough that the truck's cab cleared the gate.

Mark scrambled to his feet, his body aching from the abuse. Leaning over the roof gave him a view of the compound. He turned toward the left and fired at the men standing along the cars. Return fire was withering. Jarrod stuck a shotgun out the window and blasted away until empty.

The planned entry had failed. Instead of breaking through the gate and deep inside the grounds, they were stuck like sitting ducks, caught between two sides of fire. They couldn't survive there long.

Unable to withstand the barrage, Jarrod reversed, but caught up on the other vehicle, the truck refused to move. Mark spun to his right, finished off the magazine, slamming home the last one. They were at a momentary standoff, but only as long as he still had bullets.

BOBBY STOPPED SHOOTING TO WATCH THE PICKUP TRUCK attempt to crash through the gate. His hand still clutched the radio. Seconds before, he'd tried to call his father to warn him the defenders had anticipated their strategy and had driven a pickup truck behind the gate for added support, but no one answered.

Helpless, he gripped the radio tighter as the trucks collided. His frustration increased knowing his father was taking heavy fire, but he had no targets to reduce the threat. Movement to the left of the gate made him drop the radio to the floor and raise the rifle. A man's leg came into view, then disappeared. He stepped in again, then back. He must be leaning forward to shoot, then ducking back out of sight. Bobby lined up the spot the leg had been and waited.

He drew in a cleansing breath and released it in a slow exhalation. The leg appeared, he jumped, overanxious and slackened his finger. The shot would've been rushed and missed. He needed to stay relaxed to anticipate the movement. Bobby missed the next chance too.

Ready, his finger tightened. He pulled the trigger at the first sign of movement. The leg kicked forward and a body fell into full view across the roof of the car. The wounded man slid down the windshield clutching at his calf. Bobby's next shot punched through the top of the man's head.

Jarrod smashed the vehicle forward again. Bobby's father lifted into the air and disappeared behind the cab. The impact had driven the blocking truck backward enough to open the gate, but now they were taking heavy fire.

A lone man ran across the compound firing at the truck. Bobby took him down from behind. Scanning left to right, and back, no other targets presented themselves. "Sorry, Dad, that's the best I can do."

BECCA STEPPED FROM THE CAR AND SLID ALONG THE TRUNK, hugging the rear quarter panel. Lincoln was fast behind her. She opened fire right, he went left. She took out two men from behind before they had a chance. The third one got off a quick shot that ricocheted off the trunk, inches to her side, before she put him down. She had no more targets.

A quick glance to the right showed Lincoln had similar success. The other two members of their team joined Lincoln. Becca turned toward the back fence and ran for the cover of a line of cars, parked in u-shapes. A woman and two kids were huddled in the back of one hovel created by the cars' formation. The small space was full of belongings. These were their homes, Becca realized.

She turned her gun on the woman. The inhabitant covered her children with her body but never let out so much as a whimper. Becca held the sights in place, then lowered her arms. "I'm not going to hurt you unless you come out of there. Stay inside. If you come out, I'm going to think you're a threat and shoot you. You understand?"

The mother looked over her shoulder, her eyes wide with fear, and nodded. Becca moved on. Many of the living areas were vacant. A few had women, some of those also had children. It was a community, just like theirs.

Well, no, not quite. They never held anyone against their will. She moved on.

Lincoln had not followed. She guessed he'd taken the other direction. She hoped he had and was not lying wounded, or worse. She didn't have time to look for him. Creeping to the end of a row of sectioned living spaces, the lined-up cars giving new meaning to mobile homes, she peered around the corner and choked on her angst. Her father and Jarrod were trapped and under heavy fire.

Men fired from above and from the cover of cars on the ground. She had to even the odds, and fast.

Locating the first man, ahead and to the left of her position, across a twenty-foot-wide aisle, Becca, temper aflame, dashed into the open. Her gun barked, jumping in her hand. Her shots were off their mark as she ran. As the distance closed the bullets crept on line.

The shooter spun, a wild, crazed look on his face. He found Becca, tried a desperate snapshot, then danced against the car as bullets riddled his chest. His body slid to the ground.

Becca took up his position, picking up his weapon, a .45. She frowned. The bullets would not work in her gun. She changed out the magazine in hers and slid it into her belt. Using the .45, Becca sighted on one of the men near the fence shooting at Jarrod and her father.

The gun kicked too much, the shot flying high. It missed so badly her target was unaware he was in her sights. Lowering her aim to his feet, she gripped the weapon with both hands, tighter than she should. The gun kicked again, but this time the shooter ducked.

Becca cursed. Her opponent, aware he was in danger, wedged himself between two vehicles. She couldn't hit him, not with the .45. Becca moved, looking for a new victim. She found him at the end of the next row of housing. He stood, leaning against an old El Dorado, taking pot shots at the pickup's doors.

Becca crept to within ten feet of the man. No amount of bucking would make her miss this shot. The bullet ripped through the unsuspecting man's torso as though he'd given birth to an alien. Becca felt no remorse, only satisfaction. Taking up his vantage point, she found two more men standing on cars shooting at her father. The sight angered her even more.

In an open shooter's stance, her legs shoulder width apart, arms out, she unleashed the remaining rounds at the two men, sending them scurrying for cover. She tossed the gun aside when it was empty, saying, "Piece of shit!" She withdrew her 9mm and found cover.

She might be crazy, but she wasn't stupid.

Chapter Fifty-Seven

MARK MOVED FROM SIDE-TO-SIDE TRYING TO KEEP ANYONE from getting a good bead on him.

So far, his efforts were working, but by his count, he was down to his last five shots. Twice in a row now, he had no targets to shoot at, on either side. However, he couldn't afford to cease his movement. To stand still was to die.

He switched to the left side again. Was it his imagination or had the rate of fire decreased? The man who had been dogging him was nowhere in sight. He hadn't fired at him in a minute or so. He took the opportunity to call Martha and motioned her to get under the truck.

Pivoting to the right, he swept the barrel in a wide arc looking for movement. Nothing. A lone shot sounded on the far side of the yard. To his right, someone moaned. Beneath him, Jarrod shouldered the crumpled door open. He stepped out and fell more than leaned against the truck. His face, streaked with blood, made him look like some Neanderthal after a hunt.

Moments passed, the tension from inactivity putting him more on edge than the firefight. In the back of his mind, the thought remained that at any second that one bullet still may find him.

A voice drifted across the grounds. "Don't shoot. We surrender."

Relief swept over Mark, but he refused to let down his guard. "Toss down your weapons and come out where we can see you. Keep your hands empty and away from your body."

A different voice shouted, "Don't do it. They're just gonna kill you."

Mark frowned. The end couldn't be easy, could it? "You have my word, we will not shoot you."

"And what good is anyone's word, nowadays?" the same voice said.

"Well, I guarantee, if you don't come out, and we have to hunt you, we're not going to take any chances. We'll shoot, regardless if you surrender. The only way you survive is to give up now."

The echo of a distant shot broke the spell. He ducked and tightened his muscles. A man to Mark's right pitched against the fence and slumped over the hood of a car. His rifle slid down the hood to the ground.

Mark looked toward the house. One of Bobby's group just saved his life.

The assassination attempt ignited new anger. "Last chance. I'm moving my people inside now. Anyone I don't see in the open here in the next minute will be hunted and killed."

From the left, Lincoln came forward pushing a man in front of him. The man's hands were in the air, Lincoln's gun pressed to the back of his head. He gave him a shove and stopped.

A rifle arced in the air, landing on the open ground. A short, thin man stepped out, his hands up. "Don't shoot. I'm done."

A few more stepped into sight, cautiously. Mark repeated his ultimatum but didn't hold to the time threat. Over the next few minutes, men, women, and some children, fleshed out the crowd.

Jarrod radioed for some of their people to come inside to watch the prisoners.

"Tell Bobby to keep his people in the house and watching," Mark said.

Once they had the numbers to ensure control, they commenced a systematic search of the grounds. One man resisted and was shot. Three others were found hiding and dragged out.

Mark sat on the roof of the truck, the adrenaline ebbing. His head throbbed as though he had caffeine withdrawal. Lynn climbed onto the truck bed and stood behind him. Someone had given her a shirt to wear. He gave her a weak smile and reached a hand back. She took it and he squeezed. "You okay?"

She nodded. Though her eyes watered, she held back the tears. Lincoln came forward and stood next to Jarrod. His arm hung limply at his side. Mark said, "Lynn." He didn't have to say anything else. He helped her over the roof. Jarrod lifted her to the ground. There she examined Lincoln's wound.

"I think that's everyone," Becca said, striding to the truck.

Mark looked at his daughter. "You all right?"

"Of course, Daddy."

He wanted to smile, but the cold detached way she said it furthered his headache's progress. He rubbed his temples, then stood on the hood. Perhaps fifty people were gathered. The majority women and children. The defenders had suffered heavy losses. How many had the assault cost them?

"Listen. This is how things are gonna go." He paused to make sure everyone was listening. "We're taking your weapons."

An instant uproar arose from the men. Mark waited for a minute. He knew what their fears were. To be unarmed in this new world meant death. However, he wasn't prepared to chance them following and causing more trouble. There had to be a punishment inflicted for their actions.

He held up his hand. Jarrod's whistle pierced the din and quiet resumed.

"We are taking your weapons. End of discussion. We will deposit those weapons at the Air National Guard base. I will leave word with the General that whoever shows up to claim their weapon can have them. If you ever turn those weapons on us in any way, including kidnapping any of our people, we will come back and wipe you out to a man. That, I promise.

"If you don't bother us, we will not bother you. However, if you decide that you wish to form a relationship with our community either for safety, or for trade, or just social, that can be discussed at a later date.

"We are not here to destroy your community, but it stands to reason that if you abducted our people and held them against their will, that you may have done the same to others. If anyone wants to leave, you should do so while we are still here. If you decide to stay it should be your choice to do so. We guarantee you safe passage. No one will be forced to come with us, but if anyone wishes to join our community you are welcome. No one will force you to do anything against your will, but everyone is expected to contribute to the workload."

"There you are, you bastard."

Mark looked down in time to see Becca land a punch on a man's face. He staggered back; she stalked him, hitting him again. He cried out in pain.

"Help! Make her stop. She's crazy."

She landed a kick to the stomach, doubling him over. With both hands interlocked Becca clubbed him to the ground.

"Becca," Mark called.

"This is the asshole who tried to rape me." She planted another kick, this time to his ribs.

"No, it wasn't me! Someone help me."

Becca lifted her foot to stomp on the man's head.

"Becca! Stop now."

She froze. Her face red, her rage obvious.

A tall woman stepped from the crowd toward Becca's victim. She stopped, looked from Becca to Mark, then down at the man. In a flash, she lifted her foot and planted it in the man's groin. A high-pitched wail exploded from his lips. He rolled, clutching himself.

The woman walked away. Becca looked back at Mark, shrugged, and smiled sweetly.

Mark pointed at the writhing man. "This man will be banned from living here. If I ever find him back inside these grounds, I will kill him and anyone harboring him. There is no place for his sort in this new world."

Mark motioned to two of his people. "Drag him from the camp and leave him out there." As they did so, Mark said, "Is there anyone who has anything further to say?" No one spoke, but low grumbling sounded. Mark was too tired and still had too much anger and adrenaline flowing to put up with any complaints. "Hey," he shouted. "Shut up! We didn't start this. You did. You should be happy we're not like you or you'd be dead or enslaved. If you have a problem with how you're being treated we can make some adjustments. How 'bout I put one of the three women you held captive in charge of deciding your fate. Or better yet, the mother of the boy you tried to hang and then shot down? Do I hear any other murmurs of dissent?" He listened, scanning the crowd. "Yeah, didn't think so."

Mark pinched the bridge of his nose between two fingers and tried to calm his rising rage. The memory of Matthew being tossed over the wall like garbage was too vivid. His life had meant nothing to these people. Looking up, he viewed the assembled defenders through a red mist. He wanted nothing more than to lash out in fury, to seek revenge for Matthew, for his mother, and for Caryn and Lynn. His fists clenched.

"Mark," Jarrod's voice, though low and calm, cut through his anger. "It's over, my friend. Let it rest. Maybe we can all find peace."

Mark looked up. As his vision cleared, he sent a silent prayer skyward. Inhaling deeply, he shook his arms, hands and fingers, as if the act would rid him of the urge to punish. To kill.

"Anyone wishing to leave has fifteen minutes to pack up their belongings and meet back here. Go."

Mark climbed from the truck. He spoke to a group of his people. "Would you pick up all the weapons, please, and put them in the back of Jarrod's truck?"

At the same time, the sound of engines reached his ears. The radio crackled to life in Jarrod's hand. He listened, spoke, and issued a tight-lipped smile. "Guess who decided to join the party?"

A sudden rush of panic hit Mark and he reached for his handgun.

"Whoa there, boss man. Relax. We are all saved. The General and his troops have arrived." He waved a finger in a circle. "Yay!"

Chapter Fifty-Eight

MARK SENT TWO MEN TO THE FRONT OF THE CAMP TO OPEN the gates. Minutes later a parade of military vehicles, including two jeeps with mounted 50-cal machine guns, swept into the grounds and fanned out. General West, as if looking to make a grand entrance, sat in the command vehicle for several minutes before stepping out.

Mark met the man and they shook hands. "It's all over, General, but thanks for coming."

"Looks like you have things well in hand here."

"We do, but unfortunately, not before taking casualties."

"I'm sorry to hear, that, Mark. Truly."

Mark didn't respond.

"So, what do we have here?"

Mark allowed an inward smile at the 'we.' "There's about twenty men and thirty women and children. You might find some recruits in their midst."

"Oh?" The thought interested the man. He bugged Mark's group monthly for recruits to fill out his small band of soldiers. He lost nearly half his men in a battle two months earlier and could not find adequate, or for that matter, any, replacements.

"General, if you don't mind, I'm going to leave these people in your hands. I did promise that anyone wishing to leave could do so. I suspect many of the women have been held against their will. But, make your pitch, you may have a few takers.

"Oh, and Jarrod's truck is full of their weapons. I told them they had to see you to get them back."

"Is there anything we can help you with?"

Mark gave that some thought, then shook his head. "No, I just want to get my people home and take care of our dead. It's been a long night."

"I understand."

Four soldiers began offloading the collected weapons. Although it protested from the abuse it took, with a little assistance getting free, Jarrod coaxed his truck from the gate. Within the fifteen-minute deadline, most of the women and children, and a few men, had gathered at the gate.

"For those of you who wish to leave, you are free to go. If any of you wish to join us, follow Jarrod," he pointed at the truck, "to those cars in the field. If you're undecided, you can meet with the other members of our family and make up your mind later."

A woman raised her hand.

"I'm sorry. You'll have to forgive me but at the moment, I don't feel up to answering questions. Direct them toward the people at the cars. Okay, everyone, go. And wherever you go, remember we're all we have left. Respect other survivors."

The crowd moved on and Becca came to stand next to him. "Nice pep talk, Daddy."

He laughed despite the situation. Wrapping his arm around his daughter, he pulled her close. "Guess I'll never make coach of the year."

She hugged him and said, "No, but you will make dad of the decade."

He smiled.

"I don't know how you do it," she said.

"Do what?"

"Control the anger. I felt such rage for what they did to us, I wanted to strike out and not stop until I had nothing left to hit. You get mad, I know you do, but you always seem to be able to stop when it's appropriate, as if you have a switch."

"I think it's the last vestiges of my humanity, perhaps, that prevents me from going too far. It's not that I'm not angry enough to do more. God, forgive me for the thoughts that plague my mind. If I ever give in to that urge, then I'm no better than these people. I'll be lost forever. Although, there are times when I think that's already happened and it's too late for me to be salvaged."

"Daddy, you're the best person I know. I wish I could be more like you. But if anyone is lost, it's me. If you hadn't stopped me, I would have pounded that asshole into the dirt he was." She shuddered. "Even now, I want nothing more than to track him down and make him pay. Make sure he can't hurt anyone ever again." She looked at him, her eyes large, soft, and watery. "I get so angry sometimes I can't see straight." A fat tear tracked down her face. "Is it too late for me, Daddy? Have I lost the last bit of humanity I had?"

Mark stroked her hair. "The fact that you are still capable of asking that question tells me no, it's not too late. You still recognize the difference. I'll admit, there are times you worry me. I'm afraid for you. You've been forced to do things no one should ever have to. The upheaval in your life has affected you, but it has everyone. We all cope with the brutality of this world the best we can. Survival is an endless struggle, but then, it always has been … just not to this extreme. Situations like this don't help, but being with family and around others who care, will help us all remember how life used to be, and perhaps one day will be again."

"Now that was a coach of the year pep talk." She smiled, took his sleeve, and wiped her eyes.

"Why, you little brat."

She laughed and pushed free. "I love you, Daddy." Laughing, she trotted off.

Mark watched her go. Though he smiled outwardly, he worried about Becca. Since arriving at the farmhouse, she'd been much more stable, but there were signs of some deep-rooted problem. He hesitated to use the term illness. With enough time, and no more deadly confrontations, maybe she'd return to normal; or as normal as this new world allowed.

Chapter Fifty-Nine

MEL WATCHED THROUGH HER SCOPE AND WAITED FOR THE word to be passed that they could safely leave the house. Then it was decision time. She was anxious to talk to both Tara and Caryn. To find out how each one was and get their opinions on their next move.

She was of two minds. She liked having other people around her. The benefits were obvious and right in front of her. However, had they been on their own they never would've been in this fight. They'd have fled and hidden, staying safely out of sight. Hiding was easier to do when there was only three of them and on the move.

Staying in one location made being discovered more likely. On the other hand, if these people had not been there and so willing to help, Tara would surely be dead. Perhaps they all would be.

With no threat imminent, she allowed her thoughts to wander. Images of the various members of the family came to her. Bobby and Caleb here in the house and, to a lesser degree, the strange wild-haired boy with the bow. Lynn reminded her of Caryn. Mark was nice, but knew he was also tough. Although she hated that he ordered her around, she understood it wasn't personal. She had a grudging respect for him.

Others she had met also welcomed her and treated her as an equal and with respect. Mel had to admit, being part of a group again did have its merits. Decisions. Decisions.

"Mel?"

She started, smacking her eye against the scope. "Damn, Bobby. Give a girl some warning."

He stood in the doorway, smiling. "Sorry, Mel. I called you twice, but you were either asleep or lost in your thoughts." He reached a hand down and helped her to her feet. "We just got the all-clear. The army will handle things from here. Let's go join the others."

She stretched. "Sounds good to me."

Caleb and Myron joined them at the car. They piled in and drove across the street. Arriving, Mel climbed out and went in search of Caryn. After asking after her, Mel found her huddled behind a car parked in the open field on the far side of the camp. She had her knees drawn up tight to her chest. Someone had given her a windbreaker that was too large for her. She stared straight out in front of her.

Caryn?"

The woman did not respond.

"Caryn, it's me, hon."

Caryn shifted her gaze. Her eyes looked blank. No expression marked her face. Mel squatted next to her and placed a comforting arm around her friend's shoulders. "You okay?"

She nodded.

"It's over now. We're safe."

Caryn shuddered. "Are we?" Her voice was weak. "Are we really?" Her tone grew in volume and intensity. "Will we ever truly be safe?"

"I don't know. Maybe you're right, we never will be, but what's the alternative? To quit? To lie down and die? We survived all that this crazy world has thrown at us. Who knows what tomorrow will bring, but we'll stand tall and face it."

"I don't know, Mel. You're so much tougher than I am. I'm not sure how much more I can take."

"Hey, don't sell yourself short. You're a lot tougher than you give yourself credit for. Look how far you've come.

Look how you stood up to those assholes who wanted to hurt Tara. I misjudged you and for that, I apologize. This world is never gonna be the same as it was, but we can make the most of it. You faced your fears and are still here. I'm proud of you."

"You didn't see me inside the compound. They sold me, as if I was dinner. They would have … they would have done terrible things to me and I wouldn't have been able to stop them. Is that any kind of world you want to live in? I don't."

"What are you saying? You're giving up?"

Caryn wiped her tears away. "I can't take the fear and the uncertainty anymore. If I have to live in fear then maybe living no longer holds any appeal."

"Tell me, when they came for you, did you fight?"

"I was going to, but Mark showed up before I had to."

"If you were willing to fight, then you aren't ready to give in yet. Otherwise, you would've just let them do what they wanted. The world is only going to be what you make of it, but wasn't that the case before all this insanity happened? Maybe we need to give these people a chance to show us there's still something worth living for."

"I don't want to be afraid anymore." Her voice held a haunted quality.

Mel looked toward the woods. They were so close and held the promise of freedom. She could get up right then and leave everything and everyone behind her. She could make it alone, couldn't she?

Whether sensing her thoughts or just in need of further comfort, Caryn lowered her head to Mel's shoulder and cried softly.

Mel sighed. "I'm not willing to quit, nor am I willing to allow you to. We're still alive. There has to be a reason. I don't know about you, but I want to know the purpose for my survival. Let's find out together." With those words,

Mel understood she had made her decision, if only for the time being.

Chapter Sixty

THE NEXT FEW DAYS WERE BUSY. THE COMMUNITY TOOK IN fourteen women and children, and two men. Finding homes for them in the already crowded grounds proved to be a challenge. One Mark was willing to leave, not without some guilt and relief, in Lynn's capable hands.

He stood back while Lynn sat the new arrivals down for induction. Work crews were set up to do quick renovations of the two other unoccupied houses on their block. One was across the street, the other a quarter mile down the road.

Martha took in a woman and her two children. The loss of her husband and son left her alone in their house. The companionship would go a long way to helping all of them adjust and heal.

Once the new members were settled in, the sad duty of burials took place. The community had lost four treasured people in the battle. The entire assembly joined for the funerals. Several people stepped forward to tell stories about each of the deceased. Mourning as a family made the reality of the losses bearable.

Mark looked around the gathered community. They were growing, but so was the graveyard. Was the trade-off worth the loss? Did they have any other choice? Could he have done anything different? The questions assaulted him nightly as he tried to sleep. The main nagging query refused to be set aside. If Lynn hadn't been involved, would he have been so aggressive in the attack, so careless with other lives? Maybe he wasn't fit to lead. His decisions always brought death.

No one ever came out and accused him but in his mind, he assigned meaning to their looks. They blamed him for the losses. The burden weighed heavily. He became sullen. Lack of sleep and loss of appetite drained him further.

How much more could these good people endure? How much more could he? The answer was as unknown as the future. They had no choice, but to live each day, ready to face the next and what may come. Their existence was an endless struggle, their survival the only sign of victory. Resuming a normal life was an endless hunt.

Other struggles would come. Other new roadblocks would be placed before them, but in the end, they'd face them as a family.

MEL GAVE CARYN A STRONG HUG. "I'LL MISS YOU, CARYN. Remember, we're not far away."

"I know. It's the right thing for you to do. I'll be fine. I hope you understand my decision to stay."

"Of course we do," said Tara. Though bandaged and still weak, her color and energy had returned. She offered a broad smile and a softer hug of her own. "We'll still see each other. You've become a sister to both of us."

Caryn smiled. A rare thing. "Well, I'm glad you didn't say mother."

Mel and Tara laughed and headed for the jeep that waited to take them to the base. Tara was determined to go back to the life she had known before the world changed. She was military through and through. Mel decided to join her, although she hadn't yet decided to enlist. She held no illusions that the general and his staff would do everything in their power to convince her to do so, but she was allowed to live on the base for now without making that choice, as long as she did her fair share of the work. A concession the general allowed because of his lack of manpower.

He was also very excited to have someone with Tara's flight experience, even if it was only helicopters. That desire gave Tara leverage in making a case for Mel to stay on base with her. She parleyed her skills into a promotion and was now an officer, assigned to the training of the five new recruits enlisted from the camp.

If anything, Mel figured this new adventure was going to be interesting.

She watched Caryn's sad and frail figure as the jeep backed down the drive. She'd miss the woman. The whiny burden had come a long way, much of it not good, to be sure, but she was in the best place right now. Lynn would look after her and Doc had been training her on the equipment they recovered from Smahl's office. They had a real clinic now. Mel hoped Caryn's duties gave her a new purpose and kept her mind off her fears.

She reached an arm out the window and waved. Caryn waved back. Was she making the right decision? Tara elbowed her in the side.

"You ready for this, girl?"

Mel smiled. "No."

Tara's laugh filled the interior. Her dark skin glowed with delight. "You're gonna love being in the military. Maybe I'll even teach you to fly."

Mel thought about that possibility. That'd be cool. Perhaps she'd stop running for a while. She had friends now. Family, a sense of purpose, and, just maybe, peace. What more could there be? She was afraid of the answer.

ABOUT THE AUTHOR

Ray Wenck taught elementary school for 36 years. He was also the chef/owner of DeSimone's Italian restaurant for more than 25 years. After retiring he became a lead cook for Hollywood Casinos and then the kitchen manager for the Toledo Mud Hens AAA baseball team. Now he spends most of his time writing, doing book tours and meeting old and new fans and friends around the country.

Ray is the author of forty-four novels including the Amazon Top 20 post-apocalyptic, Random Survival series, the paranormal thriller, Ghost of a Chance, the mystery/suspense Danny Roth series and the ever popular choose your own adventure, Pick-A-Path: Apocalypse. A list of his other novels can be viewed at raywenck.com.

His hobbies include reading, hiking, cooking, baseball and playing the harmonica with any band brave enough to allow him to sit in.

You can find his books all your favorite sites.

You can reach Ray or sign up for his newsletter at raywenck.com or authorraywenck on Facebook

For a free book, visit raywenck.com and sign up for the newsletter.

Random Survival Book 4 A Trip to Normal
https://www.amazon.com/Trip-Normal-Random-Survival-Book-ebook/dp/B07M5979H2/ref=sr_1_20?crid=2X854HE0A2BIE&keywords=ray+wenck&qid=1639010888&sprefix=ray+we%2Caps%2C171&sr=8-20

Other Titles

Random Survival Series
Random Survival
The Long Search for Home
The Endless Struggle
A Journey to Normal
Then There'll Be None
In Defense of Home
(Coming soon) A Life to die For

Danny Roth Series
Teammates
Teamwork
Home Team
Stealing Home
Group Therapy
Double Play
Playing Through Errors

The Dead Series
Tower of the Dead
Island of the Dead
Escaping the Dead

Pick-A-Path Series
Pick-A-Path: Apocalypse 1
Pick-A-Path: Apocalypse 2
Pick-A-Path: Apocalypse 3

Stand Alone Titles
Warriors of the Court
Live to Die Again
The Eliminator
Reclamation
Dimensions

Ghost of a Chance
Mischief Magic
Twins In Time
When the Cheering Stops

Short Stories

The Con   Short Stop-A Danny Roth short   Super
Me   Super Me, Too

Co-authored with Jason J. Nugent

Escape: The Seam Travelers Book 1

Capture: The Seam Travelers Book 2

Conquest: The Seam Travelers Book 3

The Historian Series

The Historian: Life Before and After

The Historian: The Wilds

The Historian: Invasion

Jeremy Kline

The Invisible Village

The Lost Tribe

Bridgett Conroy Series

A Second Chance at Death

Traveling Trouble

Ray Wenck

Ray Wenck

Made in the USA
Coppell, TX
01 July 2022

79466607R00157